ALL THE

BROKEN

THINGS

ALSO BY

KATHRYN KUITENBROUWER

Way Up
The Nettle Spinner
Perfecting

KATHRYN KUITENBROUWER

ALL THE

BROKEN

THINGS

RANDOM HOUSE CANADA

PUBLISHED BY RANDOM HOUSE CANADA

COPYRIGHT © 2014 KATHRYN KUITENBROUWER

www.randomhouse.ca

Random House Canada and colophon are registered trademarks.

This book is a work of fiction. Names, characters, places and incidents either are the product of the author's imagination or are used fictitiously. Any resemblance to actual persons, living or dead, events or locales is entirely coincidental.

Excerpt from Sir Orfeo reprinted by permission of HarperCollins Publishers Ltd. Sir Gawain and the Green Knight, Pearl and Sir Orfeo © The J. R. R. Tolkien Copyright Trust 1975

LIBRARY AND ARCHIVES CANADA CATALOGUING IN PUBLICATION

Kuitenbrouwer, Kathryn, 1965–
    All the broken things / Kathryn Kuitenbrouwer.

Issued also in electronic format.

ISBN 978-0-345-81352-7

    I. Title.

PS8571.U4A64 2014   C813'.6   C2013-900734-2

Text design by CS Richardson
Cover images: (figures) © Elisa Noguera / Trevillion Images; (bear silhouette) © pio3, (bunting) © pashabo, both Shutterstock.com
Printed and bound in the United States of America

10 9 8 7 6 5 4 3 2 1

My Boys

The strangest of the truths in this novel are the facts of a bear wrestling circuit in Ontario, the production of Agent Orange in the small town of Elmira, Ontario, and freak shows at the Canadian National Exhibition (CNE).

Ontario outlawed bear wrestling when a bear mauled the trainer's fiancée to death in 1976. Freak shows were a huge attraction at the CNE, with many freaks making their international debuts in Canada, and only ended in 1979. Agent Orange was produced by Uniroyal (now Chemtura) in Elmira under contract for the U.S. military for the purpose of defoliating the jungles of Vietnam during the war.

Chemical manufacturers knew that the dioxin in Agent Orange was both carcinogenic and mutagenic. Some 83 million litres of the poison was dropped onto South Vietnam from 1961 to 1971. The victims of Agent Orange have not been properly acknowledged and the legacy of Agent Orange continues, as the chemical works its way through a third generation of exposed Vietnamese citizens. Canada has never admitted any responsibility for this.

I have played a little with time because I felt the story needed a carnival.

Bearward

Middle English Dictionary: bēr(e-wǎrd(e n. Also bar(re)warde. [From bēr(e n.(1).] (a) One who takes care of or trains bears, bear keeper; one who has charge of the bear in bearbaitings.

For some there stood who had no head,
and some no arms, nor feet; some bled
and through their bodies wounds were set,
and some were strangled as they ate,
and some lay raving, chained and bound,
and some in water had been drowned;
and some were withered in the fire,
and some on horse in war's attire.
And wives there lay in their childbed,
and mad were some, and some were dead;
and passing many there lay beside
as though they slept at quiet noon-tide.

From the Middle English Romance *Sir Orfeo*,
translated by J.R.R. Tolkien

1984, BEAR

LOOK AT THE BEAR licking Bo's toes up through the metal slats on the back porch. Bo is fourteen years old, and the bear not a year. The bear is named Bear. When the boy spreads his toes as wide as he can, Bear's mottled tongue nudges in between them and this tickles. Bear craves the vanilla soft ice cream that drips down Bo's cone and onto his feet. Bo imagines it must be glorious for Bear to huddle under the porch— her favourite spot—and lap and lick up the sweet cold treat. He imagines himself tucked in down there pretending to be a bear, and how wonderful it might be, after a day alone, to have someone drip sweet vanilla ice cream right into his mouth.

Bo crouches, peeps down between the corroded slats, holds the cone over his feet, and waits as the ice cream melts and then slides through his toes. The first drips shock, but then his body warms the liquid up, and it is a velvety feeling, the ice cream streaming everywhere, making a mess—of himself, the porch steps, and Bear's fur. Squatting, Bo waits with his free hand for the long piebald tongue. Bear curls back her lips to smiling and presses her fangs up against the bottom of the porch, and there it is.

Bo grabs the animal's tongue and feels it slip wet from between his fingers. "I got you!" Bear shakes her head, banging it against the porch, and huffs at Bo. She knows this game.

Still, determined to taste the ice cream and salty boy-skin, she shoots her tongue out again anyway. Bo bides his time until the tongue is so busy probing between his toes and up along his foot that he is sure Bear has forgotten about the game, and then, Bo nabs the tongue at the base and hangs on, laughing. Bear tries to swing left and right but she is caught. And then a great paw comes up, sliding along the porch slats, and Bear begins to moan so plaintively that Bo lets go.

"Oh, Bear," he says. "Oh, Bear."

Bo loves the tongue sweeping coarsely against his skin, he loves talking to Bear and being sure that he is understood and also that he is understanding her. He loves

Bear's stink, her thick coat and the way her body lumbers around the backyard and through the house when he lets her in. He loves the expressions on the faces of people when they first see her, and he loves when Bear swats him so hard he falls over, and that it is play. He makes a couple more attempts at grabbing Bear, more to feel the soft tip of her tongue than to win the game.

When most of the ice cream is gone, Bo sits down on the edge of the porch with his legs dangling and lets Bear clean his ankles and up his calves and thighs. She's come out from under the porch. Bo coos and pets her head and behind her ears and down her muzzle to where the skin hangs along her throat. He marvels at the way the fur swirls over her eyes, parting in the middle, and how elegant that is. The animal loves to be touched—she moans with pleasure.

Bo holds out the cone, tells her, "Gentle, soft," and gives it to her when her teeth get too close. Bear places the cone on the ground and licks all the ice cream from it, then eats the sweet cone, along with the sticky napkin with which Bo held it.

Bear is three times as big as she was when Bo first got her. Soon she won't fit under the porch and Bo will have to construct a shed for her. Besides, the weather will eventually turn and she'll want to hibernate. But now it is May and they are enjoying the first ice cream of spring.

Bo cups Bear's face and draws her sleepy eyes up to meet his. "You're mine," he says. "Do you understand?"

The bear tosses her great head—she does not like to be held still for long—and then she gently mouths the hem of Bo's T-shirt, sucking at it like a nipple. Bo jumps down from the porch. "Okay, come on," he chides. "Well, come on, you."

He dances around Bear and she sits back and watches him, her front paws begging. Bo steps in close and lunges out a palm and swipes at her ears, but Bear just ducks and shifts position, shakes him off. The boy gets cocky and comes in closer.

Bear presses up onto her hind legs and roars and wraps her arms around Bo and shifts from one foot to the other—a shuffling dance-step. If Bo's mother happened to be looking out the back door, she wouldn't be able to see her son. She might see the flap of white that is his cotton T-shirt and she might see the stripes that are his shorts, but Bear has grown so large that she more or less covers Bo. She lifts him up and thumps him down. It is a pro wrestling manoeuvre and Bo is impressed. Bear pins him and straddles him in no time. She licks his face, places where the boy had been untidy with the ice cream.

Bo hears the screen door squeal before he hears his mother's "No!" She stands on the porch and shakes a mop. She does not need protection, but she always brings it. "Shoo," she calls. "Shoo." She pokes the dried-out mop toward them as if it is a lance. "Go away. Go away." She could have tried to scare the animal away in her native

Vietnamese but she is convinced Bear is exclusively English-speaking.

"Cut that out, Mum," says Bo. But Bear knows not to defy Bo's mother. She gives Bo one last long lick and huddles under the porch. "Mum," Bo says. "Why did you do that? We're playing." He grabs the mop from her, glares at it, then her, and hands it back.

"It's dinnertime," she says. "We have company."

Max Jennings is sitting at the kitchen table, again.

CHAPTER ONE

BO LAY IN HIS BED and stared at the ceiling, at the wallpaper, at the drawings he had made there. How should he begin? Once upon a time, he thought. Yes. Once there was a war that went on for years and years, and no one went unscathed, neither the side that lost nor the side that won. It went on and on, and some say still lingered in smaller ugly ways, passing from generation to generation.

In the country where this war took place, there lived a boy and his mother and father, and because of their ingenuity, and their luck, when the war ended, they were able to escape. They fled on a small wooden fishing boat, and were lost at sea, with some hundred or more other people.

The father soon fell ill, and even though he had survived treacherous battles, he was only human. One calm day, only three days into the voyage, he died. The people on the boat slid his body into the sea and tried to console the mother, who wailed and keened and reached her hand toward the ocean surface to try to grab at his shirt as he sank. Below deck, the boy pulsed his angry little body against a stranger who clung to him to keep him from seeing his father disposed of in this way.

Days passed, and they landed safely. They lived in a camp with others like themselves, and then the boy and his mother and the baby she was growing found a new home in a faraway country where no one knew them and they knew no one. And now they'd lived here for years, and it was like a dream where some things were real but you were never sure.

THE COCK WAS CROWING. A day like every other. A Friday in September. Bo would get out of bed, he would dress, he would go to school. And he would fight. Bo did not know why the fighting had started or what exactly he was fighting over or about or for. He only knew that without the fights he was invisible. He'd been fighting all of the four years he'd been here, every day it seemed.

The neighbour to the west had a brood of hens and a cock. The cock and the fact of no curtains on his window were the main reasons why Bo never needed an alarm clock to get himself up and why his mother, whose real name was Thao, but whom everyone called Rose, never had to wake him. The cock's crow tore the day from the night, and gave Bo enough time to watch, from his bed, the light edge up from the horizon, like the slow reveal of the movie screen at the Humber cinema when the velvet drapery began its ascent. Something—anything—could happen in a movie, even if nothing ever happened in real life, or nothing new. Still, this did not stop Bo from wondering if something could, and what this new something might look or feel like.

A sharp ray of light reached his eyes, and he shut them, then pushed his body to get out of bed. His T-shirt lay where he left it the day before, crumpled on the floor. He put it on, and also his jeans, which had been donated by the church people and, for once, were not too short. He pulled his shoes on. The shoes had been a gift from Teacher. They were Adidas, which in spite of being the height of fashion, did not improve his social standing. Sometimes when he looked at himself in a mirror he wondered how every kid at school knew that he was abnormal. He looked so normal to the naked eye.

He stretched in the middle of the kitchen. He did thirty squats and then thirty jumping jacks and then thirty push-ups. He wished he had a bar for pull-ups.

It would be easy enough to mount one in the doorway to the hall but his mother had said no, that it wasn't their house and it would leave holes in the wood trim. The tiny bungalow belonged to the church group and his mother paid rent.

He heard her clearing her throat as she emerged from her bedroom and walked to the end of the hall. He heard the tap run. Bo curled his fists and held them in front of his chest, moved them up and down as if he were doing pull-ups, his body tense. It was a training day and he wanted to be ready for Mr. Morley.

"What have you eaten, Bo?" His mother had come into the kitchen. Her small figure bent toward the sink. She peered in at the dishes she had not done the night before.

"Nothing."

"There's food in the fridge."

Rose had made an ugly casserole from the recipe on the back of the mayonnaise jar. She did this, he believed, to feel more North American. Bo opened the fridge door and looked at it now. It was caved in. Cheese and sauce congealed around the edges of the pan and it did not look edible. Glistening orange-yellow tubes of crisped macaroni had dried up—their little round mouths pleading. It hadn't been that awful warm, but sitting there between the fish sauce and the eggs, it made him think of underwater creatures—squid and octopi—and how they could grab and squeeze you dead.

"Eat something!" his mum said. She reached in past him and pulled an apple from the keeper.

He could smell her. She smelled of puke.

"Mum."

Rose was heading to the little ancestor altar in the corner, but she turned and squinted at him, indignant—she could be like that in the mornings. Bo put some macaroni in a bowl and spread it out, then cut it and cut it until it no longer resembled something so unspeakably dreadful. Then he ate, staring out the window, away from his mum. He heard a whistle and listened for the train that ran on the tracks near the house. The ground shifted and the rumble went up through his body. He loved this feeling, even if he knew the trains were bringing farm animals to the stockyards to be slaughtered. Sometimes, the trains would stop and he would hear a sheep bleating or a cow bellowing. He loved to hear them in spite of everything he knew.

"I have track and field this morning," Bo said. "And also after school." He was reminding her that his sister would be alone for a short time. Rose worked shifts. In Vietnam she had been a housewife but here she cleaned at the hospital to make money.

"Okay."

They spoke English in their home—she wanted him to fit in. His mother knew English from school, had been a good student, but now, in Canada, in public, she sometimes pretended not to understand.

Rose crouched at the altar. It was a painted, six-inch medallion of the Buddha shoved into a sand-filled red metal box. It sat on the floor in the corner of the kitchen. Rose lit three sticks of incense, nestled them into the sand in front of the Buddha, and then placed the apple beside them. She made a hasty little prayer, then said, "I'll make something for lunch."

"Can we have soup?"

"Yes. But I won't be home for dinner, remember. I'll be late. Ten-thirty maybe."

"Okay."

Rose looked away from his food, averting her gaze on purpose. What you choose to see, Bo thought, and what you pretend not to see. He thought of the pieces of his past, and how he held them like photos, and the way they did not flow. The past lay in snippets, little nothings not adding up. He was picturing Rose in a doorway, somewhere. Where?

He whispered, "Mum, remember before?"

"I am lucky to have a bad memory," she said.

Then she smiled. It was nice when she smiled.

Bo said *housewife* when asked at school what his mother's occupation was, even though she never did anything remotely domestic if she could avoid it. She only did chores if they felt dramatic and interesting, or made a statement, like mayonnaise cheese slice casserole.

She looked back at his plate now. "Oh, Bo," she said.

His fork hovering between his plate and his mouth, the pasta screaming *Help* at him.

"It's for the dogs." Rose pointed at the failed dish. "Put it out for them."

"Okay," Bo said. Dogs wandered around in their neighbourhood in the mornings, their owners too busy or lazy to take them on leashes to High Park. If Bo fed them, maybe they would come by for visits more often. It would be like having his own pet.

Rose turned back toward her bedroom, saying, "Check on Sister when you get home." But he didn't need reminding.

Orange.

Bo's sister's name meant Orange Blossom in Vietnamese, so he called her Orange. Rose called her Sister. Orange was their family tragedy. The one they mustn't mention to others. Orange was unspeakable and unspeaking. She could not see very well and was all wrong, every part of her.

Bo barged through the front door and set the dish out on the lowest front step. No dogs were out. It was early though, and he didn't see even a squirrel.

He called "Goodbye" to his mother, then walked backwards—he had practised this—watching in case anything showed up. He moved east on Maria Street until he hit the corner, then he took a last scan for dogs and turned south toward school. It was a Catholic school, and because of the church group's generosity,

Rose had allowed Bo to be baptized so he could be sent there. She went to church herself, despite the fact of the shrine, and despite the truth, which was she didn't put much stock in Jesus. Rose put stock in gratitude.

At Dundas and Gilmour streets a boy named Peter joined him. Peter was Bo's friend from Dundas and Gilmour to Dundas and Clendenan, and down Clendenan until 86, at which point it was impossible to maintain the friendship. Ernie Wheeler lived in that little white clapboard house, so Peter lagged or sped up and occasionally punched Bo or yelled "Chink!" at him if he thought Ernie might be looking. The three blocks of friendship were worth it.

MR. MORLEY WORKED the track team hard. If a child got cramps, Mr. Morley ignored that child. Bo never complained. The easy thing with Mr. Morley was that it was unnecessary to speak much—you could be like a dog, or like Orange. By the slight flicker in the coach's eyes, or the edge of something like a smile behind his mouth, or the way his body leaned into the weather, Bo knew what Mr. Morley wanted and adjusted to please him.

Morley looked at his chrome stopwatch. "Three minutes." He meant three minutes to get from their yard to the high school racetrack. The team crossed the playground, then Clendenan, and went in through the chain-link fence to the track where they would do their laps. All the way, Bo tried to step so that he missed cracks in the pavement, for better luck. Now, he admired the shiny silver casing of Mr. Morley's stopwatch.

Mr. Morley held the watch high, clicked down the starter, and nodded at the team. They began jogging around and around the track. Bo controlled his breathing, felt the hardness of pavement tremor up his legs, and worked to absorb and soften it into propulsion.

A mandatory ten laps to stay on the team, but Bo did more. He lost count. He didn't care that this infuriated some of the other kids—the running removed care. Different things came and went from his mind: his mother, his father, sharks, Orange—her protruding eyes, and the way her body bent and twisted, and what she could be thinking. He wished he knew what she thought about when he was away.

Mr. Morley blew his whistle. Practice was over. An hour had passed inside the space of no time.

TEACHER DREW A wooden ship with a beautiful prow on the chalkboard. She wrote in cursive: *History*. She told stories about Cabot and Columbus. The one Bo liked best was a story about a boat with horses on it and how they eventually ran away and made all the horses in North America.

"Like Noah's Ark," said Emily.

"Yes, a little like that," said Teacher. She smiled at Emily. "Imagine how magical finding a new land must have been. I wonder if any of you has ever been in a boat on the ocean?"

Bo shrank down in his chair, but Sally stretched her hand skyward, like her shoulder might dislocate if she jammed it higher.

"Yes, Sally."

Teacher always smiled a little when she listened. Her bobbed hair touched her shoulders. He'd known her for a long time—since he and Rose had come to Canada— and he had to pretend he didn't know her all that well. It wasn't cool to know the teacher. Bo didn't know why this was, just that it was. But Teacher knew everything about him. He practised a neutral face.

Sally said, "We took the ferry back and forth to Ward's Island over the summer. Twice." Her arm stayed waving in the air as she spoke.

"Thank you, Sally. Anyone else?" Teacher tilted her head toward Bo. "That's Lake Ontario, of course, a ferry boat. A lake is much smaller than an ocean, and it has sweet water in it, not salt water. Most of the animals that live in a lake cannot survive in the ocean. They cannot master the salt." She looked directly at him.

She knew he had been in a boat on the ocean. She and ten other families had sponsored Rose and Bo to come to Canada. And even though her name was really Ann Lily, his mother called her Teacher, out of respect, and in his mind, so did he. And now, after four years, she was his teacher. Grade eight. He preferred not to think of that boat. Sweet water or salt water.

"Have you ever been on the ocean, Bo?" she asked.

Everyone knew already. It was the source of much of the ridicule he'd endured from the class and even from some of the younger children in the school. At fourteen, Bo should be in grade nine; he'd been held back in grade five to learn to speak and read and write in English.

Teacher said, "Bo?"

He stared into the middle distance, and answered. "I was on a boat on the ocean." He did not say that everything about the boat and the ocean shamed him. The memory of it was like a monster, but just the feeling of a monster, without the actual monster, so he couldn't fight it. That there was no actual monster made it much worse. The bad feeling settled in if he let it.

"Can you tell the class how it was?"

He knew she wanted only and very badly to make him real to the class, but adults didn't understand real. They understood nice and kind and the rest they tried to ignore. In this way, they were far worse than the children, who at least teased him about the rest. The odd thing about the teasing was it made him real to the other kids for the duration of the mockery. That might be the only kind of real he would ever have.

"I don't remember very much, Miss. It was windy some of the time. There were fish following the boat." In fact, he remembered everything about it. He lived those five days over and over, the looping horror of them.

"Oh, lovely," she said, stretching out the word, blinking, "and did you fish?"

"No."

His mother made him stay far back from the side of the boat because they were a waiting kind of fish. They were sharks. He'd seen how fast they took the dead when the living shoved them off the deck. The ocean housed another world you couldn't see unless it came to the surface, or where the water was very shallow.

When his father died, his mother asked one of the men to keep him below deck. Bo thrashed to get away but the man held him, until Bo was panting, furious. He had a right to see his own dead father. His mother told people—if they dared ask—that her husband had been lost at sea, but he was never lost. She *gave* him to the sea.

Bo's face must have showed some of this, for Teacher put her hand to her mouth, then changed the subject.

"Okay, class, eyes up at the front." She yanked a map down and picked up her wooden pointer. They named all the oceans until they could reel them off in any order.

It was a kind of apology, he knew—the class was lulled
by it. Teacher had a way of entrancing them: Indian,
Atlantic, Pacific, Arctic, Antarctic, Indian, Atlantic,
Pacific, Arctic, Antarctic. The class had the oceans memorized, but they did not really know them, did not know
the flat expanse of shimmer, did not know their boredom
and how they held the key to whether they might find
land and live, or just sail on forever, like some of the other
boats had, never to be found, the people dying one by one.

"Bo," Teacher said, finding her way again.

He'd been looking at his desk, and now he looked up
fast. "Yes, Miss?"

"Can you show us on this map where you lived?"

Bo preferred not to. But he got up and located Toronto
on the map. "Here," he said, and the class erupted into
laughter.

Teacher smiled. "Okay, but before, where?"

"Vietnam," Bo said, and traced his finger across and
across until he got there, "is here."

"The other side of the world, class. Bo, you may sit
down." Teacher began to pace down one aisle. "Vietnam
had a terrible war," she said. "And many people had to leave."

The whole class could feel that this was not part of the
lesson. This was something else. They looked into the air,
and some of them at Bo, as if he could stop her. The class
seemed to tighten—not just the children, but the walls,
windows, knotting around Bo. And still she went on.

"The U.S. wanted to stop communism and they did horrible things to fight the North Vietnamese Army. For one thing, they sprayed poison over their forests, and killed everything."

Teacher had stopped pacing and was standing halfway between the back and the front of the class, going on and on. From where he sat, Bo could smell her perfume. He stopped listening to her. He just smelled her, and tried to find space. He imagined the chalk and the chalk brushes and all the little things in the room hurtling toward him as if he were a magnet, and then, without him even knowing it, he whispered, "Stop," and she heard and looked down at him and seemed to awaken from whatever trance she'd been in.

"Class," Teacher said, through that tunnel of waking. "History lesson is over. Moving on to something very important." She unhooked the ocean map scroll and rummaged for another one, an old-times map that she pulled down, fidgeting until the locking system held. Smiling at them all, she pointed to Ancient Greece. "The play we are going to put on for this year's Variety Show in June has its origins in Ancient Greece. We are going to start studying this old story now because it fits nicely with our study unit *What Is a Hero?*"

There came a heaving groan from the class. It was a reaction to the words *play* and *Variety Show*. The class felt itself too old for plays, too old to be corralled into such a thing, even if secretly many of them loved both the idea of a play and the annual Variety Show. These students were smart enough to hide their enchantment. Teacher tried to rally them.

"The play will be based on an old *hero tale* from the Middle Ages, the story of Sir Orfeo." She plunked a mimeographed and paper-clipped stack of papers on the first desk—Emily's—and indicated she wanted them passed back. "By Monday, you will have read the poem, and memorized the first ten lines. It's a poem about a hero. It's a fairy tale. There's magic."

Everything changed about her when she said that it was magic. She looked beautiful. She didn't speak for a while, and Bo stared. He wondered what she was thinking.

"What's it about, anyway?" said Peter.

And she told them about how Sir Orfeo loved his Queen Heurodis, and how one day she had such a terrible nightmare while asleep under a tree in a garden that she ripped her clothing to shreds and also her skin. She dreamt a Fairy King kidnapped and stole her away to his fairy kingdom. Orfeo set up guards but it didn't matter—the dream came true. Anguished, Orfeo went barefoot to the forest and for ten years searched for her, playing on his harp to keep himself company. Orfeo loved to tell stories and sing, and even the animals came to hear him. One day, he spied Heurodis with a group of fairy ladies and even though he looked terrible after all that time in the forest, she knew him. He followed her to the Fairy King's underground castle and sang for the Fairy King. The Fairy King loved his songs so much he offered him any reward he wanted—and, of course, Sir Orfeo chose Heurodis. The King didn't want to give her back, but in the end, he relented. Orfeo and Heurodis returned to their land, were crowned, and lived happily ever after.

"Sounds retarded," said Ernie, so that only Bo and a few others near him heard.

Bo thought of Orange, and watched how Teacher's face lost its strange enchantment and went back to normal. She had not heard Ernie.

She said, "It's a very old story." And she turned her face a little away from them. "It has survived because people keep telling it."

It was as if some secret was hidden in her face that no one would ever uncover. He must practise not caring. Bo's shoulders lowered at the sound of the lunch bell ringing.

IN THE PLAYGROUND, Emily stopped Bo. "Why did Miss Lily say all that?"

Bo looked at her with only his eyes and not his whole face. Emily was too pretty to face. "Say all what?"

"About Vietnam."

"I don't know," he said.

"Come on. Yes, you do."

"I don't." But what he thought was that it was none of Teacher's business. She had once said to him that he ought to know about the war and where he came from, but her attentiveness felt like pity. It was pity. Bo said, "You never talk to me usually."

Emily shrugged. "Can I have the red tab from your jeans pocket?"

Bo knew there was a contest on, that if Emily could collect fifteen red tags from Levi's jeans she could cash them in for a free pair. But he was still surprised that pretty Emily would ask for his. His tag should be off limits, tainted in some way. He only had them from a donation bin at the church. Some of the other boys had dared the girls to twist and grab and pull them off the pockets while they still wore their pants.

"Sure," he said.

"I've got nine already." She handed him a small pair of nail scissors and watched as he tried to reach back and cut off the red tab. But he was awkward and people were now watching. "Forget it," Emily said. "I'll get it from you tomorrow."

Bo nodded, tucked the scissors in his pocket, and walked home for lunch.

Even the dogs had spurned the macaroni casserole. Bo left the dish on the stoop and went in the house. He ate soup with his mother, but they hardly spoke. "Thank you," he said, when he finished. Rose smiled at him.

He found Orange in her bedroom on her mattress, rocking. Her eyes were pushed so far out of their sockets, she looked Martian. He might look weird to Orange through her convex eyes, he thought, flattened out, unreal. He lay on the mattress and curved in toward her. He hoped this made her feel safe. She was four years old.

She had sailed over in his mother's belly. Bo imagined her in a boat—a tiny half-walnut-shell boat—in his mother's womb, dancing waves, skirting danger. Hurry, he thought. When she was born they had only been in Toronto a short while. It was winter, and cold, and he and his mother barely knew where they were—where the hospital was and where home was, or how anything related to anything else.

Orange looked like she was sneering, her body kicking back and forth, the momentum bringing her nowhere. He watched her twitch and rock. She sometimes pummelled the floor, and bashed at the walls. She hated. One of the new English words his mum and he had to come to understand was *monster*. And another was *pity*. Certainly none of the sponsor families had expected to be caring for such a hideous thing, had not reckoned on the depth of pity they might have to feel. Orange rocked such that Bo could tell she was moaning even though no sound came. Her rabbity head stretched out behind her, and her eyes were veined, wrong. There was nothing the matter with her mouth but her tongue wasn't right. The doctors predicted she would scream out of frustration, but she never did. Her shoulders pinched up too high and she was so skinny it looked like her body belonged to a different head. She had only thin wisps of hair falling over her forehead. He thought: ugly means when you don't love something.

"Orange!" Bo said. "Hello!"

Orange swivelled her eyes toward and around his face and then commenced rocking again. She lifted her arms and tucked her stumpy-fingered hands into her T-shirt sleeves and wound and wound them into the cloth. She slid down from the bed and turned and heaved herself to stand using only her crooked legs. Bo sat down beside her and waited to see if she would come to him.

It wasn't a good idea to try to handle her.

"Little Orange," he whispered, over and over as she rocked. He had only thirty minutes left in his lunch hour and he would like to pet her if she would let him. He did not look directly at her, but pretended to be picking at something on the bedspread. This sometimes worked as a decoy. Orange was now crouched to pounce. She looked mean.

Regularly, in catechism at school, there were stories

about healings and the miracles that Jesus performed and that the disciples wrote about in their books. There was the leper, the bleeding woman, the mute, and yesterday Teacher had read the story of the restoration of the dead man. Lazarus. He looked sad in the picture in the textbook. In all the pictures, the sick were pitiable and everyone was pleased to have them cured. Bo could never figure out if Jesus performed miracles out of grace or to prove that He was the Son of God. It seemed to make a difference, but this was never discussed.

The mute person and the leper were interesting, but once they were healed they were like everyone—a great sea of people all the same. He would like his father back, but surely a dead man's soul would not like to be sucked back into his body. If Jesus could make Orange a normal four-year-old, she would not be Orange. All of these thoughts unsettled Bo and he would have liked to ask someone, but adults hated to be asked questions they could not answer, so he kept them to himself. Sometimes when he was running at track, the answers came to him as feelings, driving right up from the earth through his legs to his brain.

Orange bit him like a dog. He did not like to think of her as an animal, so he shook his head to rid himself of that thought. She bit often. Her mouth clenched hard until blood sprang from his hand, and he sat very still until she forgot to bite and let go. The blood congealed right away, a small dribble along the teeth crease on his hand.

She slumped down now with her head in his lap, and lay there looking into nowhere. It must be strange to never be able to properly close your eyes. He wondered about sleeping and whether Orange could dream. Maybe all her life was a dream or maybe none of it was. Bo traced a finger over her ear. He could tell by the weight of her body against him how she felt. She was really lovely if you gave her the chance.

When he walked back through the house, he saw his mother staring out the kitchen window. "I'll see you after work," she said, but did not look at him. He must not notice his mother crying.

"Okay."

He looked at her through the glass once he was out-side, wondered if she saw him, and made a face. No. She didn't see him.

All afternoon, until track practice, Bo paid no atten-tion. He drifted.

AFTER TRACK, Bo found a quarter jammed in between two sidewalk paving stones. He slipped the quarter into his pocket and felt Emily's little folding nail scissors nestled in there.

He'd taken a different route home along Evelyn, which meandered in ways that did not seem to make sense given the landscape, but he liked it, and felt strongly, once he found the coin, that it had been the correct path for him to take. There was a caribou embossed on one side. The antlers were especially impressive. Bo wanted to take the money to the store and buy a popsicle but the scissors reminded him of the promise he had made Emily, and then promises in general, and then Orange, who had been alone for fifteen minutes by now. His mum left for work at four. He shuffled faster toward home.

ORANGE HAD COVERED HER FACE with a piece of flannel Rose had trimmed from a diaper, and was asleep, her breath lifting and collapsing her rib cage in a calm rhythm. Bo said, "Hang on." He spoke to himself.

He shimmied his jeans down as far as he could with his hands and then jogged his legs to get them lower so that he could use his feet and ankles to twist them off entirely. He scooped them up, found the scissors in the front pocket, and, holding the jeans by the tag, cut it off, then let the jeans fall to the ground in a heap.

He laughed, holding the red tag up in the air. He opened the little sheaf of cloth like a tiny book and turned it every which way. *Levi's*, it said, in black thread. He kissed it, whispered the name "Emily," and then shot a look at Orange in case she had woken up. She had not.

"Orange," he said, as he tugged his jeans back on. "Stay."

He wanted to bring Emily the tag and give her back her scissors. He told this to his sister's bent and sleeping body. He tucked pillows on each side of her. He did not want her to fall out of bed and hurt herself, and he thought she might like the feel of being hugged. Emily, he knew, lived on St. Johns Road in a huge Victorian with peeling gingerbread. The house looked haunted. Ivy swept up the red brick, twining along the arched portico, and a wooden veranda seemed to dangle off the main building. It was said there was a swimming pool in the backyard, an idea that frightened him. He would not go near the backyard if he could avoid it. He would be there and back before his sister woke up. He ran.

Bo could hear a flute being played. When he knocked, the music stopped and Emily opened the door. He handed her back her scissors and the red tag, and she thanked him.

"Do you want to come in?" she said. Emily had green eyes and a face daubed with freckles.

He did want to. "No," he said. "Was that you playing?"

"Yeah, my parents make me take lessons. They claim it's edifying." She thrust her hip out, and he didn't really

know what he should do. Finally, she said, "So what part
do you want?"

"Part?"

"Sir Orfeo? I'm trying out for Heurodis. All the girls
are." She struck a pose tearing her nails along her face.
"Well?" she said.

"That's pretty realistic," Bo said.

"I looked up the Greek story in *Britannica*," said Emily,
meaning the encyclopedias at the school library. "It's
old, like Miss Lily said. Orpheus—that's his name—has
to promise not to turn around when they are leaving
the underworld. He breaks his promise and in the end
he loses her forever. I looked it up," she said again, as if
he hadn't heard or believed her. Then, "Are you sure you
don't want to come in?"

Bo shook his head.

"Suit yourself," she said, and laughed. And when he
didn't leave, she added, "By the way, I am going to close
the door now."

"Okay," Bo said. He stood there until the door was fully
shut and even after Emily pushed her fingers through the
mail slot and waved goodbye, giggling. Even when she
said, "Really goodbye, this time, Bo," with a tone.

Only when the mail-slot cover clanged shut did he
bolt down the stairs and over to the corner store. He had
enough for Pop Rocks, and ripped the pouch open as he
left the store. He licked his index finger and shoved it

into the candy crystals and then into his mouth. It was wild the way they sparked along his tongue and up to the roof of his mouth. He decided to save some for Orange, and folded the pouch shut.

At home, Bo licked his finger and stuck it in the packet, placed the red and blue sugar on his tongue. He lay alongside Orange on the mattress and took the covering off her face. The little crystals took off pinging inside the dark space of his mouth. He wondered: was she awake or was she still sleeping? Either way she would watch this beautiful thing and it would be real or it would be a dream.

Over and over he dipped his finger and placed the candy onto his tongue until the surface of his tongue went first blue and red and then so blue it darkened to black. Finally, Orange made a gesture toward the packet, then toward her own mouth. And so he dabbed his finger into the candy, and onto her tongue, and watched her jolt about until she got used to it. Then she opened her mouth again, and he fed her more of the miracle of Pop Rocks.

What would he audition for when the time came? Certainly not Orfeo. That was a part for one of the other boys. He would offer to pull the curtain cords. He had touched them once before and remembered the way the silk rope slid through his hands, and how good it felt to pull and have the curtain respond. He could watch the action from the side, from the arch the curtains made over everything.

AT EIGHT, AFTER TRYING to get her to sleep for half an hour, Bo left Orange skidding across the bedroom, back and forth on her bottom. He set a doll and a stuffed donkey down for her to play with, but when he shut the door on her, she thumped against it.

"I have to go, Orange," he said. "Please!"

She thumped and banged as he left the house.

Now he waited at the corner of Maria and Gilmour, his fists stuffed in his pockets. He looked up and down the street.

"He's going to really give it to you this time." Peter had come up behind him, tall and gangly. "Maybe you should have stayed at home," he said.

"Why?"

"Ernie means it this time."

"Means what?" Bo said. Ernie never meant anything except the contact of his body on Bo's and the way that pain ricocheted back and forth between them.

Peter faked a left hook; his messy hair bounced a bit. Then he said, "Oof," and doubled over as if he had punched himself. "What if he kills you?" he said when he'd recovered.

Then I'm dead, thought Bo, and they'll have to deal with that. But Ernie couldn't kill him. He knew. He would let Ernie win before anything like that could happen. He'd seem to go wild and it would fool everyone.

Well, it would fool everyone except Ernie. You can't fool the guy you are fighting—the guy you are fighting can feel the fake. That guy, Bo knew, was the only one who really truly knew your capacity, or if not your capacity, he would know if you weren't full-on. Bo was never ever at capacity, and Ernie never let on.

Bo and Ernie had fought regularly since Ernie moved to the neighbourhood four years earlier. It occurred to Bo once when he was shadow boxing in his room that in some way, Ernie was his best friend, the human closest to him in the whole world. Bo and Ernie were addicted to one another.

Bo barely ever said a word to Ernie as they sparred and scratched and belted one another, but Ernie was a talker. They knew each other's moves, each other's bodies, their various smells. If they stopped, Bo would miss the fights. In fact he loved them, and by extension he loved the immense hatred Ernie had for him.

"Well, well, well," called out Ernie, "here you are." An entourage of children trailed behind him—some of them mimicking his walk and his particular snarl. What he said made no sense. Bo always showed up.

"Fight," one of the bystanders murmured, and then louder: "Fight!" The children herded them in, encircled them. "Fight! Fight! Fight!"

Bo shifted from foot to foot, not letting Ernie see which way he intended to swing or which way he might deke. Meanwhile he watched everything about Ernie, especially his eyes. The eyes always looked in the direction the brain planned to move the body, and they were fast—you had to pay close attention.

"You move like a faggot," said Ernie, and this brought snickers.

I move like a butterfly, thought Bo, thinking of Ali, though he knew not to say anything out loud. He reached out, cuffed Ernie on the neck, and then held on. This brought their chests together in a clutch. Bo had him tight and out of the corner of his eye saw that Ernie's face was growing red. He was trying to buck Bo backwards, but Bo had planted his feet and bent his knees, and he thrust into Ernie using his leverage and momentum.

"You dance, you hug—"

"Shh," Bo said. The talking. It drove him crazy.

"No, you little chinky fairy."

Ernie swung his arms up and around and tucked his head down, releasing his hold, and then grabbed Bo's waist and swung, nipping him from behind and toppling him. Bo's shoulder hit the sidewalk, his ear slammed down hard, and he was winded. He lay there huffing as the circle of children moved, forming again around the shifting fight. Ernie waited for him and then not. Bo saw his shadow first.

Ernie tried to roll him over and pin both his shoulders. But Bo tucked his toes into the road, imagined them shoved deep into the concrete, imagined all the force of the earth, every layer, even the molten core, anchoring up his propped legs, and then he used that force to buck his back and neck and head up into Ernie's. Ernie fell back and Bo rolled on top of him. The crowd whooped.

Now Ernie was beneath him, spitting mad. He tossed his torso to and fro, trying to unsettle Bo. Both boys slowed to catch their breath.

"Chink," said Ernie.

"I'm not a Chink," said Bo, but he might as well be Chinese for all Ernie cared. It was just a way to get at him. "Shut up. You talk too much."

"Boat Boy."

This hit home. Bo moved his forearm up under Ernie's chin and pressed in and down. "Take it back," he said.

"No."

Bo applied more pressure. "Take it back."

"No." Ernie's voice wheezed out—he was struggling to suck in oxygen.

He tried to edge one elbow out from under Bo's knee and Bo let him, feigning inattention. And then came Ernie's open palm at Bo's face and then the other palm, so that while Bo struggled to keep pressure on Ernie's windpipe, Ernie forced Bo's head back so that now neither of them could easily breathe.

It was as if, then, everything fell away. There was no space nor was there time and the two boys floated toward death. It did not feel so bad. But then Bo released his hold, lifted his body, and slammed it back down onto Ernie's midriff. He slammed Ernie's body again, felt it shudder.

Someone yelled, "Hey!"

The circle wavered and, and in that split second of wavering, Bo shifted focus—he let himself shift focus— and Ernie slid out from under him and with his leg, toppled him.

"Adult. Shit. Run!" someone yelled. It sounded like Peter.

Ernie leaned down, the sweat and stink of him enveloping Bo. He leaned so that his lips were almost brushing Bo's lips, so when he spoke, Bo not only heard the words, but also felt the puffs of air entering his mouth— Ernie's breath—and surely, Bo thought, Ernie also felt the warmth of his own struggling breath.

"Tomorrow," Ernie said, and he stood up, checked to see who was left to see, and horked on Bo's cheek.

Then Ernie stumble-ran away—Bo watched the wreck of him finding strength to just leave.

Bo CURLED OVER ONTO HIS SIDE, tried to catch his breath. He saw no one. He wondered if maybe Peter had fabricated an adult in order to stop the fight. Bo's nose dripped snot and blood. He hadn't noticed Ernie hitting his nose but it might have smashed in any number of ways. Bo felt his head for lumps.

A small pool of blood congealed on the pavement under his face. Bo wiped his nose with the tips of his fingers. His nostrils had already started crusting up. From where he lay, he could see clear down Maria to his house. Orange, he thought. For years, this fight had played itself out in one way or another. In a moment Bo would get up and go to see Orange. She would be asleep, he hoped. He had better get back before his mother got home. She did not like it when he left Orange.

"Up," he muttered, and heaved himself onto hands and knees.

Bo noticed the trouser cuffs of a man standing beside him. Beige dress pants. Bo looked up. The man's belt: black leather and almost worn out. The buckle displayed a nickel-plate grizzly bear head, roaring. The man's shirt was a blaring sort of white and reflected the street light so that it seemed made of sun, and his jacket was yellow and dirty, the shoulder pads sunken.

"You can fight," the man said, his hands on his hips, his head cocked.

Bo sat up on his heels, staring at him.

"Sorry," said the man, shaking his head. "I'm rude. The name is Gerry—Mr. Gerald Whitman." He shot his hand out and pulled Bo up to standing. "Golly," he said. "I would have thought you'd be bigger! What are you, all of ten?"

"Fourteen."

"Gerry. Please call me Gerry."

Bo nodded.

"You ever thought of making some money from that?"

Bo wondered what *from that* might be and the confusion must have washed over his face.

"You ever considered working in the circuit? Fighting? I can set you up."

"No—"

"What's your name, boy?"

"Bo."

The man smiled, his mouth shot full of decay and gold, and something else—happiness, goodness, times past, Bo wasn't sure—but he liked the man straightaway, and so smiled back.

"Well, Mr. Bo Jangles. What you may not have noticed while you were scratching and pummelling the life out of that shithole of an excuse for a kid, was that money was changing hands. Green was flowing." Gerry glanced up at the darkening sky, at the moon poking up in the east. He turned to catch a glimpse of the last of the orange orb of the sun sinking in the west. Then, he sniffed. "Moolah," he said. "I smelled it all the way from Dundas Street and Keele."

Bo squinted at the strange man. He *was* strange.

"Tall kid with glasses?" Gerry said. "He made a fiver off your loss. He would have made more if you didn't lose every time—"

Kid with glasses—that was surely Peter.

"Kids'll bet more risky if you win some, lose others."

Bo stared at him some more.

"Oh, you're wondering how I knew you lost on purpose? I saw you pull back, that's how I know. You were, what? Seventy-five percent, eighty? Holding at least twenty percent back, right?"

Bo considered the shininess of Gerry's shirt buttons. "I have to go," he said.

"Go, then," Gerry said. "See ya." He pulled a pack of cigarettes out of his jacket's inside pocket and tapped one out. Craven "A." Menthol. He looked up to see Bo still standing there. "The cigarette of choice for quitters," he said, smiling, gesturing with the smoke at Bo. "Don't ever start, Bo Jangles."

Bo said, "Nice to meet you," and headed down the street toward his house. Gerry's eyes followed him the whole way.

"It is approximately one hundred years since the end of the American War," Bo said to his sister. "I am Orange!"

He looked over to see her reaction. Gleeful—that was good. He was trying to cheer her up before Rose got home. It was a game he had played with her for forever. Not a game exactly, but a kind of storytelling. She watched more than listened, he figured. She loved it when he was animated, and he loved the words and the thoughts scrolling out of his head. It relieved him of them.

Orange was snotty with misery—he'd been away too long. "When the doctors caught me," he said, "they shrieked. The nurses shrieked, my mother shrieked, my brother shrieked, and so was I born amid shrieking." He could say what he liked because she didn't understand him. She gave no sign of understanding. "In the worldly hierarchy, I am below the vulture. I believe I may be below the dandelion, which is very low indeed. I have no earthly use. But do not worry for I am quiet."

Orange rocked back and forth on the bed but made not a sound. She wanted to hear what Bo was saying. He stopped to see what she would do if he stopped. She rocked for a while and turned herself toward him, so that her bulging eyes could—

"I am hideous!" he screamed, and her lips slid around like a smile. "I am ugly!" Her lips curled back, revealing gums and teeth, and there was her tongue plastered down and stunted. Even her tongue was bent. "Do not feel sorry for me," he whispered. "For I am powerful. I am the great-great-great-great-grandchild of chemical number 2, 4–D plus 2, 4, 5–T."

He flourished his hands like a conductor of a symphony. He leaned over her, for effect. "I am that which scares you the most," he said, his eyes narrowing. "I am the pure ugliness of love. I am melancholy. I am joy. I am the BIG MISTAKE you once made."

Orange swung her arms—fleshy cudgels—and Bo pulled back for fear of getting punched. The words were flowing. It felt fine to him and he continued, whispering this time:

"I am Orange, and I have a girlfriend. Her name is Emily and she loves me. I am Orange and she sucks in breath when she sees me. She sucks in one breath and pulls a tornado from me—she takes my roof right off." Bo stopped, his finger swirling the air, cotton candy, air.

Orange stood on the bed and put one foot in front of the other and did not fall. She did this two or three times and then threw her arms up above her head and bounced them back to her waist so fast she made wind. Was this walking?

"Orange, Jesus. Stop that."

But she wouldn't or she couldn't, so the arm-throwing went on for a long time before she slowed, panted back her breath, and fell in a heap. He lay beside her. Stared at the fancy toile wallpaper, its luxurious embossment, paper that had been put on the wall long before Bo had even known there was a wall here, so long that it had turned yellow, and brittle. There were sections torn right off, others peeling. But the images! Men on horses and women with parasols—there were centaurs and deer. In between them, over the years they'd lived here, Bo had drawn small shadowy men with big guns taking aim at the men on horses, at the women with parasols. The deer and centaurs frolicked all around them, oblivious.

A golden deer lay every few feet transfixed by an arrow and dying. "Little sister," Bo said, and carefully placed his arm over her, so as not to startle her even the slightest. "You can walk." He looked straight into her eyes and he felt like she must see him. She saw something.

He looked at the wallpaper again, entered its flat forest, traced his finger along the paths between the figures. He said, "I am Orange! I am ugly! I wander in the painted forest. So long has passed since the end of the war. The soldiers have all been forgiven! I am a princess now and I was a princess then. I wander in the forest of paint. One day I will be paint, too, and that day will be glorious. Even ugly things become beautiful."

He liked the feel of English words roiling around in his mouth, how you could build them up to make something that hadn't previously been there. "My brother rocks me until I fall asleep," he added, squinting at her, wondering if she would fall for it.

And then he did rock her and then she did fall asleep.

IT WAS AFTER TEN O'CLOCK when his mother pushed open the door to the bedroom and woke him. He'd fallen asleep beside Orange.

"Come," she said. "I warmed the soup."

Bo and Rose sat at the table and ate. She smelled of lemon floor wax and antiseptic and gin. She'd pulled a bottle from the space behind the dish detergent under the sink and poured some into her glass. Always between them there were questions, but never were these questions asked. For Bo it was as if the air thickened in the space between his thought and his voice. He could not ask about his father; he could not ask about the family they'd left behind in Vietnam.

"How was work?" he could ask.

A crazy woman died. First she went crazy and then she died.

"How was work?"

It was quiet today.

"How was work?"

I don't remember.

Every time he asked her this same question, it was a variation on these: Do you love me? Did my father love me?

The TV droned from the little living room—it went to test pattern, the volume low, dull static to keep them company—and his mother so tired. The trains punctuated time with their irregular passage—a loud clanging outside of himself. This was helpful.

"How was Sister today?" Rose asked, this question loaded with some awful truth Bo could not fathom.

It was said that children with severe birth defects, true monsters, often had shortened life spans. They could not expect to live to be one hundred, or even five, and sometimes not even one year old. A doctor stood beside Bo by his mother's hospital bed four years earlier, while Rose nursed Orange, when she was just born, and said this, with a tone that suggested relief, that suggested they might be happy to know.

"She walked," Bo said.

"No," Rose said. It was not a no of surprise, it was a no of will, as if Rose could stop this from happening. Her statement held such vitality, Bo's body shocked at it. He was not used to anything so forceful from his mother. Rose slumped at the table, always tired, so *not* right, with no expectation that happiness would ever visit her. She did not seem to think of it or else had given up on it. Maybe mothers did not require happiness.

"Yes, she stepped forward and backward on her bed. I've never seen her do that. It wasn't like my walk or yours but she was on her feet and she went like this—" He showed, with his fingers on the table, Orange's weird walking.

"Then she has walked." Rose closed her eyes, so deeply inside herself.

"Yes," whispered Bo.

Her eyes opened. "Sister may not go outside," she said, glaring at him as if he had taught her to walk. Had he?

Since she was born, he'd swaddled Orange and smuggled her out into the yard. It was a small transgression—even smaller if he considered that his mum had never actually said she had to stay inside. It was just that he knew Orange was to stay inside. And so he disobeyed. In the night, through the various stages of the moon, to the heartbeat of the trains pulsing through the backyard, he unwrapped her and let the night air breathe over her, let it whisper, let her know it. He looked at his mother. Of course she had seen.

He said, "No one else ever saw her."

Rose sucked air in through her teeth. "I don't want her to cause problems for you, Bo. It's already so hard," and then: "Sister walks."

Bo started to say something, but Rose lifted her palm to indicate she didn't want to talk anymore. She didn't want to think about Orange out in the world. She didn't want to think about Orange at all. Once she had called Orange the devil that came out of her body. She planted a picture in Bo's mind then of a deformed baby emerging from between her legs. Bo's mouth dropped open recalling the image. "I made you," she had said. "And I made Sister. You are both mine."

But now, she just looked over at him, weary-eyed, sad—his beautiful mother—and said simply, "No one must see her."

CHAPTER TWO

SATURDAY MORNING, Rose answered a knock at the door, and there was Gerry on the porch. Bo watched them from the kitchen table. Rose wore her blue cut-silk sarong, its worn spots almost grey. On top she wore a pink T-shirt and Bo saw she had no bra on. Gerry looked everywhere but there, which Bo understood to mean he had noticed too. Gerry was much taller than Rose so that she had to look up. Orange was asleep. Bo had already checked on her twice.

"How can I help you?" Rose said.

"Are you the mother of one Mr. Bo? I would like to talk to him." Gerry had a different jacket on, one with stripes, and he wore a huge bow tie the colour of trout meat. He put his hand out to shake Rose's, but confused, she bowed.

"Bo is sleeping," she said.

"I'm awake, Mum," Bo called from the kitchen, from where it would be easy for Gerry to spot him anyway. Of course she knew this.

"Bo Jangles," Gerry called, neck craning.

Bo came to the door, not sure what to say, how to bridge this stranger and his mother. But Gerry took over.

"Mrs. Bo," he said.

"Rose," said Bo. "Her name is Rose."

"Mrs. Rose," Gerry said. "I have a proposal."

He said he wanted to take Bo for the day. They'd drive west and north to Fergus. Gerry took a map out and showed Rose the exact route, even where they might stop for a gas-up and a doughnut. He outlined how he would feed Bo lunch and possibly dinner, how they'd be home by nightfall.

"Fighting," Gerry said, "but more *play-fighting*. Theatre."

Rose waved her hands as if to make him stop. "How do you know my son?"

"I met him just yesterday," said Gerry. "I thought he might want a job."

"I don't want Bo to fight."

"Well," said Gerry. Bo could see him thinking, *Too late for that, lady.* But instead he said, "You don't understand, Mrs. Rose. I'm paying him. Now it's true I can't pay him a full salary today, since he's just watching. But if he thinks he might want to work with me, he'll get more. It's a fine deal, and I wouldn't like for you to pass it up. Ten dollars for today—" And here he slid his wallet from the pocket of his trousers, pried the leather carefully open, wet his thumb with his tongue, and separated one bill out from the rest, making sure that Rose had seen the wad of money nestled there. "But double should he fight, and triple should he win. It's a damn fine deal." He stooped over her, and for Bo, the world seemed to wait. "My boss and me, we're looking for a more permanent home for the events, of course. Someplace classy, you know?" He seemed to think this might weigh in her decision.

"No," said Rose. Her cheeks twitched a bit and Bo did not know whether she was torn about the money, or upset to be reminded of his fighting. "No fighting."

"No fighting," said Gerry, mimicking, trying to figure a loophole.

Then, Teacher peered up at them all from the walkway: she had just appeared. "Is everything okay?" she asked.

Gerry turned to look down at her. "Well, hello!" he said. He took her in, glanced from Bo to Teacher.

She dressed differently on the weekends. She looked messier, younger. It was like she was two people. Teacher carried a placard upon which was written something about peace, and No Star Wars. Bo knew she protested down at City Hall or somewhere most every Saturday.

She had once asked Bo whether he knew that Canada had supplied the United States with the defoliant Agent Orange. She said it just like that: *the defoliant*. As if he cared. "Are you angry?" she said. He didn't know why he should be. "Your sister," she added, to be helpful. But Orange was Orange. Why would he be angry?

Gerry ruffled Bo's hair, then stepped down onto the sidewalk and extended a hand to Teacher. "I'm Gerry," he said.

"This is Miss Lily," said Rose. "She's Bo's teacher." She made a little bow toward Teacher and Miss Lily returned this in a clumsy sort of way.

"Teacher?" said Gerry. "Well, nice to make your—"

"Nice to meet you too," said Teacher, but her eyes narrowed. "Thao, do you need any help here?"

Gerry smiled wide at Teacher.

Bo said, "Mum?"

Rose looked down at the ten in her hand and frowned. "He wants Bo to fight." It was like she was talking to the money.

"Fight?" said Teacher.

"It's more theatre, really," said Gerry. He kept his body still and his smile so real, and his eyes shone. Then he cocked his head and said to Rose, "Forget about it." He reached for his ten-dollar bill.

Rose pulled it back, Teacher watching. Rose turned to Bo. "Be back by night. For Sister. Good day, Teacher."

She did not look back at Teacher as she turned away.

Bo knew she was ashamed to take the money. But she also did not want to be beholden, did not like to owe—they needed any money he might earn. Bo ran in behind her to get his shoes. His mother was slouched over the sink, running her fingers along the surface of the oily dishwater. She smiled at him, a tiny sad smile.

"Bring a coat," she said. "It will get cold." He wore cotton running shorts and socks to his knees. It was a warm day.

"I'm okay."

"Bo, it will get cold."

He weighed pleasing her, and then grabbed his jacket. He went to his room and came back with his school rucksack, put the jacket in there with a few other things he thought he might need.

"Be careful, Bo," she said. Worry veiled in worry.

He could hear Teacher's and Gerry's voices outside. "Mum," he said, "I am not fighting today. Don't worry."

Rose ran the kitchen faucet instead of answering, and handed him the ten-dollar bill.

"No, Mum."

"Take it," she said. "It's not mine. I don't want it." Owing was terrible, he knew.

"Okay." He took the money, stuffed it in the pocket of his shorts, and went outside.

Teacher's placard was leaning upside down against her leg. She blinked when she looked at him.

"Bo," she said. "Do you want to do this?"

He felt the money in his pocket, and said, "Yes, Miss Lily."

"Are you sure?"

Her asking made him feel more strongly that he did. "Yes."

Teacher looked at a small business card she cradled in her palm. Bo looked too. On it was the head of a bear with writing in fancy script: *Gerry Whitman, Carnival Proprietor.* Under that a phone number. Teacher nodded.

"Okay, Bo," she said. "Do you know what a collect call is?"

He did not. And so she explained to him how to reverse the charges, and how he should call her if anything went wrong and she would help. She looked directly at Gerry as she told him all this.

"Do you understand?" she said. It was as if she were asking Gerry, and so they all laughed when Gerry answered that he did understand. She wrote her number with a ballpoint pen on the back of Bo's hand so he wouldn't lose it. She told him to have a great day, and looked at Gerry's card again, then at Gerry.

"NICE MUM YOU GOT THERE," Gerry said, leaning forward to turn the keys. Bo grabbed the door handle and swung up. The height of the cab pleased him in spite of the fact his feet dangled an inch from the floor. He plunked his rucksack beside him, kept his hand on it. Gerry winked and said, "Nice teacher. Pretty too. She said if she were your mum, she'd never let you come with me."

Bo's tongue pressed at his teeth. He was too shy to shrug, not sure at all how to respond. "She's a peace activist."

"Uh-huh."

As the truck bumped down off the curb, Gerry's laugh suggested something Bo could not even imagine. To correct this, he said, "She saved my life. She sponsored us," wondering why he should feel the need to defend her.

"Nice work if you can get it."

Bo didn't know what to do with that either, so he stared at the windshield. The truck was a Chevrolet, greasy blue, with flecks of other colours so that it was also gold and purple and silver. Bo hunkered in the bucket seat—it was cream, cracked leatherette, seamed in four-inch-wide strips. The stick shift came out of the floor, and the whole cab reeked of minty smoke. The ashtray was open and full, the smelly butts of a deck of mentholateds stumped out there. Gerry navigated through the Junction toward the highway, and Bo felt the sideways movement of a swaying boat. Sometimes, his dad was everywhere. He worked to shut down that line of thought.

"You check out the box, boy?" Gerry jabbed his thumb over his shoulder to indicate the back of the truck.

Bo cranked his head to see a covered cage of some sort. There was a small tear in the canvas tarpaulin wrapped around the cage bars and he tried to see in. It was pitch black.

"What's in there?"

Gerry laughed. "You'll see soon enough," he said.

Something sparkled deep in a corner of the cage—eyes, maybe, but Bo couldn't be sure.

"How far is it?" he asked, and Gerry told him, so he settled into an almost-comfortable spot between the seat and the door, tucked his hands into his armpits, feigned sleep, and struggled and failed to stop himself from recalling the boat, always the boat. There was a girl huddled against her mother, younger than Bo by a few years, and she sniffled and cried the entire five days. He'd wanted to smack her for it. Later, in the camp in Malaysia, they became friends, played at hiding from the soldiers. At the end of three months, when Bo and Rose were about to leave, she ran up and gave him a candy twisted in a piece of plastic cellophane. He wondered how long she had saved it. He told her he would not forget her, but he almost had. He didn't like to think what had happened to her. He didn't like to think how she might have gotten that candy. He wished he was not thinking of this now.

Gerry turned on the radio and they listened to music. They drove west, the radio going over into talk shows and news and weather, until finally Gerry cleared his throat, reached in and switched the radio off.

"You got the change going, Bo Jangles?" he said.

Bo cocked his head at Gerry, confused.

"Your dick growing?" Gerry clarified. "You got hair? In your armpits and all that? You know what I'm saying?"

"Sure, I know," said Bo, to shut him up. Geez.

"Why'm I asking, you might ask?" Gerry laughed. "I'll tell you, Bo."

Bo shoved his hand into his pocket, felt the crumpled ten-dollar bill, and thought how he would not ever tell anyone this part.

Gerry switched the radio on again then off, reached over to the glove compartment for his Craven "A"s. He pushed in the lighter, waited for it to pop, and snuggled it into the end of the cigarette that sat waiting between his lips.

"I can't have no little boys in the ring, is what." His inhale was deep and full of knowledge. "You a virgin, kid?" He opened his window a crack and exhaled up toward the gap.

"Virgin?" said Bo.

Gerry crinkled his eyes against the smoke and broke into a cheeky smile. He looked directly and purposefully out the windshield. "You need me to break it down for you?"

Bo snorted and stared out in the direction Gerry stared.

"I lost mine at twelve," Gerry said, "to Amy, who was supposed to be babysitting. Well, I wasn't a baby, but she did sit." He burst out laughing.

"Lost what?"

"My innocence," said Gerry. He rolled his eyes like he was swooning and made a strange guttural sound.

Bo had not lost anything.

"Kid?"

"Yeah?"

"What's in the bag?"

Bo realized he was clutching his rucksack tight, and let it loose. "Nothing," he said, and then, "a camera." Teacher had given it to him. Bo had gone to her apartment one day when Rose was just home from the hospital with Orange. He could already speak a little English but it felt strange to hear it coming out of his body and he was shy. He followed her down the street to her place. Her walls were painted bright colours, and there were tapestries and paintings everywhere. There was no spot that did not hold some new object or picture to inspect. He walked around slowly and looked at her things. She had a typewriter and this fancy camera that lay on a little table strewn with photographs. The camera had dials and different lenses.

"Do you want something to drink?" she said. "Some Coke?"

"Yes, please."

She noticed him staring at the camera, so she showed him, letting him look through the lens. She pointed out how to focus, and how to set the aperture, the rate of light coming in. And then, "You press here." She put her own finger on the place. "I'll show you." She pointed the lens at him and twisted the dials on the camera. He heard the *click* when she pressed down on the button. "Now, you try," she said, handing it to him.

Bo rotated the dials until he could see the line of her face so sharply cut from the walls and the other things behind her. She wore lipstick.

"Hold the camera as still as you can."

He clicked the camera at the exact moment she put her hands on her waist and leaned toward him, laughing. And then he looked at the camera for a while, admiring its shiny casing. He loved the weight of it.

"Photographs," she said, "are absolutely marvellous, don't you think?" She riffled through her scattered pile and pulled one out. "Here's a funny one of me," she said, and handed him the picture. She was standing in a wide green field, except she wasn't standing, she was hovering off the ground a few inches.

"It's nice," he said. Teacher was wearing a pretty white dress with little lacy holes in it. "How did you do it?"

"Oh, it's magic," she said, and laughed.

He just blinked at her.

"Okay," she said. "I jumped." She jumped to show him and then they both laughed.

But still, it was a kind of magic.

She pointed to the camera, then. "Would you like it?"

There was a charmed waiting between them. He read the word *Nikon* in raised plastic letters on the casing. "Yes, please," he said, softly. He did want it. "I could borrow," he said.

"Sure," she said. "Or keep it." She emptied the film from it, and gave him some fresh rolls. She showed him how to load it. "I never use it," she said. "I have a newer one." She smiled. "Maybe you can make a photo album."

Weeks later she had given him the photograph she had taken of him, and the funny one, of her floating. Bo had taped them into his journal.

"You see that sign?" Gerry was pointing to a billboard for Fergus.

"Yes." It was huge. You couldn't miss it.

"Your life won't be the same after today," said Gerry. "After today, everything changes." And then he said, "Come to think of it, you might want to take a picture or two."

Bo moved the rucksack to the floor and pushed it behind his feet. He hardly had money for film, and processing was so expensive that when he finished a roll, he rarely could afford to develop the photographs. The finished film rolls nestled like secrets in a box under his bed, with his journal and a few other treasures he kept hidden.

THE TRUCK LURCHED INTO A FIELD, the trucks and trailers lined up in a makeshift parking lot. Gerry swung the truck around so the back end faced a cage set up there. Choking dust rose up around them as they got out. Bo pulled his rucksack onto his back, felt the soft thump of the camera against his spine. Gerry spoke to two men, gave them some instructions and the keys to his vehicle, and then put his arm around Bo's shoulder and spun him around to face the barns. People milled everywhere.

"Let's go look around, Bo Jangles. You ever been to a county fair?" And when Bo gaped back at him, Gerry said, "I didn't think so."

The tour of the animal barns never felt like more than a diversion, but just the same Bo enjoyed the stench of animal droppings, hay, oats, and straw, and he loved the costumes some of the handlers wore. The stockyards near his house were the closest he'd come to this, but there was nothing bucolic about the yards, just the baying of beasts sensing some awful approaching truth. He would return to the city, he would tell Orange, and maybe Emily if she would listen; he fantasized about this, smiled.

Eventually, Gerry led him toward a ring set in a grassy field, around which a large group of people had formed. Their chatter wound up to the sky. Bo couldn't hear a word, just talk-noise and the occasional sputter of laughter. A man in a striped jersey grinned in the corner of the ring—the referee. Beside him, a man in a silky housecoat hopped on his toes and then loped around the ring, gesturing to the crowd and roaring.

"Wolfman," said Gerry, squinting into the middle distance, something—love or respect—softening his face.

Wolfman beat his chest, and some of the people in the crowd—adults!—beat their own chests back, laughing, mocking. The fighter ripped his housecoat off his shoulders and let it hang from the tie at his fat waist, and there was his massive bare-naked chest, black hair already matted with sweat, and a belly round and hard. Downy hair started at his neck, went down across his back—he was so like an animal.

"Where is she?" Wolfman roared, spit flying. "I'm in a fighting mood." His housecoat unwrapped and fell as he pranced about, and he kicked it out of the way.

The crowd cheered, and Gerry said, "The thing to remember, Bo Jangles, is that all the world's a stage, and wrestling is no different."

Everything Gerry said seemed to have some laughter in it, some deep-down joke Bo did not get. He smiled in spite of this. He rummaged in his rucksack for the camera, thinking to take a picture of Wolfman, but Gerry saw him and tapped his arm and said, "Wait for it, kid," and pointed. Bunting decorated the outside of the ring, and a wide temporary ramp led up to it on one side, kitty-corner from where Bo and Gerry stood.

Bo wondered only briefly what that might be for, before the two men from the parking lot, now clad in shiny red underpants and wearing shiny red and silver masks, yipped like dogs to get the attention of the crowd. They stood in front of a cage and sprang the door open. And then Bo saw it poking out—a bear, its eyes alive and seeking.

The sparkle he had noticed cowering at the back of the darkened cage in Gerry's truck.

Gerry watched him, his grin cracking dimples in his cheeks. "That's it, Bo. Now you begin to see."

The beautiful creature came out scenting the air, its nose sky high. Bo's first bear. And what a fine thing. The creature was three and a half feet or so at its back, he figured, and up to his own neck. It took its time lumbering out of the cage, stopping to scratch itself—a place on the rump rubbed raw to the skin. The wrestler was not so hairy after all, for between the matted fur of him, Wolfman's awful pink skin showed through. Bo felt suddenly repulsed at the vulnerability of that skin—it was miserable, miserly even, compared with the bear's coat, its shagginess, the refined swirls of hair along the beast's muzzle and down its chest.

"Wow," Bo said. He watched the bear through the lens of Teacher's camera, struggling to find the perfect frame, while she moved, and shook herself out, and moved again. That ripple of fur when she shook. Bo tracked her beauty.

"That there's Loralei," said Gerry. "Girlfriend to many, lover to few."

"Loralei," repeated Bo. The name sounded like a song.

He shifted as close to ringside as he could and snapped another picture. The bear turned to face him. He let the camera hang from its strap and just watched. She rubbed and rubbed at the outside of the cage and seemed not to notice that anyone else was there. And then, she bounded directly up the ramp and into the ring. People began tossing drink cups, fistfuls of dandelions, anything they could grab. The referee yelled down at them and held up his hands. And then it was like in church, that stillness that can come over a crowd looking up.

"Usually the trainer is required to hold her by a chain," said Gerry. "Just in case. But Wolfman is special, see?" Gerry rolled his eyes. "His courage knows no bounds."

The announcer now repeated this exact same thing through the crackle and feedback bleat of the cheap microphone, and Gerry said, "Now you watch carefully and earn your ten dollars."

Wolfman circled Loralei, taking time here and there to throw the garbage out of the ring and make fists at the crowd. "Don't mess with my bear," he yelled, and, "Leave my girl alone!" Loralei was nosing a weed someone had thrown at centre ring when all at once Wolfman bumped his chest against her side and grunted.

The bear rose onto her back legs and settled on her haunches, twisting about to take in the view, the smells. Gerry waved to her, his hand partway up and the wave noncommittal—a signal maybe, thought Bo.

"Howdy, Lora," Gerry whispered.

Loralei came to her full height and Wolfman reeled back and fell, from the sheer shock of it, it seemed to Bo. And down she came over him, the skin flaps at her armpits stretching like wings. The great stench of her wafted out into the audience as she worked to pin Wolfman.

"Whoa!"

People reeled, the magnitude of her body odour hitting them in waves. But the referee leaned in close.

Under the bear, Wolfman squirmed and bellowed, making jokes the whole time: "Let me on top, girlfriend! How is this polite? This ain't right."

Bo felt he would need a lifetime to sort out all he was seeing and feeling as he watched this.

"Look at her now," said Gerry. "She's smelling us, and everything else—french fries, wieners, that nice lady there."

It was hard to believe the bear could smell anything over her own stench, but Loralei rolled her head back and around, taking in the scents the crowd gave off, her body rocking a bit as Wolfman tried to slip out from under her, and when that failed, tried to buck the huge creature off.

Bo recalled his last fight with Ernie. *Feet*, Bo thought, *feet*, but it was too late. Loralei shifted to the side, her front paw now holding Wolfman, and sniffing, always sniffing. She rotated so that now she was back to front, pushing her great dreadful butt into Wolfman's neck. The crowd went wild.

Wolfman was struggling for breath. His arm was caught against his own chest, which meant he was surely not choking from much but the odour—he had built a bit of space between himself and the bear. The crowd was now laughing hysterically, and Bo saw Wolfman's face show astonishment then indignation then fake pleasure. What *was* this?

"A show," said Gerry.

Bo moved so he could see better what the crowd was laughing about. Loralei had pulled back, her great paws on either side of Wolfman's legs and her face nestled in between them, the pink of her tongue curling in and out of her mouth as she licked his crotch.

"It's honey," Gerry whispered behind Bo, then leaned in. "Loralei has a penchant. She loves honey."

"Honey?"

"Yeah, he's smeared down there with it. The crowd loves it."

People sobbed from laughter, tears streaming. Wolf-man's eyes rolled up in his head. The great bear licked and licked, would not stop licking, her leg muscles rippling whenever she dug in for more sweet. Bo supposed a bear would lick anything covered in honey, so what was so funny about this? He frowned—Gerry caught this.

"Come on," he said. "Not so serious, okay."

Bo shrugged. He felt sorry for the bear, who had no idea what was going on and was just enjoying the sweetness.

Gerry heard him thinking so hard, and said, "People laugh at whatever makes them uncomfortable. It's the surprise of it that makes them laugh. See the referee, Bo?"

The referee had made his eyes big and was jerking his face up and down, to the action, to the audience, apparently incredulous at what he was seeing, and also apparently completely incapable of stopping any of it.

"Barry Gillis, a has-been and an also-ran. Bit-part actor, can't get a job for love nor money these days so he plays the circuit. Crap in the movies, but look at him. Lord, just look at him."

Bo did. Barry had taken on a tortured look, as if the bear were doing to him what she did to Wolfman. Lora-lei had now grabbed the edge of Wolfman's underpants between her teeth and was suckling on them.

"Stop," Wolfman yelled. "Geez, stop her, ref."

Gillis stood up, faced the crowd, shrugged. He mimed that he had no idea what to do. The announcer chuckled into the mic, then said that Wolfman should have opted for the chain and trainer after all.

Bo saw it then.

He watched Wolfman's arm separate itself from the jumble of body and creature, his hand clenching something. Bo saw the hand unclench off to the side, beckoning the bear. But the Wolfman's feet and legs told a different story, and the ref, with his antics, covered for him. Wolfman's lower body found purchase on the mat, just as Bo had against Ernie the day before. This created the sense that with leverage, the body of Wolfman could overcome the body of Loralei. It couldn't—of course not—but it could appear as if it did. Wolfman bounced, forced himself into a crowbar stance, and grunting, pushed hard. For those attentive enough to see, and few would have been, the hand jostled and cajoled, some treacly smell enticing the bear toward it.

Wolfman timed his jounces so that when the bear lifted, it seemed as if he was responsible. Loralei now looked, to the stupid, as if she might be eating his hand, as if she might tear him to bits. The referee danced around, fake-grabbing her collar and pulling, working the decoy role. She twisted against him and faked him right back, throwing her head and stabbing her paw at him, and in faux fear he stepped back and back into the ropes.

"You see that?"

Bo nodded.

"I saw you seeing it, boy. You'll make a fine contender, you know that?"

"I saw everything," he said. "What was in his hand?"

"A blueberry Pop-Tart."

"She likes that?"

"It's Loralei's favourite."

Bo grinned now, watched the crowd react. "I like them too."

After the Wolfman was free and the Pop-Tart all gone, the bear did not want to go back into the cage. She bustled around the ring several times, lapping the perimeter, and Bo recalled track and field, and wondered what that would be like with a bear—who would win, could he win? She ran rolling from the back legs to the front, her gait a fluid canter. The crowd yelled and shrieked at her but she did not seem to notice. Her eyes now looked dull, her gaze inward.

Gerry swung himself up over the rope and held his arms out, murmuring gently to her. "Loralei," he said. "Loralei. *Hmm . . .*" The hum was a thin dark song coming from his throat. She stopped running in circles and made a slow turn around him and then came closer, him murmuring the whole time.

"Loralei," he called. "*Hmm.*"

She stopped, nuzzling into him, under his arm, begging him for a pat. Gerry scratched her roughly behind her ear, the soft purr of his words seeming to calm her, drug her, and she rocked against him. It reminded Bo of

Orange, only her small self could never topple him as Loralei seemed about to do to Gerry—the bear leaned on him like he was a tree and he pushed back for balance.

Gerry laughed at her antics, and she tossed her head up and pulled her lips back into a grin. Could bears smile? And then Gerry held aloft his arms and waved them. She responded by moving in the direction of the cage. It was clear she wasn't happy about this trick of his but didn't feel powerful enough to contest it.

She lumbered to where the two masked men stood, and when they unclasped the ropes, she walked down the ramp and into the cage, where she was rewarded by another Pop-Tart. Bo watched her from the opposite end of the ring as she turned and turned and turned, seeking some comfort, before she landed and curled in a ball.

It was—strangely—her stench that enticed him. She smelled of nothing he had ever smelled. Bo approached, pushing through the now-dwindling crowd until he was beside the cage, beside Loralei. He moved his hand toward the bars, and had it pulled away. Bo hadn't noticed the strange man behind him.

"She'll take your fingers, kid." Wild black hair flew in all directions from the man's head. He wore a fitted suit, which shone, and had on the pointiest-toed shoes Bo had ever seen. He was holding a bowler hat in his hand. He was handsome, Bo thought, like a movie star, and there was not a spot of dirt on him despite the dusty field all around them. The man's eyes regarded him and he never blinked once.

Bo tucked his hands in his pockets. Gerry was already next to him.

"What's up, Bo?"

Bo looked at the man who had reprimanded him and then back at Gerry. "I wanted to pat Loralei."

"Well, go ahead." Gerry fielded a look from the man. "Caged, she wouldn't hurt a fly," he said, more to the wild-haired man than to Bo.

"Jesus," muttered the man. "I don't want to see it." He put his hat on and scissor-walked away, shaking his head. He didn't look back until he was past the crowd, and then only briefly.

"Who was that?" Bo asked.

"Ach, it's just my boss. Never mind." Gerry turned to the bear. "Loralei? Meet Bo. Bo, Loralei."

Bo pushed his fingers into the bear's shoulder. The oil coming off her fur was so strongly scented, Bo gagged a bit and laughed when Gerry caught him.

"A rose by any other name would smell as sweet," Gerry said. The bear got up and began to pace around her enclosure until she came to face the two. She scented the boy, nose vibrating. "Look at her. Watch her nose go. She's learning you."

"Where did you get her?" Bo thought if he knew, he could maybe get one too.

"Found her. Taught her everything she knows—didn't I, Lora?" Gerry reached in and scratched her chin.

"Found her where?"

"Never you mind. She's my girl."

Bo had known this from the moment the cage opened. Loralei was Gerry's bear. You could own a bear, Bo thought. Own it and train it up. It was a wondrous thought.

"She was the sweetest thing. She came lolloping into the world with my heart on her sleeve. Watch this." He lifted his arm and Loralei sat to beg. He snapped his finger and she poked her snout out of the cage and made to lick him, licking the air near him instead.

"Neat," said Bo.

"She'll do most anything I want her to do."

Behind them, a crowd had gathered again. With his chin, Gerry indicated the ring, and Bo looked up, away from Loralei, to see two masked wrestlers now grappling, hands clawing and sliding along each other's huge, greased-up torsos. It was the men who had let Loralei out of the cage earlier, the men from the parking lot, Bo now saw.

"Tweedledee and Tweedledum," said Gerry.

"What?"

"One as stupid as the next. But they can move."

Gerry jammed his index fingers in his mouth and whistled. One man held the other man and, squatting slightly, heaved and lifted him so he hung upside down. Sweat rolled along the hanging man's sternum and dripped onto the mat. The holding man shook his opponent, once, twice, three times, and then threw him to the side and watched as he clutched himself in what must have been agony.

"Real-life twins," Gerry said.

Yes, they were twins. Staring at the wrestlers, Bo leaned on the cage having forgotten what was in it, but Gerry was watching. He laughed even before Bo felt the wet tongue sliding behind his ear and jumped away, gasping.

Gerry patted Bo's shoulder. "She wouldn't hurt a fly once she's caged."

"Will she fight again today?"

"After the main fights, I offer the crowd a go. You'll see something then, Bo. A lineup of idiots paying to fight her. Paying good money."

Bo held his hand up for Loralei to lick, trying to grab hold of her tongue. It was a game he'd played with the neighbourhood dogs, which they liked. Maybe a bear was a little like a dog. Loralei eye-rolled just like the dogs, and stuck her tongue out for more. "Let me fight her."

"No."

"Why not?"

"You're not ready."

Bo said, "You said she wouldn't hurt a fly. Please."

"It's twenty minutes I could be earning money. No."

Bo searched around for something he could offer, but there was only the crumpled bill in his shorts pocket. "I can pay—"

"I'll pay." The voice came from behind him, and Bo turned to look. It was the boss whose clothing shone. Those shoes scared Bo a little. "I'll pay to see the bear fight that kid." The money was already thumbed out of the man's wallet. A twenty and a ten.

"Max," Gerry said, waving him off.

"My money dirty, or what?"

"Jesus," said Gerry, but he took the money and nodded at Bo. "Take a walk, Bo Jangles, and get your mood on. I don't want to see you for a while. Come back in a couple of hours. Loralei needs a nap."

"You'll let me?" said Bo. "Really?"

"Go." Gerry made to chase him, but Bo didn't stick around, didn't want any minds to get changed. The fur, he thought, the fur right next to him.

Bo walked without caring where he was heading, just away so that Gerry would not have a chance to call him back and cancel. The midway sugar nestled into his nostrils, cotton candy swirling there just as surely as it swirled around its paper hub. Bo jostled through lineups for the bumper cars, the Ferris wheel, the merry-go-round. He did not think these were for him.

He perched on the rail of a steel fence designed to keep a queue in check, no one lined up behind it. The ride looked busted. A thin boy stood behind it and off to the side. Bo picked a bit at the chipped paint on the rail, blue over yellow. The boy did not seem to mind him being there and so he settled in to watch the surge of young people vying for this or that ride, arguing, gossiping, whatever they were doing. It was about ten minutes before the shiny man, Max, was in front of him.

"I like your moxie," he said, extending his hand. Bo did not know what this word meant, and the man must have guessed. "Your bravery," he added.

His hand was firm and warm, a good handshake. Bo had never seen a man with more perfect eyebrows. They looked almost pencilled on.

There was a brush of cloth or skin up against Bo's back. The boy guarding the ride had come up behind him. "Mr. Jennings?" the boy said.

"Yes, sir!"

"My name is Keith. I want to say thank you. I run the whirligig." He gestured to the ride behind him, added, "When it ain't broke."

"You're welcome, Keith, though I do not entirely know for what."

Max let go of Bo's hand to shake the hand of the other boy.

"You own the whole fair, I think."

"Well—"

"The freak show is pure genius, sir."

Max nodded curtly at the boy and muttered, "I prefer the term 'sideshow.'" He tipped his head at Bo indicating he should follow him, and left.

They walked for some time, wending in and out of the teens, the mothers, the small children, the dads, in behind a tent that held the bingo.

"Don't mind my home," said Max, pointing to a silver trailer. He opened the door and ushered Bo into a strange plush living space. It was upholstered in soft red material, even on the ceiling. "I live here on and off," Max said. "My real house is sometimes too far to drive home to. Sit down, sit down!" He gestured to a red Formica table that was bolted into the floor. "For the record," he said, "I did not start the so-called freak show. The freak show has an ancient history, of course. Lazarus Colloredo and his twin John Baptista must take full credit. They made a fortune, even if they could neither move very fast nor entirely enjoy the gifts of wealth. They were joined at the waist, young man!"

Max's voice mesmerized Bo. Bo had no idea what Max was talking about but he wanted to keep hearing that voice. He sat at the table watching Max's fingers dance while he spoke.

"Can I get you a drink, kid? A pop or something?"

"Yes, please."

Max pulled a ginger ale out of the tiniest fridge Bo had ever seen and plunked it down on the table. He stood there smiling at Bo and scratching his neck. "I do like your moxie, kid."

Bo pulled the tab on the pop can and took a sip. "Thank you," he said.

"I meet a lot of kids looking for work," Max said. "I tell them to go home to their mommies. But you? You've got something. A little glimmer. A spark. And Gerry says you like to fight."

This was not true. He did not like to fight. He just did it. "I've never fought a bear," Bo said.

But Max was not listening to him. "That teenager at the whirligig? I'll fire him this afternoon. Calling it a freak show. The audacity. I curate. I am a curator of humankind." Here he waved his hands about and hit the tips of his fingers on the upholstered ceiling of the caravan.

Joined at the waist—Bo pictured something terrible. He sipped the cold pop and waited for what would come next. He took in the space—the blood-red interior—a miniature home, with a kitchen; the eating booth Bo sat at was like ones he'd seen in diners in his neighbourhood, but smaller. Through an open door down a short corridor, he spotted a toilet. The place smelled of bacon, and Bo realized he was hungry.

Max said, "I do not—ever—call it a freak show. People deserve dignity, don't you agree?" He was now rummaging in a drawer. Pure propulsion, he seemed to Bo. Max muttered, "Dignity at any cost." He pulled out a sheaf of papers, glanced at it, put it back, rummaged some more and pulled out another, smaller batch of papers. "Gerry and I would like to give you a contract," he said, frowning a little. He leaned down, his eyes very large as he met Bo's stare. "Now, I want you to look at it and think about it before you sign it. A contract is serious—it's a very serious document."

Bo nodded. He wished he had some idea what this man was talking about, and looked at the paper for clues. The contract said "Jennings' Magic and Carnival Enterprises Unlimited" at the top and there was the bear-head design from Gerry's card right underneath.

"I'd like to see you fight first, of course," said Max, "but do have a read-through."

Bo stared up at Max—at his hair, that smile, and the eyebrows—and then when he began to feel rude for staring, he surveyed the walls, the many framed photographs screwed to them so that, he supposed, they did not whip about when the trailer was in motion. He focused in on one of them. A boy not much older than he was, with another person growing out of his stomach.

Max followed his gaze and intercepted his thoughts. "The handicapped are simply differently gifted," he said. He caressed the frame of one of the photographs as he spoke. "The bearded lady is a scientific phenomenon! The cod boy, half-human, half-fish, is billed unfairly— for he is perfectly at home in the water. These are humans, not freaks. I call them"—and here he again flourished

his arm, this time careful not to bash the ceiling—
"curiosities!" His voice had gone very low. Max grinned
into Bo's face, and drew his finger along the words in the
contract, where Bo was to sign. "Who are we to judge?"

Bo shook his head, then focused on the colour photograph to the right of Max's head. It wasn't more than half
a foot square. He tried to identify what it was. A jar full
of something curled into itself, pink, fleshy, limbs locked
around it.

Max followed his eyes and pointed at the picture.
"This?" he said. "A true oddity, isn't it."

"It's—"

"A fetus," said Max quietly. "With an abnormal
growth, see?"

"What's—?"

"A stillborn human monstrosity. The hospital would
not sell me the thing itself, just allow me to arrange for a
studio photograph of it. No matter. I found another,
better specimen. I've made a hallway of photographic curiosities as well as the specimen jars. It is one of the fair's
most popular attractions. Also, inexpensive for the peep-
ers. A cheap thrill. We plan to expand the operation—
more of it and better curiosities—and, well, we're hoping
to get the Canadian National Exhibition concession for
next year. I tell you, kid, it's looking good."

Bo's eyes were still on the photograph. "A baby," he
said. It came out of him like a sigh.

"Well, no." Max pulled himself up tall. "Technically not. A baby," he said, "would be alive, of course. Naturally."

"Orange." Bo thought he'd only thought it, and was surprised at the thick silence gathering in the caravan.

Max had stopped moving and was squinting at him. "What is orange?"

There was no air in the trailer. "Nothing," said Bo. He looked down at the contract. "Can I take it with me?"

But Max wouldn't let go. He cocked his eyebrow. "Tell me, really," he said.

Scanning the room, Bo now noticed one horrific photograph after another. The tallest man next to the shortest woman. A boy with three thumbs. A child whose face looked like a dog's, all fur, and sorrow. A man with breasts. A woman with a beard. Some other awful thing he couldn't quite understand. What was all this? Who might love these? This was what the whirligig operator had meant by "freak show," what Max had called a sideshow.

Bo got up from the table and said, "I better be going. Thank you for the ginger ale."

"Wait, kid," called Max.

The trailer door swung out and Bo stepped down into the grass. The camera in the rucksack banged against his back and the thought of taking another picture made him sick. He was glad to be outside. The air in the caravan had been too still, and out here it was so crisp. How lost in Max's voice he had become.

"Sweet Jesus, I'm sorry. I've frightened you."

Bo turned back to see Max's face squished between the closing door and the aluminum trim of the doorway. He had forgotten the contract inside and now was too shy to say anything about it.

"The bear," said Max.

"Yes."

"She's a southpaw. Watch her left hook."

"Thank you."

"And boy?"

"Yes?"

"It's all a show, you know that, right?"

Bo nodded. He had certainly heard this enough today.

"Because if you know that, you will always, always, be safe."

Bo stared up at Max, and there behind him, glowing on the wall, was that dead baby. It couldn't be normal that people *liked* to look at these things, would pay to look, but when he considered that Gerry had said that people laughed at what troubled or surprised them, it made some sense.

"My sister," he said, like a pin dropping.

"Your sister?"

"I guess she's a so-called freak show." He was figuring this out himself in that moment. "It isn't right to show them like that."

"Kid," said Max. "I'm sorry—"

But Bo pulled the door wide and then slammed it as hard as he could in Max's face to let him know what he thought of his freak show. The caravan wobbled on its concrete block foundation, and he heard Max inside yelling, "Hey, hey."

The feeling of telling Max about Orange—the brazen feeling Bo had got—dissipated the farther he got from the trailer, until his running became a walk, and his breathing calmed to normal.

Bo queued for a hot dog and had already slathered it with ketchup when he heard Max behind him, apologizing again. He turned to find him sweating through his lovely jacket.

"I'm so sorry. I have—clearly—offended you. Your sister. You must love her very much." It was hard to tell whether this man was kind or evil. And in the space of thinking this, Bo heard: "And may I ask?"

Max crooked his neck and made his eyes soft. "What's wrong with her? In what way is the poor thing handicapped?"

Bo plunged the end of the hot dog into his mouth and took a huge bite, stood there glaring up at Max, chewing, chewing. "Bad," he blurted through the food. Max was shaking his head, as if in sympathy. And then, Bo saw how blue the man's eyes were. They held such clear intention.

Max smiled. "I could meet her."

Bo wiped his face with his sleeve. He said, "No

thanks." Rose would never allow it, for one. And second, there was no way he wanted this man seeing Orange.

"Listen, call me Max, would you?" Max flapped his jacket to air his armpits. "Kid," he said. "Look, how bad off is she?"

"This is—" Bo wanted to say "stupid" or "ridiculous" but couldn't find the word straightaway.

Orange was bad, Bo thought, really bad if he compared her to the freak show pictures on the walls of Max Jennings' caravan. "She's a monster," he said. "And not for sale."

Max looked affronted. "I wasn't offering to buy her," he said. "The curiosities have *contracts*, child." He went thoroughly red in the face. "Well then, what about a photograph? Fifty? Seventy?"

"No," said Bo. No photograph.

"Come on, boy. Everyone has a price."

"No."

Bo pushed back through the midway to find Gerry. Once he got to the ring, he saw a huge man clad only in sparkly blue trunks prancing around the ring with his arms aloft, hands fisted, chanting, "Me, me, me," and another man slumped in the corner covering his face in a cape fashioned out of a Canadian flag and rocking in exaggerated lamentation. Watching took Bo's mind off Max. His eyes followed the ruckus in the ring, but when Bo slowed his thoughts and pulled his gaze to waist level, he saw men opening wallets, men accepting money, nods and shrugs. Green flowed. He did not know exactly what it meant, but he knew that Gerry saw in him a green flow.

Every so often the sad wrestler lifted his eyes to watch the huge man, then launched into another bout of crying. This the crowd loved. They shook their heads, yelled, "Come off it, get over yourself." Bo overheard someone say, "He ain't called the Clown for nothing, eh?" And then the wrestler who had lost the match unwrapped himself to reveal the dregs of face paint melting off his cheeks and a rubber nose hanging around his neck from an elastic band. The Clown.

The announcer peered from the ring into the audience. "And now it's your turn, people! Who here is a ninety-eight-pound weakling? Who here has something to prove?" On the other side of the ring, Gerry rubbed Loralei's neck, latched the chain to her collar.

Look at her, Bo thought, she's beautiful.

The announcer swung the mic around and around, grabbed it and crooned, "Prove your strength with the lovely Loralei! Who's gonna be the first nutcase?"

The bear scrambled up the ramp, Gerry restraining her with the leash. Bo thought of those Junction dogs lucky enough to get walked to High Park, dragging their owners. The bear did not seem to know she had a person attached to her. But no, Loralei scented back; her nose danced to the left and right to track Gerry. Bo saw this. He thought back to his first sight of her, her butt-scratching anxiety, and knew she felt safe. She trusted Gerry hanging there at the other end of the leash as she joyously dragged him along.

Bo thrust his hand upward, as the other children sometimes did in school, eager, pumping, stretching his arm to the sky. As if he knew something. He did. He knew he had to cling to the bear in the ring, find her spot, bring her down. It would not be so much a fight as a play fight, a show.

"You Chinese?" The announcer queried over the mic, over the ropes. "How much do you weigh, kid?"

"Ninety-eight pounds," Bo said. "Exactly."

"You couldn't hurt a flea."

"I fight every day at school."

This brought waves of laughter. Someone patted his head, and one young mother with a baby in a stroller said, "The poor—" but did not finish her sentence before she began to shake her head.

"The bear'll eat him," someone yelled.

"Good riddance."

"Aw, nice talk."

"Little nipper, step back." A man in a ripped T-shirt and jeans pushed Bo to the side, trying to get the attention of the announcer. He seemed to think the battle would be between Bo and him. He hopped, jabbed at Bo. "I'll fight the slant. I'll fight him."

"Shut up."

"Drunk," Bo heard someone mutter. And the man in the ripped T-shirt was. He reeled around to smash someone, anyone, but the reel was too far, too fast—dizzy, he stopped to bend and vomit.

Gerry hugged Loralei in such a way that it appeared as if he were forcibly restraining her. But the bear looked almost bored, sniffing the midway sugar and salt combination.

The announcer shot a look at Gerry. "What do you think?"

"I don't know."

"Me, me, me!" Bo tossed his arms up as he had seen Wolfman do earlier. He stomped widening circles from his spot at the ropes until he had a space in the grass roughly the size of the ring itself. He dropped the camera and rucksack to the ground beside him, began to beat at his chest and rip at his clothes. If he had to get down to his underwear to get his fight, he would. Then he roared, and the announcer, wiping tears of laughter from his eyes, turned again to Gerry, who only shrugged and half smiled.

"Thirty dollars, kid," the announcer demanded.

But Gerry called out, "Forget it. The kid fights for free. Come on. Look around you."

An immense crowd had formed, double or more the size it had been, pushing toward the ring. The referee pulled Bo up by both his arms and into the ring, set him down in the corner, draped him with a housecoat, squirted water down his throat, swiftly massaged his shoulders.

"Geez," he said, shaking his head. "I dunno, kid." Then he slipped into centre ring to begin officiating.

Bo watched his own feet lift his body up off the stool and jig him around the bear. He ran giddy in the circle, thinking of Ernie, back in the Junction—who would, pathetically, fight *only* him, while *he* would fight this immense beautiful thing. The pleasure of it overwhelmed him. When Gerry sent him a signal, he held his fists up and hopped around the ring, roaring at the people, white knee socks flashing, mimicking what he'd seen on Saturday television.

The announcer's voice was so smooth: "Our own Little Nipper, folks! You saw it here first." He shook his head in mock incredulity, wiping a non-existent tear from the edge of his eye. "I love this kid already, and so do you. Don't you, folks!"

Gerry dropped the chain at Loralei's collar and stood back, keeping a grip only on the leash handle. Loralei did not move from her spot in the middle of the ring. She simply sat and watched Bo as he leapt from foot to foot, gesticulating at the crowd and at her, leaning in sometimes to test the extent of her calm, to test her ability to just sit and wait.

The more tempestuous men in the crowd began to insult her now, yelling that she was chicken. Then more joined in. Their derision caused a shift in the crowd, and all leaned in now and yelled. They wanted to *see* something.

"Give him a slap, Loralei," someone called.

"Give us a show."

"Give 'er!" yelled someone else, and people laughed, breaking the tension, and this is the moment when Bo bounced against her.

His whole weight meant nothing to Loralei. So he yelled, "Hunh!" and threw himself at her chest again and then once more. It was like running into a furry tree. He luxuriated in her smell. The awful stench reminded him of the melting spring earth in parts of High Park, of the raw of unwashed body. Loralei lifted her right paw then and drew Bo to her, sat back on her haunches, and clasped her other paw over the first.

"Well, I'll be darned," crooned the announcer.

She hugged him, the referee circling in wonderment.

Bo scissored his legs like he was running, but they were an inch or two off the ground so he ran in vain. And then Loralei lifted her great hulk and began a slow upright walk around the ring, Bo clutched to her.

Bo felt the space there between the bear's arms and his own body. He clasped onto her neck fur tight and faced her as best he could. Then Loralei released him in a heap on the ground and tried what she had accomplished with Wolfman, but Bo saw it coming.

He twisted right and got to his feet, got behind her and pulled on her shoulder. She tipped, and then she was on her back, rolling. He took the opportunity to kneel on her belly and pin her arms and legs as best he could. Strange to straddle a bear—he tried to imagine it was Ernie as she writhed back and forth, which did test his imagination what with the smell and the glinting fangs.

She held back, he knew. She pulled her punches. She was letting Bo win. Bo glanced over at Gerry at the end of the chain and caught the wink meant for Loralei. She pretended to struggle while the referee counted to ten, and Bo pretended to hold her. Then it was over, and the bear went to Gerry for treats, and the love of the crowd washed over him.

Bo was a star.

The referee held the squirt bottle and let him drink. He was parched. The water went over his face and down his body, washing away some of the bear fur stuck to his sweat. "Good work, kid."

The thing was over before it had really started. But still. Bo looked out into the swarm of clapping people, and there was Max Jennings, smiling, shifting a wad of money from his fist to a money sac on his belt.

ON THE WAY BACK, it was quiet for a long time in the truck. Bo knew Gerry was pleased, not angry, and that the quiet was contentment. He looked back through the cab window at the bear, trying to spot her through the tear in the tarp. He knew he could not see her but he looked anyhow. He hoped Loralei would notice him checking on her.

"She pulled back, Gerry," Bo finally said.

"She's five hundred pounds, Bo Jangles," Gerry replied. He shook his head, once, and smiled at him with his eyes. "I pulled her back."

"How?"

"I trained her. Like I said, you can train the wild out of most any creature if you get it young enough."

"The chain, then."

"It's a prop, is all. The people in the audience feel safer if she's chained. The truth of the matter is that if my darling wanted to, she could bound right off the chain and I'd never see her again. She doesn't follow the rules of the chain. She does what I want. She looks at my hands. She can read most any signal I give her by now. She's four years old." He grinned, and added, "She's all mine."

"Where do you keep her?" But Bo was thinking, how do you keep a bear? And more, how might he keep one?

"She lives in the yard by my house. Outside Grimsby."

Grimsby. It sounded so desolate, like in a horror movie. But "in the yard." That you could keep a bear in the yard, he thought. That was marvellous.

"Grimsby," he said.

"She's staked. On a rope. She has her own kennel. She's comfortable."

The truck hurtled down the highway toward home, images whipping past him—trees, rocks, signage, the flit of deadfall—Bo imagined a beautiful bear walking in circles in his backyard, a groove forming under her as she satellited the hated peg.

"That guy Max—"

"What about him?"

"I don't like him."

"Well, he's very unlikable but he pays the bills."

"He's really your boss?"

"You could say."

"So he owns the fair?"

"He owns the sideshow, and that's a lot." Gerry looked over at Bo. "Hey," he said. "What did Max Jennings say to you, anyway?"

"Nothing," Bo said.

"He told me to give you this." Gerry opened the glove compartment and pulled out a stack of papers that turned out to be the contract Max had showed him earlier. Gerry handed it to Bo, and said, "Me and Max are both hoping you'll sign on for the rest of the fall season."

THE FOLLOWING DAY, coming out of church, Father Bart stopped Bo. He bent down to whisper, "You took something, Bo."

It was true. He had slipped an extra Host off the plate at communion. One had melted on his tongue, the other was by now likely crumbled in his pocket. He took one regularly for Orange.

"I'm sorry."

"Stealing is very serious," said Father. "Stealing from the church is especially sinful, of course. Where is your mother?"

Father Bart knew very well his mother did not linger after mass.

"She went home before Communion," Bo said. "For my sister."

"Please tell her I need to speak to her. She'll likely know what I want. It's urgent." Father Bart pursed his lips, then let out a long breath and seemed to relax. "Why did you take the Host?"

"For Orange."

"She isn't old enough. You know this. She has not received the Sacrament."

Bo went back into the church to stand in front of the crucifix. He said three Our Fathers and two Hail Marys, which was in excess of Father Bart's suggested atonement. The priest said he wanted to make Bo fully aware of the mortality of the sin he might commit if he did not atone for this one. Sin was a slope, slick and irresistible. While Bo chanted the prayers, he thought of Loralei—how she smelled, how she'd hugged him, how easily she could have killed him, but that she had not.

"You understand," said Father Bart, when he came back out into the glinting autumn sun, "every one of our actions has a consequence."

"Yes," Bo said, and Father nodded down at him.

Mercifully, when he reached home, the Host was intact. He placed it on Orange's tongue, said, "The Body of Christ." She stood, rocking to keep her balance, her butt stuck way out, her legs bent, her feet far, far apart. She stretched her mangled tongue out as the Host slowly fractured and dissolved there.

Bo watched, wondering for the first time whether her ugliness might have a value. It was strange to consider it. After Bo's bout with Loralei, Max had sidled up to him to whisper, "I would pay for a decent photograph. I'm serious, kid. Good money."

Good money. What was bad money?

CHAPTER THREE

I T WAS MONDAY and Teacher stood at the board in white pants and a white blouse, a strip of shiny black belt slicing these. A chalk drawing of a man in a sheet took up the full height of the blackboard beside her. He carried a little harp shaped like a tulip. A strange animal stared at him from the third blackboard—three enormous dogs' heads, the fangs sharp and their mouths open. The animal was so huge, Teacher had run out of blackboard near the top. The class chattered.

Bo huddled Loralei in his mind, the fight, the fair. He'd signed the contract even though he hadn't understood all of it, and he'd got Rose to sign too. Then he'd tucked it under his mattress in case Gerry ever came back for him.

"Sit down, children." Teacher waited until they hushed, then began to tell them about how this man Orpheus had lost his wife Eurydice when she was bitten by a snake.

"This is the Greek story! I looked it up," called out Emily. "It's the story *Sir Orfeo* is about, right, Miss?"

"Yes, Emily. It's an old, old story. I wanted to tell it to you." Teacher walked back and forth in front of the class. She got more animated if they paid attention, as if they had fed something in her. They were all soaking up the story—and watching her. She pointed to her drawings like they might come to life. Bo imagined her pacing back and forth at City Hall with her placard.

"Everyone has a talent," Teacher said. "And Orpheus's talent was singing. He played this lyre, and he sang beautifully. When Eurydice died, he was so very sad that he went to the underworld—"

"That's like Hell," said Emily, and Teacher hushed her.

"The Greeks believed the underworld to be a very treacherous place. Orpheus had to traverse a dangerous roadway, and cross a river with a ferryman named Charon, and somehow pass by"—here she pointed to the animal she had drawn on the board—"this monster named Cerberus."

"A monster?" blurted Bo.

"Yes, Cerberus is also called the three-headed dog. Orpheus sang it to sleep."

Bo shrank down in his chair. Teacher came to stand over him. "Maybe the dog was not as bad as he looked," said Bo. He was thinking of Orange, and of Max wanting her for his sideshow. His face crumpled, and when Teacher touched his shoulder it was too late—tears came. Bo watched Ernie scribbling a note that would be passed to Peter and on through the class. This was who Bo was, a boy made up in the stories of others. He tried to think only about the weekend and how he had fought the bear.

Teacher bristled beside him and stared at Ernie. And then back at Bo. She had seen something transmitted, not the note but the idea of the note.

"Ernie and Bo," she said. "I want to see you both in the hall."

Ernie glared over at Bo. The rest of the class raised eyebrows, giggled.

Teacher followed the two boys out and shut the door behind her. They stood ready to hear Miss Lily's reprimand. She crossed her arms and was silent for a good long time. Bo looked up into Ernie's sneer. It would be better to fight than to just stand here.

"I want your help," Teacher said, finally. She looked to Bo and then to Ernie. "Actually, I need your help. We will be viewing a film."

"Miss!" Ernie's eyes lit up.

"Hush," she said. "The film is on a reel in the A.V. room, and so is the projector. I want you two to go to the A.V. room and fetch the projector and the reel. Bo, I want you to hold the reel. It is rented and needs to be returned in perfect condition. Ernie, you will roll the cart with the projector on it. You will not twirl, or spin, or ride on the cart. Do you both understand?"

"Yes."

"Do you know why I asked the two of you to do this?" she added. There was clearly a trick in this question.

"Yes," said Bo, hoping to stop her.

"Tell me."

Bo shook his head fast. He did not know at all.

"Ernie?"

"Because you can rely on us?"

"No," she said. "I most certainly cannot rely on you. I asked you because I want you to work together. I want you to cooperate. Do you understand?"

They both nodded. Bo did not know what Ernie thought but he thought that he would never be able to work with Ernie, and that to have to do this small errand with Ernie was already worse than the torturous silence of Teacher. But still, a film—they would see a film.

"Teacher's pet," Ernie said as soon as Teacher had gone back in the classroom.

"Shut up."

"Did she buy you right off the boat?"

"She didn't buy me. Nobody bought me."

"That's not what I heard."

Ernie and Bo arrived at the A.V. room, located the projector on its brown steel rolling cart. The reel came in a beautiful green round metal box, clipped together at the sides. It was like a huge shoe-polish tin. A piece of masking taped across it read: *Toys, Grant Munro, 7 minutes, 46 seconds, 1966.* Short, Bo thought. But still, it was already a perfect thing carting a real film down the hall, along the terrazzo floor, carefully avoiding stepping on the steel grouting between the tiles.

Ernie jumped on the lower shelf of the cart and pushed with one foot, riding it until they reached the classroom door. "Don't tell," he said. It was an order not a plea.

When they entered, Teacher was saying how the most important thing about the two stories—Orpheus and Sir Orfeo—was the risk they both took in going down to the underworld to save someone they loved. This was their heroic deed. "Over the next weeks, we will speak more about this story, but for now, I wonder if anyone can tell me what makes a person a hero?"

Ernie's hand shot up, which surprised everyone. "Someone who sings dogs to sleep," he said, and many in the class laughed.

"Very funny," said Teacher. "But children, really, what makes a hero a hero?"

"He's someone who loves so much, he does valiant deeds," Sally offered.

Bo watched the back of her head, the perfect part of her hair, and the long brown braids, one on either side.

"Yes, class. Did you hear what Sally said?" Sally's shoulders softened and her back straightened.

"Yes," they answered together, grateful for Sally's answer. The class breathed out a breath they'd been holding hard. They looked toward the film projector.

"Sally, you get the lights, please, and, Emily and Peter, pull the blinds down."

Teacher was now leaning into the projector, squinting, trying to find the right feed. "I'm fitting this film in before the lunch bell, but really it is part of the history lesson. I would like you to think of heroes when you watch it, please." She was nervous about working the projector and the class loved her more when she was like this, a *real* human, like them. "I think it goes here," she said, fiddling with the film.

"It goes in there, Miss," said Bo. He showed her the right slot in the receiving winder. She smiled at him in a way that made Bo forget for a second that she was his teacher, and he smiled back. He was glad they weren't talking about monsters anymore.

She hit a switch and said, "Now sit back, class."

The theme song, full of trumpets, rolled over them. There were little kids in the film watching a museum display of toys. Laughing. Suddenly the toys began to do things, and the children laughed harder. Then there were G.I. Joe dolls in camouflage. They were just dolls at first, but then they began to move, doing what soldiers do, and the children in the film became serious, because now they were watching a war through the display-case glass.

Teacher stopped the film and asked, "What is happening?"

Bo heard Emily say, "The children's imaginations are coming true."

And Teacher said, "Good," and let the film run again, and now the G.I. Joe dolls killed one another, a jet dropped bombs, there was a river of blood, and the movie-children stared and stared.

Bo swallowed, and held his breath. For him it was memory.

Teacher began to speak over the credits.

"War," said Teacher. "Why do we have war?" The film flapped against the reel and someone turned the lights on.

Bo sat very still and tried not to blink. He sent his mind to wander in Orange's blue castle. He fought knights on her behalf, and then he ran and ran around the track, and thought about Loralei and smelled her and fought her again and again, and in this way he stopped himself from listening to Teacher and the class speak of war. Then it was quiet, and Teacher was looking at him and he realized they were alone.

"The bell rang," she said.

He got up and gathered his things.

"Bo," Teacher said, as he was about to leave.

"Yes, Miss Lily."

She was biting her bottom lip and looking worried. "I'm sorry," she said. "It's in the curriculum."

"Okay." Bo nodded, but he felt sick. He had to get home to Orange. But he could see that Teacher wasn't done with him.

"Remember I once told you where I worked before becoming a teacher?"

He did. Her summer job for two years before teachers' college had been in a chemical plant that made Agent Orange in a small town outside Toronto. "It doesn't matter," he'd said.

"It does matter. It's important for everyone to understand that their actions have consequences. War is bad."

Bo turned away. He thought of Father Bart saying this same thing to him about stealing the Host. War is bad, he thought. But war also made Orange.

"I have to go take care of my sister," he said. "I'm sorry." And Teacher just nodded.

BO'S MUM HAD ALREADY LEFT for work when he got home and Orange lay on the floor of her room splashed in her own vomit.

She slept, her breathing thick with mucus. He lifted her so that she would not wake, put her on the mattress. He washed the sick from her cheeks and from the wispy hair near her ears. Vomit congealed inside the curl of her ear too, and he took a damp cloth and wiped it away. When she was tidy and he'd cleaned up the mess on the floor and made sure she was peaceful, he called the hospital, asked for Rose Ngô. It was some time before she picked up.

"Mum, it's Bo."

"Bo," she said, and he could hear surprise in her voice. "Why are you calling me? What is the matter?"

"Sister is sick, Mum."

"Tell me what's wrong and I'll bring some medicine home."

"She's very sick. I have to go back to school, Mum. Her face is all red and she's burning hot. She needs to see a doctor."

"Bo, no," said Rose, and here she switched to Vietnamese. "No more doctors, Bo." She hissed this into the receiver and then she hung up the phone.

Orange didn't wake up when he propped the window open, or when he tucked the sheets around her to try to keep her in one place until he got home. The whole house stank of sick. Before he called the hospital a second time, he watched Orange's flushed face, the red only making the shape of it more marvellous and strange. His mother would not come to the phone, and the Muzak infuriated him so he hung up. He wiped Orange down once more with a cold cloth.

"Sorry, Orange. I have to go."

TEACHER SAID, "Take out your copies of *Sir Orfeo*. How many of you read the poem over the weekend?" All of the girls put their hands up, and a few of the boys.

Bo saw that Ernie did not raise his hand, so he decided it would be better not to admit he had read the poem even though he had read it through twice. When the time came, he would vie for the role of the Fairy King, who said almost nothing except "Truly it is so / Take her by the hand and go / I want you to be happy with her!"

Then they began a reading, going around the class taking turns until the entire poem was read. It took almost the whole period, with Teacher stopping here and there to ask them questions. She wanted them to understand everything about the poem and its story so that when she rewrote it as a play, they would truly enter the spirit of it. "A play is a little piece of magic," she said. "If it's done well."

Emily had her hand up.

"Yes, Emily," said Teacher.

"In the Greek story, Orpheus has to promise he won't turn around when he leaves Hades. But he does. He turns around to make sure Eurydice is there, and she dies again."

"That's right."

"Why doesn't that happen in *Sir Orfeo*?"

"It's a really good question," said Teacher. "I don't really know. No one knows. But one thing is true. Whenever someone retells a story, bits get added and bits get lost."

"I like this version better," said Emily.

Teacher said, "Me too."

When they were done reading, Teacher doled out parts, the class's anxiety and excitement pressing them into one great feeling. A boy named Michael had got to read the Fairy King section and had said the lines with such conviction, Bo had no doubt who would be King. He thought again about working the curtain, how pleasant that would be.

Several of the girls cried when Emily was picked for Heurodis.

"And I've given the role of Sir Orfeo to Bo," said Teacher.

The class fell silent. It was like Bo had entered a shadow. His classmates could not see him in this role. They would not. But Emily's face lit when this was revealed.

"It's a play," said Ernie, to snap her out of it.

"Obviously I know that," she said.

The class erupted into laughter, and then chatter, and Teacher let it get wild.

Bo looked at Teacher. "It will be too many lines, Miss," he said.

"It will be a challenge," Teacher said, tilting her head and smiling.

"I don't want the part." He had said it louder than he meant to, and now the students quieted and looked at him. It was as if they had never considered he might want or not want anything.

Teacher sat on the edge of her desk and gazed at them all. "I gave you each a role that I think will be good for you. That I hope will help you develop into good adults. I've given a lot of thought to this. I also want you to know your character so that as we study the poem and its history this term, you will come to know these characters even better. That will happen as we begin to look more closely at the Greek myth of Orpheus and compare some of the stories, and the people in them."

Peter's hand shot up.

"Yes?"

"Ernie and I play a tree."

The class burst into laughter again—even Bo laughed, careful not to catch Ernie's eye.

ERNIE HELD BO'S LARYNX with the palm of his hand, shoving him again and again into the gym wall. Bo strangled as Ernie whispered, "Orfeo, Orfeo, Orfeo." They were in gym class, and Mr. Morley was late. Peter watched like they were on TV, his eyes glazed, entranced.

Shut up, Bo thought. He hadn't wanted the part. He slammed back with his torso, pushed Ernie away long enough to adjust his position, make himself less vulnerable. He made like he was recuperating, then rammed his head into Ernie's stomach, pushing through and, when Ernie fell, landed astride him. He pinned Ernie's arms to the ground.

"Jesus," said Peter.

Mr. Morley's head appeared just above the horizon of boys—his tawny hair, some of which he had already lost, and a blush of angry pink rising on his face.

"What's this?" he said.

He sentenced the whole class to ten minutes of fast laps. Mr. Morley sat on a chair in the middle of the gym until they were done. He went from visibly furious to calm in those ten minutes, and when he called for them to stop running, they came to him, panting, out of breath. He gestured and they understood. Bo expected to be sent to the office. He wondered if Ernie would be sent too.

"Today," said Mr. Morley, "you'll learn to fight properly. Peter, twenty push-ups for blaspheming. Bo, get the mats. Ernie, help him."

"Cobra Clutch!" someone squealed.

"Wrestling," said Mr. Morley.

They hauled out an old mat set, pieced this together in the middle of the gymnasium. It was a bull's-eye, a huge dartboard laid out on the ground. There was something ceremonial in setting it up, amplified by Mr. Morley's quietness.

"This is an old sport," he said. "The rules have evolved over centuries." He showed them how to enter the wrestling arena, how to shake hands. "No oil, no sweat." He dried his own arms with a towel. He wore an undershirt and shorts. "Next class I will bring singlets."

Morley kept his feet apart and held his hands out with palms to the sky. All the boys found their positions. "Okay, Ernie." When Ernie stepped toward him on the mat, Mr. Morley wrapped his arms under Ernie's armpits and came in for a hug. His head tucked into Ernie's shoulder. He shifted his back foot in beside Ernie's front foot, so that his feet pinched Ernie's and held them in place. "I pull my body weight into the ground," he said. "And sit back." Mr. Morley flung his head back and twisted then, still holding Ernie, so that together they arced back, flying and then falling, with Ernie somehow landing on the bottom.

Anger contorted Ernie's face, but it subsided almost before anyone noticed. He laughed. "Cool move," Ernie said. "Do it again."

Mr. Morley moved off the mat, nodded to Bo. "You," he said. He blew his whistle when Bo hesitated.

Bo took his position on the mat, his legs wide and solid, his hands ready to take Ernie's hands.

"Bo," said Mr. Morley. "Let him take you the first time."

Bo let Ernie curl his arms under his own, tuck his head down.

"Feet," said Mr. Morley.

"Oh, yeah." Ernie slid his back foot forward, held Bo's locked, and sat, throwing his head and shoulders into a twist.

Perfect. Bo sailed, and was pinned, breathless.

"See, boys. Greco-Roman wrestling. Counterattack? Anyone know?"

Bo put his hand up.

"Bo."

"Keep your weight deep down, lean to the opponent's outside foot, and when his weight follows, drop and roll."

"Okay. Maybe. Try it."

So the boys locked again, but this time when Ernie shifted to throw himself back, Bo sank and pinned him instead. Mr. Morley smiled.

He had each boy in the gym class try to make the manoeuvre. "No throw. You are to stay upright. Feel your opponent's vulnerability. Feel it, and act upon it."

For forty minutes the class of boys attempted to perfect this. The boys took turns on the mat, half listening for the thump beside them, turning to see who had mastered whom. Bo imagined throwing Loralei, the bear arcing across the mat, flailing fur, even though he knew it wasn't possible.

Rose was home—early—and Orange sat in the kitchen sink, frothy suds billowing around her. She slapped the water when she saw Bo so that it crested over the sides and onto the linoleum. She was too big for the sink but Bo knew she was too much for his mother to handle in the bathtub.

"Shh, Sister. She likes to splash." Rose was drunk, the only time she could be so lovingly fluid, so motherly. Her body swayed.

"Thank you for coming home, Mum."

"How was school?" she said.

"Good."

"What did you do?"

"Nothing."

Rose put her head down on the counter, let Orange splash her. She said, "I gave her medicine to bring the fever down. Hopefully she'll be better tomorrow. I wonder if she ate something bad. Did you feed her anything strange?"

"No," he said.

A Host, even if you were not consecrated into a Sacrament, could not give you a fever, Bo thought. It was only flour and blessings. But if God was angry there was no telling what He might do. He was erratic. You never knew what He would like or dislike. If God sought vengeance it would be upon him, though, and not his innocent sister. *If she died*, he thought, and then he stopped himself thinking. She mustn't die. He would pray for her tonight, tell God that if He killed Orange, He'd lose Bo's faith.

"Help me," said Rose, and Bo lifted Orange's tangled red body out of the sink.

She did not want to get out, and kicked and thrashed. She liked to make sounds, smacking flesh against the water, ugly music. She made a wet mess of Rose, who laughed at first and then got annoyed, and finally spanked her, holding her with one fist and hitting her on the bottom with an open palm, so that the sound mimicked Orange's own music. Orange's little mouth rounded to scream but nothing came out, though Bo knew she screamed with all her body and soul. He saw small pustules along her legs.

"What's that?"

"It will heal, Bo. No doctors, right?"

Bo said, "I will take care of her." He had to stay calm or Rose might turn angry, he knew. Or start crying. She had already started crying.

"Sister needs to eat," Rose said.

Bo said, "I'll dress and feed her."

His mother's face flickered with emotion when she handed Sister over: disgust and misery hidden behind stoicism. Pity mixed in there too, which he could stand even less than disgust. At least disgust did not pretend to righteousness. Orange had come out of her body. It was this creation that formed the disgust, he knew. If it had been someone else's child, his mother might have had more compassion. As it was, she simply hated herself for making this. And he hated her for it too, a hate mixed with love.

"In the forest . . ."

Bo whispered up close to Orange's malformed ear, bent into her as she rocked herself to sleep. "In the forest you are a princess. It is a beautiful forest—yes, all blue and white, made entirely of paint—and in it there is a grand building. It might be a castle or a palace. For many it looks impossible, all brush strokes and colour. But you live in the palace and are famous for living there.

"There is a horse just your size and you ride upon it. It is also blue and still smells of oil, as if it was just created by the artist, just for you. Your horse is named Bucephalus and it is upon this horse that you carry out your greatest deeds. For you are endowed with superpowers. You are a hero."

He would write about Orange for his assignment What Is a Hero? He would write about how daring it was for her to allow herself to be born, and maybe Teacher would understand about Orange, then.

"Once there was a man riding through the forest who came upon you. He thought you the most hideous creature his eyes had seen. He called you 'loathly.' The loathly lady." Bo was stealing from King Arthur but he didn't care. Stories wanted to be stolen.

Orange stopped rocking to listen.

"It was Sir Gawain. Another one. A future one," Bo said. "He did not know your powers. He found you seated on a log in the forest and asked your hand in marriage. You thought it was a joke!" Bo looked up at the ceiling and then around the room, stopping here and there at the scenes on the wallpaper. "And then Sir Gawain kissed you," he said, and turned to kiss Orange.

She flailed her arms, wildly, so he caught them and held her. He looked right in her eyes. "He kissed you and you stayed just the same."

AFTER ORANGE HAD FALLEN ASLEEP, Bo found his mother at the table, asleep over her evening tea. Bo woke her by gently touching her back.

"Bo," she said.

"Go to bed."

"I need to talk to you. That man Gerry made me nervous. What if you get hurt?"

"I won't get hurt. And maybe he won't come back." Bo wanted him very badly to come back.

"Remember, I need you." She wrapped her arms around herself.

"It's not real fighting, Mum. It is like a show except there are some people in the audience who don't realize it's not real. A person could only get hurt if they made a mistake. And I won't."

"Bo—"

"Mum, it's like a puppet show, nothing more than that. If I make enough money, you can stay home. You can take care of—"

He stopped because she had got a look in her eye. He had wanted to say, *take care of us*.

Rose's hand lifted and she slapped his face. He blinked from the sting of it, but said nothing.

In the night, he woke to his mother wailing. When he went to her room, he found her crouched on her bed, tearing her face with her nails. She'd gouged long wounds into her skin, and beneath her nails was her own blood.

"Mum," he said. "Mum."

She was asleep. She didn't wake up as he pulled her hands down and pinned them until she relaxed. She didn't wake up until the morning.

"Who did this?" she said, bewildered, gesturing to her face as she came out of the bathroom.

"You were dreaming," Bo said.

She started, then said, "I remember a nightmare." But she would not tell him how it went.

She went back into the bathroom and powdered over the rents in her face, but it was easy to see them. They ran like frozen tears down her cheeks and her neck.

CHAPTER FOUR

I~T WAS FRIDAY~ after school and Rose was at work. Bo wished Gerry would come by. He had memorized the phone number from the contract but didn't dare dial it. He was playing with Orange on the floor in the small living room. He galloped her stuffed donkey toward her and then, just as she grabbed it, he pulled it away. He crouched for a long time playing this game, sometimes letting her win, and then his legs cramped and he stood. A shadow fluttered at the window and he looked out at the porch.

It was Emily—her hand made a tiny nervous wave, her manic smile was painted on too late. She'd seen. Bo slammed himself in front of Orange anyway, to hide his mother's shame and now, perhaps—and this feeling grew—his own shame, as Emily witnessed the horror of his sister, her skewed self, her snot, her ugly. In the tiny unwinding moment, Orange *was*. Emily tapped at the window, and Bo shook his head, even though she surely could not see him.

"Let me in, Bo," she called, the glass shunting the words off into watery dreaming. "Open the door, for heaven's sake." She was banging on the door.

"Don't move," he whispered to Orange, but as soon as he got up, she began to flipper around the living room, throwing herself over and over, in her new freedom. He thought of seals, and then gathering fishes, and then tried not to think. "Please, Orange. Be still. Jesus."

She looked up at him, swinging her head. She made a face and he was chastened. Then, just as suddenly as she had made the face, it was gone and she was a seal again and then she was a cow or a horse, always some sort of animal, transforming. Some aberration of an animal. Some wrong-beast. Orange had become wild from playing, and then being held down—this had only exacerbated her need to move.

Emily tapped on the pane and demanded he open up, for crying out loud.

Bo belly-crawled to the hall and stood to open the door, first brushing down his clothes, straightening things. He peeked around the jamb before Emily saw the door had in fact been opened for her.

He said, "How can I help you?"

"What?"

Bo blinked. Emily pushed in and dropped her rucksack. She moved past him and turned to the living room, looked down on Orange, who was now sitting, flipping her head side to side, tossing her arms around herself in a rough hug.

"Wow," Emily said. "The rumours are true."

"Rumours."

Emily shot him a look. "Cool," she said.

"It's a fucking freak show," he whispered.

Emily made a face to indicate to Bo how incredibly stupid he was, then said, "Freak show is cool," and looked back at Orange.

A hole had been cut from under him. Not a hole through the floor, like in the cartoons, but a hole in the Earth, a hole in the universe, and this hole was pulling a portion of his body into it; it was not unlike a punch, but a punch that takes forever to land, and then as it does it thins all the flesh around it into a long elastic bubble. Nestled inside this bubble in his gut was Emily, and nestled in with her, Orange. *Freak show is cool.*

"Yes." It was all he could think to say.

"What's her name?"

"My mother calls her Sister."

"And you?"

"Her Vietnamese name means Orange Blossom. I call her Orange."

"Wow," said Emily, and squatted down closer to Orange. "I'm Emily," she said. "Hello there."

Orange swung her head side to side as if not to notice Emily, but Bo could see she was taking it in, the shiny novelty in her midst—a new person. Emily twisted her smiling face up to Bo.

"My mother works with disabled kids. Did you know? She teaches swimming. It's therapeutic."

"Swimming," repeated Bo, and felt sick. His toes were clutching at the edge of the deep end, the water surface oscillating, flicking light at him in a fearful enticement. Sharks.

"Maybe Orange would like it. Not everyone is afraid of the water, you know."

"I'm not afraid," Bo said.

"Come on," she said. "Remember grade five—the field trip to Sunnyside pool?" and then, "If someone held her on a flutter board, though."

"She wouldn't like it. She doesn't like other people to touch her." At Sunnyside, he had sat tucked into himself against the chain-link fence, claiming a stomach ache.

"Well, you could hold her."

All the cells in his body built tight walls around themselves and he stood there thinking of standing in the water holding Orange, his father sinking into the murky dark deep end, shirt billowing. Bo's head began— of its own accord—to shake back and forth. Emily reached out her hand to push a strand of Orange's wispy hair back off her cheek. And Orange did not move. She let Emily move the hair behind her ear, and she kept very still. A marvel.

"She doesn't let anyone touch her." Bo moved beside Emily and squatted down on his haunches. "Orange—"

"My name is Emily. Do you like to dance? I do. Very much." Emily spoke very quietly, the words tumbling over each other. Orange let her inch closer. "Do you like to swim? Does she, Bo?"

"I don't know. She's never—"

"Does she like to bathe?" said Emily, then turned back to Orange before he answered. "If you like the bath, you will like the pool. I'll take you one day. Emily." She repeated, nodding, "Emily," and touched her own collarbone, "Me."

Orange, sweaty and dirty, leaned her torso against Emily. Her breath purred. Bo edged over to sit beside his sister, and when he put his hands out, she began to bash him with her stubby fists. She hammered him—his arms, his shoulders, his face—so fast, hard.

"Oh my God." Emily sunk down to the floor. "That's enough, Orange. You stop that." But Orange did not. If anything she increased the pummelling.

Her hands were nothing but fists. She used them as cudgels upon him, but she was small and the damage she did was minor. Bo said, "It's okay. It's normal." He was used to it, and began to laugh a little, especially since Emily looked so concerned. "She doesn't mean it, Emily."

"Oh," said Emily. "Oh!"

Bo opened the palms of his hands and caught Orange's fists in his. He let her struggle against him to slow the momentum of her beating so that somehow he unwound her from herself, and stopping seemed like her idea. Soon she was calm and relocated, contained.

"She's like a new creature," said Emily. "Not a human and not an animal. Some new thing."

Bo liked this. It made it sound as if Orange were a rare discovery. He pulled his lips in, and held them there, thinking, then said, "My mum—" He thought of Orange butting her head and body against the door to her room while his mother twisted the dial on the TV or the radio louder and louder to keep Orange's yearning at bay. If he admitted it was horrific, he was admitting something about his mum, and this seemed equally horrific. A bad feeling, like water pushing at the back of his heart and up toward his eyes, came over him. "She thinks Orange is shameful."

"She's human."

"My mum?"

"I guess. I meant Orange, though."

"No," said Bo. "You said it yourself. She is something new."

"Next year, when the weather gets warm and our pool is open, we'll sneak her out and bring her to my house. We'll be quiet."

"No."

"Promise."

"I can't."

Emily folded her arms and turned a quarter-turn away. "Promise."

"Maybe," he said, then, "Hey, Emily, don't tell anyone you were here. That you saw her," he said. "Promise?" The limp child was now deeply asleep in his arms. "My mum will be home soon," he said, hoping that Emily would leave. He saw she was looking elsewhere, down the hallway, into his life.

"Why did you come?" he said. "I mean, in the first place?"

"Oh," she said, and twirled around. She stared at him and smiled.

Bo shook his head. He didn't get it.

"Dummy," she said.

And then he saw. New jeans. They were cigarette legs, holding tight to her body. She looked taller, and he wondered whether he imagined that or whether she really was.

"They look nice," he said.

"Yeah, I finally got them."

Bo shifted Orange over his shoulder and stood nodding

for a bit, feeling awkward, not knowing what to say to Emily anymore. "I better put her to bed," he finally said.

"Okay," Emily said. "I'll let myself out." She waved with her fingers and turned to go. "See you."

But after she left, he did not put Orange to bed, but sat with her, in the living room, a dumb sitcom flickering on the TV. He sat in the only comfortable chair they owned, an upholstered rocker, green, the Naugahyde peeling, and watched her sleep in his arms.

CHAPTER FIVE

Gerry came back for Bo in early October. "You ready for work?" he said.

"Yes."

There were fifteen country fairs scattered through Ontario. Gerry intended them to get to each one, at least two or three per weekend. Inside the cab, Bo could smell the truck falling apart, gas fumes leaking in through holes in the floor. He missed school every Friday and some Thursdays if they had a ways to travel to get to someplace that looked just the same as the last place they'd been. Loralei was stressed, so Gerry had started giving her Valium. It made her slower, which made her seem dumb, but it was better than risking her swatting someone, or so

Gerry claimed. Bo spent some of the travel time staring out the window, some of it counting his money. Today was a Sunday and they were heading to Walkerton.

Bo placed his bills in piles on the truck bench between him and Gerry—ones, twos, fives, tens—which got Gerry singing about how the king was in the counting house, counting out his money. Bo didn't mind because he loved the part of the song about the blackbirds, which always made him childishly check for his nose. The air was thick with summer still, as if no one had told October about fall, and Gerry, out of the blue, seeing him happy, asked Bo about that kid he'd been fighting when he found him.

Bo thought about Gerry "finding" him, and said, "Ernie?"

"That the ass-wipe's name?"

"Yes."

"Do you fight other kids?"

"No."

"Why only him?"

Bo shrugged, leaned in to the radio. "Can I change the channel?" he asked, which made Gerry laugh.

"Sure you can, kid." Then nodding to the money, Gerry said, "How much?"

"Four hundred and fifteen." "Rubber Band Man" began pouring out of the radio. Bo rocked in his seat to it.

"A bundle," said Gerry.

"Should I get a bank account?"

"I never bother."

There would be two fights for Bo that day. He'd fought other boys, and he fought Loralei, and he always knew who would win and who would lose from the outset. Not once had there been a bout that went wrong. When he wasn't at fairs with Gerry, he fought Ernie. He thought of it as training, that the experience was building him. He was strong. Mr. Morley had nodded and smiled when he broke a school record for sit-ups. He'd won the fitness medal, and been called a fucking slant for it by Ernie, who had red-faced it to second place. If he counted those slams with Ernie, he'd thrown his body at some other body thirty times these twenty-one days.

"I'm not tired," Bo said, as if saying it would make it true.

"Why'd you say that, kid?"

He shook his head and furrowed his eyebrows. *He would sleep when he was dead*, a line Gerry spouted now and then. The thought of it made Bo shiver, then shrug it off, since sleeping wasn't like dying, anyhow.

In Walkerton, it looked like the same kids milling around, same mums and dads, same 4-H Jersey calves, same giant pumpkin. Bo lost the first bout on purpose, at a cue from Max Jennings, who had begun to work more closely with Gerry on rigging the show. There must have been a lot of money at stake. The skinny boy who beat Bo was the son of the mayor. The kid had no sense of gravity, which made it difficult for Bo to create a decent spectacle, make it look good. It was easier to make a show with the overweight boys. They knew how to stand, and people seemed to find fat funny.

Bo had played this boy, getting him to chase, then evading his touch. He'd held the kid in a clutch, then shifted his weight in whatever direction the kid wanted it to go, so it looked as if Bo had lost his balance, which he had. The betting crowd didn't need to know he was losing his balance on purpose. He'd let the kid ram his chest with a bony knee, and even that didn't really hurt. When it got too much he slid out from under so the kid hit the boards with his knee. Bo smiled when he yelped. The thin padding on the ring floor did not forgive. Bo put on his most angry face when the referee lofted the mayor's son's hand in the air. Being a shitty loser made him hated, and hatred meant they'd bet against him with Loralei. The green would flow.

After the match, Gerry said, "You got two hours to kill, kid."

Max Jennings thrust his chin toward Bo. "How's the family?" he asked, meaning Orange. He wore a pristine, cut-silk, silver suit that glimmered. He knew how to make his face look sympathetic. "I'm just asking," he said.

"They're okay," Bo said. But it wasn't true. The family was not okay.

Max fanned twenty-dollar bills in his palm like a magician. "The offer stands." He flicked his perfect eyebrows.

Bo walked away.

He heard Max as if he were talking through a foghorn in a dream. "Jesus, come on, kid!"

Bo was through the short Walkerton midway strip in no time, so he circled back, angling past the bingo hall, and used his pass to enter the freak show. Freaks were nothing more than strangely built humans, some of them suffering diseases, all of them finding a home in this otherworld. If a person thought that humans only came in one shape, then they were fascinated by these beings. It was as simple as that. Bo knew that Orange would be excited to be here—to be anywhere. She wouldn't notice kids staring, dropping their cotton candy, spilling their pops to get a look, necks craning. That she wouldn't notice made it somehow worse.

Many of the regular summer attractions—freaks Bo had only heard about from Gerry—had already headed south for the winter, so the feature at this fair was a dwarf and his talking dog. People crowded in.

How's the family? Max's question leapt in his mind. A bad asking. His mum was vacant or drunk, his sister out of control. His own fake carnie bouts had become more real, and more reliable, than anything really real.

Bo watched the dog flip and beg and roll itself up in a ball and cry for a bone. It might have been interesting if the dwarf hadn't looked bored and resentful. His act consisted of baiting the audience. The dog was just a cog in a carefully designed routine, but it had range. It could baa and moo, and make something like a quack. The dwarf finished up, then took a long pull from a beer bottle. The spectators milled around the tent, whispered over the mummified mermaid, the bottled microcephalic baby, the hairless cats, scared and drugged in their bright yellow miniature circus-train car, and the live cow with the second head sprouting from her skull. "Wow," people said. "Will you look at that?"

Bo imagined Orange in a cage, or an aquarium, looking baffled, or worse, getting wild with that fury she had, bashing her twisted self against the floor, the walls, while these people, the normals, laughed, pointed in awe, shame, whatever they felt. He checked the time and left the freak show.

The crowd pressed in on him. Kids making their way to this or that ride, the pop of pellets hitting and missing paper targets, some toddler wailing. He thought of his mother despondent at the kitchen table two weeks before. "I lost my job." Her eyes glancing up at him at the last second.

"Did you quit?"

"No," she said.

"What happened?"

"I missed too many days."

Bo had kept that news from Gerry and Max, not wanting pity, or any sort of drama. He forgot to breathe whenever he recalled Father Bart looming at him after mass that time. "Where is your mother?" It was something he, too, wondered from time to time.

For twenty minutes, Bo stood in line for the Ferris wheel, as a snake of twittering couples fed into the dangling cars. Before his fights, Bo sometimes spent his tension on the Ferris wheel or the Loop-the-Loop, whatever ride was biggest, fastest. It was like a dare he had with himself. The operator was an older man who looked like he hadn't slept in a long time. He performed his job like a robot, shuffled Bo through the gate, then closed it, opened the bar on the ride, made sure Bo was strapped in, closed the bar, pushed a button to shift the car up. Automatic. He didn't look at Bo, though Bo recognized him from every fair in all the different counties he'd been to.

Bo watched the faces of the people entering the cars as his rose in the air. They betrayed everything—fear, excitement, sorrow, anticipation, joy and worry. He thought that maybe it was only in these moments of anticipating how a ride could be your last, when everything of life showed. And then the Ferris wheel began to turn in earnest, and Bo's body seized up. He recalled the swells under the fishing boat, and the screams of the men through two days and nights as they took turns trying to scare away pirates. There were tales of these pirates raping women and murdering men. Now, the mechanics of the ride, the slick gravity manipulation, the panic of it enveloped him. He was sweating with fear, his anxiety swelling and dying with each rotation, until it was over. He laughed at himself, then, and thought, Screw you, Max Jennings, my family is just fine.

He exited the car, and stood to watch as the others stumbled out, their eyes bright, their faces absolutely blank. He stopped to buy a burger, and ate it as he pushed through the midway crowd toward the ring, sidestepping grass muddied by the rain of the night before. He could smell Loralei as he got close.

THE BEAR GRABBED BO'S HEAD with her paw pads and pulled him in for a hug. He disappeared into her fur—the audience could see his legs and that was all, and they shrieked. Bo shouted right into her chest. They had practised this. He would shout into her chest and she would react by pushing him away. She had recoiled, frightened, the first few times he did it, until she realized it was part of the play. She thrust him to the ropes then, and he bounced around, rolling his eyes up for effect, then fell theatrically to the mat. He would have rope burns and scratches to prove he'd fought her.

She lumbered over while he lay there, and simply sat down on him.

"She'll crush him," someone yelled. "Hey!"

But she was perched, not fully sitting at all. Bo had enough room under her to press his feet into the mat and buck, the signal for her to leap up. She stood to her full height and clawed the air, bounded around the ring and made a great show for the crowd. Then she ran at Bo, head-butting him mid-body, heaving him up and onto her back. Here he was able to cinch his arm around her neck and manoeuvre her staged defeat. He pinned her with his scrawny body, and to prove his mastery over her, Loralei rolled her eyes back in her head and shot her tongue out—a cartoon death throe—until the announcer finally called it.

Gerry got Loralei to sit down. The referee came into the middle of the ring, between Bo and Loralei, grabbed Bo's hand and held it aloft. Loralei sniffed, then nuzzled Gerry. A root beer emerged from Gerry's pocket and Loralei lifted her head, opened her mouth like a baby bird, and Gerry poured it down. Her prize. The crowd's frenzy was the soundtrack to Bo's own joy.

And then in the truck, counting his cash again, Gerry said, "Nice job," and handed Bo a wad of money.

"Thanks."

"Well, kid."

Bo piled the new bills smallest to largest and added them to his stack, then wound an elastic around it twice and thrust the wad into his pocket before looking over. "Well what?"

Gerry sucked in his bottom lip and was chewing on it. He looked like he might cry or like he was trying to look like he might cry. "That's it."

"What is?"

"Walkerton is the end of the road, my friend. I got no work for you until next year. You keep yourself fit and you stand to make a load next season. Sit-ups. Push-ups. You keep fighting that arse-wipe of a friend of yours. If Max convinces the CNE to book the side-show, you might get spotted, go professional. There's no stopping you—"

"No more work?"

"Sorry, kid."

His mum at the table. Orange. Bo's ribs caved in on him. No work. He would not cry. He yanked the bundle out, tore at the elastic and counted and recounted. He thought forward to months without Loralei, his mum sick at heart, no way to pay for anything. What would they do? When he got home, he would go out and find Ernie, and he would punch.

BUT WHEN HE GOT HOME, Teacher was in his kitchen sitting across the table from his mother. "Hello, Bo."

Rose looked up at him. Her eyes gave nothing away. Orange reached out to him from the floor, and when he didn't react, she slapped the floor until he picked her up.

"Hello," he said to Teacher, and then he nodded to his mother. He knew that Rose had already seen his panic.

"Sit down, Bo," said Teacher. She gestured to the chair beside her.

"What is it?" he said. He jostled Orange and made a face at her. He didn't want to sit down. He looked at Teacher and then at his mum again.

Teacher smiled. "I think you know," she said. "You've missed a lot of school. You and Rose need to understand—"

"I'm sorry," Bo said, interrupting her. "I won't miss any more."

"I know things aren't easy," Teacher said.

How did she know? Bo wondered. How was it that even their misery was public knowledge?

"If I can help in any way—" she said.

Rose tsked, and Teacher looked over at her.

"We're okay," said Rose.

Orange had nestled into Bo's shoulder and was curled there, heavy and tired. Bo snuggled his face against hers. She smelled good. He could excuse himself and put her to bed.

Teacher glanced down at her purse hanging from the back of her chair, and Bo saw her flush. She said, "If you'd let me help."

"Thank you," said Bo. "I won't miss any more school. Really."

"Okay, Bo," she said. She pulled her purse over her shoulder and opened the zipper. "I have something for Orange." It was a red plastic bottle. *Bubble Magic* it read on the label.

Bo looked at it. He turned it around. "What is it?" he said. Orange jerked toward it, grabbing.

"You don't know this?" Teacher said. She put out her hand to take it back. She smiled. "Let me show you, okay?"

Bo nodded, so she twisted the lid and pulled out a little red wand with a round plastic ring at one end.

"Watch," she said. She gently blew into the wand's ring.

Orange leaned in, and then, as the soap bubble began to blossom from the wand, her arms flailed and Bo had to set her down. Three or four bubbles floated around them. Teacher dipped the wand into the bottle and blew again. The bubbles found little currents in the air and danced along them. Teacher laughed.

Even Rose smiled. "So pretty," she said.

Teacher dipped the wand again, and blew, and this time so many bubbles formed, it seemed impossible. They were everywhere, iridescent, perfect. Orange grabbed at them.

"Okay," said Teacher. She handed Bo the wand. "I better go." When he looked confused, she said, "You just blow softly."

Orange slapped him, trying to get the bottle. Bo dipped the wand and blew, and did not notice Teacher leaving. He had to make bubbles for Orange; she hit him whenever he stopped. He made bubbles for an hour, and when he finally put the bottle away, Orange pummelled him.

HALF ASLEEP STILL, the next morning Bo thought of the floating bubbles. Before he had put them away, he and Orange had lain down on the floor so they could blow them back up into the air as they fell. It had been so pleasant, and now he wandered in that memory. Then suddenly he remembered that it was Monday, a school day, and that he would have no more bouts until springtime.

"Mum?" he called out, but she didn't hear so he got up and stumbled into the kitchen.

Orange sat in Rose's lap. His mother was trying to get Orange to eat. There was porridge crusted on Orange's arms and splattered across her cheeks. Rose looked up when Bo came in.

"I slept in."

"I thought you had already gone to school."

"I'm late. I'm missing basketball practice."

"You must have needed the extra sleep," she said, and he knew she was right. But he wanted to be at practice, running, jumping, ridding himself of thought.

Bo took a banana from the counter and sat, peeling it all at once and eating it bit by bit. All he could think of was that he had no work, and neither did Rose. Orange lunged at him, flinging a bit of oatmeal she'd been mashing up in her hand.

"Ugh," he said, when it landed on his clean shirt. And then he lunged at her and yelled, "You're a dirty girl!"

"Bo!"

He had not known he could sound so mean. He crouched at the table and held Orange's face for a second, and smiled to her.

"Mum?" he said.

"What?"

He dug into his pocket and pulled out the roll of money. "Here." Bo put the money on the table. "Gerry told me there wouldn't be any more work until next year." He pointed to the money. "That's everything." When Rose shook her head, he added, "I'll get another job."

"No, Bo. I will get a job," she said. She slowly swallowed as if to calm herself.

"No," he said. "Orange needs you." I need you, he thought, but he didn't dare say it, and his mother and Orange did not move, just sat amazed at what he had dared say, and so he left.

He grabbed an old mop handle that was broken and lying on the front porch and, on his way to school, swung it at every object that caught his fancy. He made noises as he whacked everything, and it made him feel a little better. An old lady crossed the street to avoid him.

When he got to the schoolyard, Teacher was at the front door. "Bo," she called. She looked as crushed and sad as if he had hit her, despite the fact that he was far away from her, hitting the post of the fence that enclosed the schoolyard. The hollow metal twanged in an ugly way. "What is it, Bo?" There was no one else around. It was too early for most people, and practice was in the gym. "What's the matter?"

"Nothing," he called. Everything.

Teacher wore a dark blue blazer and white trousers under her coat. Her hair was perfect. "There must be *something*."

"No." He gave her a scorching look so she would leave him alone.

"Okay, Bo," she said. "Okay." Then she opened the door and went inside.

Bo followed her to the door, watched her through the glass, listened to her pumps click against the floor on the way to their classroom. He tapped the mop handle against the brick to the beat of them, until she was too far away and he couldn't hear a thing. He didn't feel like making practice anymore, or seeing anyone. He went around the school and did chin-ups on the geo-dome climber, over and over until he couldn't breathe. As the other kids arrived, they played around him, until the bell rang.

THAT AFTERNOON, Bo stayed on at school for basket-ball practice, his worst sport after volleyball. He prac-tised jumping so he would be able to compensate for his height in a game. Mr. Morley measured his vertical at point-seven metres, and said, "Good." Bo headed home late, and stinking of body odour, and starving. At Dundas and St. Johns, Ernie was waiting for him.

"I can't," Bo said. "I need to get home."

"Pussy-whipped," said Ernie, so Bo ran at him and thumped him to the ground.

Ernie grabbed his ankle, pulling him down on top, and they tussled. "I have to be home, Ernie," said Bo. "Really." He freed himself and stood.

"I'm gonna kill you, Bo." Ernie stood up too, and brushed off the wet leaves that had caught on his sweater. "I'm gonna kill you."

Some of the children from the neighbourhood came out of nowhere to watch.

"I can fight later," Bo said. "I can't fight you now, Ernie."

"Later then, sure." Ernie looked angrily at his fists, as if it were them and not Bo he hated. And then he swung at Bo, clipping him across the nose and mouth.

Bo recoiled. The hit was so hard it had taken his breath with it. The blood came thick and fast—a glob of it from his nose, a red trail down his chin. Someone gave a great whooping yell. It crescendoed as Bo ran away. When he turned the corner, he lost the sound in the great rumble of a train hurtling downtown.

By the time he got home, the blood had crusted along the runnels and soft hairs at the bow of his upper lip. Rose barely turned when he came in. She was tucked up in the Naugahyde chair crooning to a Vietnamese cassette tape, and smiling. Her eyes were lit up and pretty. Orange was sleeping on a mess of laundry in the corner of the living room. Bo recalled a time when his mother might have noticed two lines of dried blood roving down his face, but she was either used to it or had given up. She never really looked at him anymore. "Mum," he said. "I'm home." He went down the hall to the bathroom and washed his face, then came back to see them.

"Hi, Bo," Rose said.

He settled on the floor beside Orange, lying so that he could watch her face when she slept. He could feel the soft moving air of her breath on his face, and hear the tiny puffs as it left her lips. Sometimes, she went from being strange to being beautiful.

"The bubbles were nice," he said.

Rose nodded. "A friend of Gerry's came by today."

"Who?" But he knew already.

"He said his name was Max Jennings."

No, thought Bo.

Orange's arm twitched in sleep, like a dog's legs when it runs in its dreams. She was hitting in her sleep, he thought. Raging in her sleep. He swallowed, considering that Max might have seen Orange.

"You didn't let Max see her, did you?"

He sat up, glaring at his mum.

"I thought she was asleep, but she had toddled up to the door while I was talking. And—" Rose hesitated when she saw Bo's face crumple.

"And Max saw her."

"He was very polite. He was kind."

Bo imagined the secret glee with which Max would have regarded the distorted and warped body of his sister. He must have smiled. He must have seen the flow of green in her.

"He's not kind," said Bo.

"He said he made house calls to his favourite workers. He said to tell you to keep fit for the spring carnivals, that he enjoys working with you. Bo, he was very nice to me."

"Okay," Bo said. He did not want to tell his mother about the freak show or about anything that might make her think twice about letting him work for the carnival. He glanced back at Orange, sleeping still, and thought of Loralei, the muscles under her fur undulating as she moved, and how nice that was, and how good it was to tussle with her. How real it was.

"Mum?" he said.

"Yes."

"When the carnival gets back in the spring, I might have to miss more school."

"But Teacher—" she said.

"I know." Bo slid over to sit nearer to his mother. "I know she'll be mad, but I *need* to do this."

Rose's eyes closed and then opened. She looked up at the ceiling and her mouth twisted a little with some thought. Then she said, "Okay, but make sure all your homework is done, every day. All of it."

Bo nodded and smiled, thinking of Loralei's fur and the press of her body against his. "I will," he said.

Then his mother said, "Teacher has organized a baby-sitter for Sister so that I can look for work." She let her hand drop onto Bo's head. He stayed very still while she combed her fingers through his hair. "She noticed that Sister was alone, and did it to help us. The babysitter starts in November, in two weeks."

"Is that okay with you?"

"Not really," said Rose. "But I have to look for work. I have to find something to do. And Sister is walking; I need someone to be here to make sure she is safe."

"Maybe it's okay," he said.

Rose stopped combing his hair then, and pulled her hand away. She sang the unwinding strain that was the last song on the cassette, and when it had finished, she said, "Yes, maybe." She pushed herself out of the chair and walked to the hallway. She stopped at a mirror on the wall, straightened her T-shirt and made a face at her reflection. "That man did seem very polite, Bo."

"Mum," he said. "It's okay. Forget it."

Then she peered at herself in the mirror, smoothed her clothing again, before wandering to her bedroom. When Bo was sure she'd fallen asleep, he woke Orange. He wanted to take her through the streets and show her the dogs, and the trains, everything, but it was still light and he didn't dare. Instead, he waited a bit, and then he snuck her to the tracks, and waited for a train so that he could watch her feel the suck of air, and see all the muted colours as the cars blurred past under the industrial lights. She watched in a trance as he held her there in his arms.

It was after school on a Wednesday in November. Emily turned so fast when he shoved through the door, he realized he'd scared her. Except it was his heart racing. "What are you doing here?"

"Babysitting," she said. "I really like Orange," she added. And then she grinned so wide he thought he would fall in, and knew how awkward he must appear, because—well—this was Emily.

Bo pretended everything was fine by picking up a cloth and wiping Orange's mouth. She'd spit her food down her

chin as if to say, *don't clean me, I'm dirty*. "Don't," he whispered. He looked over at Emily. She was the *babysitter*?

"Is this your first time babysitting her?"

"Oh, no. I've been here lots of times. Your mum wasn't
sure when you'd be home. Rose—your mum? I think
she's on a date." Emily seemed pleased to tell him this.

"Date?" No. She was looking for work. "You can go
home now," he said. "I've got this."

After she'd gone, he bundled Orange into a blanket
and tucked her on his lap. He sat on the green chair and
waited, and waited, even as Orange slumped in sleep,
and even as he, too, began to drowse.

A knock woke him. He laid Orange down on the floor
beside the chair and found Teacher at the front door.

"Oh, hi! Bo!" She looked confused. "Sorry," she said.
"It's just that I asked Emily to be here."

"Practice was cancelled."

"Oh. Well, can you let your mum know I'm here?"

"She's out, Miss Lily."

Teacher sighed at this. "I'm supposed to bring her to
her doctor's appointment. She wanted to look for work,
and then we were supposed to meet back here. Didn't she
mention it?"

"She never goes to the doctor," said Bo.

"Bo," said Teacher. "Everybody needs to go to the
doctor once in a while. It's normal." And then, when he
just stared at her, she said, "Will you give her a message?"

Actually there were two. One was inside an envelope with *Rose Ngô* on the front in cursive; the other Teacher asked him to pass on: could Rose come to the school to speak with her the next day. Bo looked up directly into Teacher's face when she said this. His horror must have shown, because Teacher said, "What is it?"

"Sister will be alone," Bo said, though this was not what concerned him. He did not want his mother at the school. He did not want her to be seen.

"I'm trying to help, Bo." Teacher's face was so smooth, and kind. "It's after school. You can be here for Orange, right? Or else, I can ask Emily."

He shook his head even as Teacher pushed the letter toward him. Not Emily.

"Just give this to your mum, okay? We're trying to make this as easy as possible. Really."

Bo looked at the letter. *We*, he thought. She was delivering a letter from *We*. He knew this meant the group of people who had sponsored them, that this meant gratitude and owing. His throat constricted. He thanked Teacher and closed the door, and set the letter down on the kitchen table where his mum would see it when she got home. He went back to the living room, cradled his sister and waited.

Rose tried to tiptoe past them.

Bo said, "Where were you?" and heard her sharp intake of breath. She walked over to the kitchen table and looked down at the letter.

"I'm home now. Go to bed."

Bo stood with Orange hanging in his arms and carried her to her bed. When he was sure she had settled, he went to stand at the threshold of his mother's room. "Who were you with?" he asked.

The door muffled her response.

". . . not your business." But somehow from this he knew right away that it must be Max.

"Mum, no." This knowing felt like crying did.

"Hush, Bo. Go to sleep. I'm all right."

"Mum. Teacher came by for you. She said you had a doctor's appointment. You have to go and speak to her tomorrow at the school. Did you open the letter? What did it say?" Bo waited in the dark for her answer. He felt if she would attend to these things, she'd have no time for Max.

Finally, he heard her say, "Nothing."

Two days later, when he got home from school, Max Jennings and his mother leaned into one another at the table—Max's glass tilted mid-air—as if they had suspended their conversation and were waiting for him. Orange was splay-legged on the floor between them. Bo picked her up.

Rose looked strange. And then Bo thought, no, not strange, she looked happy. She wasn't smiling but there was something different, some freshness, and he felt only distress at this. Why should Max give her happiness?

"The prodigal son!" said Max, and added, "I have been regaling!"

"Max," said Rose. She brought her empty glass toward him and he filled it sloppily from a gin bottle. His mother saying Max's name was a hateful thing to hear.

Orange fought Bo's hold on her, and so he let her dangle to the ground to stand. She caught her balance, and then caught it again.

Rose gave him a pained look, but then stopped herself when Max put his hands out toward Orange.

"No!" said Bo, but Orange waddled over to Max and let him catch her up.

Bo noticed that Rose was holding her breath. If there were air, he would scream. And then Rose laughed, and her face was so open that even Bo could see how beautiful she was. She let all this stifled beauty shine onto Max until the laughter faded.

"Little Sister," Max said. "Little Orange." He was holding her by her arms as she bounced on his lap. Max looked at Bo. "I'm trying to help out, kid."

Bo turned to his mother. She would not resist, he could see. This gutted him. *Mother*, he thought, his thought screaming, but she wouldn't pay attention. "Stop," he said to Max, and pulled his sister away. "Leave her alone," he said to Max, but he was looking at Rose. Her eyebrows lifted ever so slightly. Don't make a fuss, these eyebrows said.

THE NEXT MORNING, Bo awoke on the floor beside Orange's bed. Bleary-eyed, he went to the kitchen. Max Jennings sat in the same spot at the table—as if he had not moved. But where the glasses had been, there were plates, and Bo saw that for the first time in so long, his mother had cooked breakfast. She sat opposite Max.

"Aunt Jemima's pancakes and syrup," said Max. "Pull up a chair, son."

Orange began to thump, a metronomic shiver through the house. Bo stared toward her room, and then turned and sat down. "Did you sleep here, Mr. Jennings?"

"Bo!" said his mother.

"Never mind, Thao." Looking at Bo, Max said, "I slept on the couch," and then laughed because there was no couch, only the chair.

Max slid a triangle of pancake into his mouth. He was

chewing more than necessary. Max had called his mum by her Vietnamese name. He had—

"Max will drive me to the grocery store, Bo," said Rose, rising from the table. "You will look after Sister."

Bo nodded. He was sorting out what this all meant, but it was too much.

"And Bo," said Max, chewing still, "I want you to understand—" and here he tilted his head to the side in a kindly way, "I find Sister a delight, a real treasure."

Bo was punching Max's face before he realized it. He slammed Max's face with his fist, all the while hearing Rose yell, "Stop!" and "No!"

Max only smiled wanly when Bo finished, as if he had known it would come to this. Then his smile turned nasty.

"You little asshole," he said, patting his clothes down. He stood up and threw his napkin down on top of his plate, then touched his cheek where Bo had hit him. "Let's go, Thao." Pointing at Bo, he hissed, "The world is perfect in its own way. As perfect as anything. You just need to let things be." A red welt was already appearing on his cheek. "You little asshole."

"Sorry, Max," his mother was saying as they walked out of the house. "Sorry, sorry."

Bo wished he had hit Max harder. He wished he had made Max bleed.

Bo fumed in the kitchen for ages before he finally went in to Orange. She wore only a messy cloth diaper, and this was half falling off. Orange's hair was sweaty and skewed, her popped eyes lined with angry veins. Her finger stumps were red from hammering the wall and her face was teary from the frustration of trying to communicate, but when she saw the camera Bo had brought into her room, she calmed down. It was a new thing and she liked new things.

"Don't move, you little asshole," Bo muttered, but she was in constant motion unless she was sleeping. He still felt so angry. He looked through the viewfinder of Teacher's camera, moving the dials to get the aperture right in Orange's dark room, making sure the flash was turned on. "You're hideous," he added. "I hate you. You're a little fucker."

He took picture after picture of her and each snap of the shutter was like the jaws of a shark smacking together, exactly like that. He told her again how he hated her but there was no truth in repetition. Orange flailed around the room and finally scuttled under the bed, trapping herself, but he did not stop. He crawled along the floor and took more pictures of her ugly face, her terrible freak-show body.

He pulled her out by the feet. "There," he said. "You're a beast." She was trying to rock away from him, but he held her down with his legs, and took several pictures of her panic, until the shutter would not click, until the camera had eaten up the film.

He opened the camera and took the roll out. He pushed the exposed film into the plastic case, and the case into his pocket. He would give Max what he wanted and be done with it.

There was a shop in Bloor West Village where they developed film. Bo ran, faster and faster, until his lungs clenched and his heart beat loudly in his head. Crying might have served the same purpose if he could cry, but he could not. The tears wouldn't come.

When he handed the film to the clerk, Bo asked, "How big can you make them? I want them like this." He showed with his hands roughly the size of the pictures he'd seen framed in Max's trailer.

"Glossy?"

"Glossy?"

"Shiny. Do you want them shiny?"

"Yes."

"Not cheap," said the clerk, and then she looked up. "About sixty dollars."

He did not know how he would pay. Maybe Max would pay for them. Or he could take back some of the money he had given to his mother. She kept it in a coffee tin in the fridge. "That's okay," he said.

"Write your phone number here and we'll call you when they come in."

When he got home, Orange was snot- and tear-drenched, and pressed into the hollow particleboard door. She had made more small dents in the wood with her mallet fists. His anger seeped out into guilt. Bo cuddled her in his arms, swayed her back and forth in wide arcs, as if she were a normal baby and he were a Swing Ride at half speed.

"I'm sorry," he said, over and over, and after a while she seemed to believe him, and fell asleep.

While she slept, Bo went to his room and crunched through fifty sit-ups, then fifty push-ups. He skipped rope, losing count, revelling in the slap of the rope as it hit the floor with each rotation. Some time midway through his workout it began to snow.

It snowed for weeks, and in that time, Bo spent more and more time inside with his sister, and his mother, and increasingly Max. Bo felt caged. He thought of running away with Orange, but couldn't figure out where to, and how they'd manage.

When the clerk from the photo shop called on a Saturday, and said, "Your glossies are in," with a tone that suggested he ought to be ashamed, he was. He hung up and pulled the tin out from behind the ketchup bottle, and counted what was left. A hundred dollars. Almost nothing. He took three twenties anyway, checked that Orange was sleeping, and headed to Bloor Street.

"These are unusual," the clerk said.

Bo handed her the crumpled bills.

"Very very odd."

Bo found himself nodding as he waited for the clerk to hand him the photographs. And when she did, Bo said, "Thank you," and turned and ran.

At home, he went in his room and pulled the images out. So many shots of Orange. He felt sick looking at them. He began to shove them under his mattress with his journal when he heard the sound of the front door shutting.

"What's that you got there?" Max already stood in the doorway of his room. He smiled like he knew everything there was to know about everything. He winked and cocked his chin. "You've been taking pictures."

Bo looked at an image of Orange still in his hand. She was standing, crooked, with her diaper slipping. Her belly bulged even though she was so skinny. She held her arms out toward the camera. Her face was so open. A picture like this must be worth something to Max.

"I'll give it to you if you leave us alone," Bo said, half knowing that Max would never now settle for a mere photograph. He knew this for sure when Max's cackle turned to a full-body laugh.

"You crack me up, kid," said Max. He shook his head. And then he stepped into the room and sat beside Bo on the bed. "Let me see the rest," he said, and reached into Bo's hidden cache.

"No." It came out as a squeak.

"Sure," said Max. "Why not?" He pulled the photos out and looked at them one after another.

They were blurred with Orange's movement, the energy of her fear. Bo watched Max as Max looked at them. His face stayed so still, but every so often he glanced at Bo as if to say, You took these?

"Give them back," said Bo, reaching for them. But Max didn't. Instead he tapped them straight on his lap and tucked them back under Bo's bed.

"I'm leaving," Max said. "I have work to do down south in the U.S., so you won't see me for a while. Don't jump for joy, kid." He flicked the corner of the one happy shot of Orange. "How much?" he said.

"Six hundred."

"Every man has his price," said Max. He stood and pulled his wallet from his back pocket. He said, "Don't tell your mum where you got this," and pulled ten hundred-dollar bills from the wallet, one by one, and handed the money to Bo.

"This is more."

"Yeah," said Max. "It is." Then he tugged the edge of the glossy and turned to go. "Your mother owes two months' rent," he said. "I tried to give it to her but she won't take it. Just so you know."

Bo looked down at the money clutched in his hand. He would simply put it in the tin and not say a word to his mother. He nodded to Max.

"And kid?" Max said, gesturing to Bo's bed. "Don't let Thao see them. Get rid of those despicable things, will you?"

All Bo could do was frown. Leave, he thought. Hurry. Go away. There would be peace. Everything would go back to normal.

CHAPTER SIX

THE DAY BEFORE the Christmas holidays, there was a knock on the door, and Gerry stood outside on his porch with an unwieldy canvas bag at his feet. "Merry Giftmas, Bo Jangles!" The porch light was broken and there was only the street lamp illuminating Gerry. Snow had drifted across the pathway to the porch, and Gerry wore a big khaki coat, the hood cinched around his face. "Your mum home?"

Bo had not known he missed Gerry, and now here he was. His mum was in the living room, staring into the corner. It was as if she hadn't moved since Max left weeks before.

"She's here, yeah."

Gerry nodded. "You going to let me in, kid?"

He pulled the door open, and Gerry stomped his boots and came in. "It's not Christmas," Bo said.

"Whatever, Jangles. I got a job for you, kid," Gerry said. "Look." He pulled the flap on the massive bag aside and yanked it open.

A brown snout poked out the canvas opening, followed by the dumb beady eyes of a bear cub. It wasn't wary or scared. It hadn't been on the planet long enough to know it should be. Bo thought his heart would thump out of his chest.

"Do you want to hold it?" Gerry asked.

The cub smelled milky and was warm against him. Bigger than Orange, but Bo could still manage her. She splayed her body wide open and melted right against him, nuzzled his collar for a bit, then fell asleep. Mine, thought Bo, and Gerry must have seen the thought in his eyes.

"I need you to train her. You up for that?"

Bo looked down on the fat paw pads and tiny claws that in so young a creature had the opposite effect of menace—they were cute. He wanted more than anything to bring the cub in to Orange. Orange would love this.

"A kind of pet," Bo said.

"Well, no. I want you to train her. She needs to learn how to dance and how to wrestle and whatever else you think you can teach her by August. She's going to be a main attraction at the ten-in-one at the Canadian National Exhibition. It's steady work and I know you people need it." Gerry looked everywhere but in Bo's eyes. "I want to help out."

"Ten-in-one?" Bo had never been to the Ex.

"It's what they call the bigger sideshows. You pay for one ticket, you get ten shows. A deal, right?"

"I'd be a freak?"

"You'd be an attraction. You and your wrestling, dancing—and whatever the hell else you can train her to do by then—bear."

Gerry had worked out all the details. He would supply food and give Bo tips on how to train the cub, and he would pay cash directly to Bo's mother. Every week, he would come by and he would pay out Bo's earnings, inspect the progress they had made.

"Max and me already spoke to your mum about this," Gerry said.

"You *and* Max?"

"Sure."

Bo considered how things stood, how Gerry and Max had already spoken to Rose. And then he looked down at the cub, felt the hard nugget of love passing from his chest to hers, and decided it didn't matter. It was work. He could help this way. He smelled the cub.

"My mum said yes to this?"

"She did," Gerry said.

So Bo went into the living room and held the cub up to her, where she sat in the green chair, and she nodded and said, "No messes." She went back to staring.

"It'll be fantastic," Gerry called to Bo, and then followed him to the living room. "Well, you'll see. You just make sure she can dance. She's three months old so you should be able to get started. These animals are highly trainable. I promised Max a damned dancing bear and now I have to provide one."

"But Max is gone," Bo said. He wished it wasn't for Max.

"Yeah, but he still knows how to use a telephone, kid. And he won the whole concession." Gerry was giddy with this news. He said, "You got until mid-August, Bo Jangles. That's when the CNE starts and that's when you have to have her ready. It's huge, kid. A break for all of us." And then Gerry put his arm around Bo's shoulder and walked him back to the kitchen, where they could be private. "You won't have to worry about Max. He won't be around for ages."

Gerry popped his eyebrows as if there were a joke he was in on. From that, Bo figured Gerry knew about his mum and Max.

"I know," Bo said. His stomach lurched and he looked down. The cub woke and bunched a swatch of Bo's shirt into a nipple and suckled on it. "Whoa," he said.

"Deal?" said Gerry.

Bo nodded. A bear cub. His own. And no Max to bother them.

Gerry went back to the truck and returned with food and the cub's leash. As he handed them over, he said to Bo, "Better if you don't prance her through the neighbourhood too much. Folks are liable to get anxious. Walk her at night on the chain, when no one is around. Otherwise keep her in the backyard, and if your mum will let her in the house on cold nights, that would be fine of her. You don't want a bear dying on you, now. They're costly, right? And mind, she's going to get big fast—real fast—real big—so be training her right from the start. You know what to do. You saw me doing it with Loralei, right?"

"I know," said Bo. He would have said anything to keep that ball of brown fur and need with him, but he knew he wasn't going to train this bear like he'd seen Gerry do it. Not that way.

"What're you going to call her?"

Bo thought for no time. He knew. "I'm going to call her Bear."

"Bear?"

"Bear."

"Hell of an original name, kid."

THE NEXT MORNING, Bo woke to this thought: bear cub chained under the porch. Rose had refused Bo's plea to keep her in overnight. He had hastily made a barrier of planks and cardboard to protect her from the cold night, shovelled the snow out and given her blankets to burrow in.

Orange began to bash her head against her flimsy bedroom door. She had grown, and even though she caught colds easily and often suffered a runny nose, she walked. She lunged and caught herself from falling. She braced her stumpy hands against furniture. It was impossible to keep her in her room unless the door was locked, and this presented another problem because she would happily throw her awkward body against it for hours if need be. It upset Rose to the point of fury.

"Shut up, shut her up," Rose yelled from the kitchen.

"I can take her outside," said Bo. He wanted to show her Bear, anyway.

"No."

"She's bored."

"Bo, for crying out loud."

It was an expression Rose had picked up from Max, and every time she said it, Bo winced. He wondered what she thought it meant. Bo came out of his room and saw Rose standing at the kitchen sink, staring out the window at nothing—the sickly birch tree and the angel-stone siding on the neighbour's house.

She said, "She's okay in her room."

Orange banged.

"The backyard at least. No one's up yet." Orange didn't mind the cold, didn't seem to notice. It was the novelty of fresh air, of outsideness.

"No," said Rose.

He went out the back door, rattled down the metal steps and crouched under the porch. The cub had torn the blankets to pieces and was in a ball fast asleep. Bo pulled her into his arms. Mine, he thought. He brought the sleeping cub inside, stood there looking toward the kitchen. His mother didn't turn around so he went to Orange's room.

When she saw the cub, she stopped slamming the wall, stopped moving. She stared for a long time. Bear yawned and stretched when Bo placed her on the parquet, her ass high in the air, her tongue curling in her mouth. She gave another gape and another, and emitted a thin doggish yelp with each yawn, until Bo was laughing.

Orange sat on her bottom on the floor in front of the bear cub, her toes curled into her crotch, so that they looked a lot like another set of arms, her left arm pressed into the floor beside her to keep her body as erect as its skew would allow. With her free hand she pumped a fist softly on the ground, and the bear watched. Bo crouched beside her and slowed her hand with his own, to show her how the bear followed the motion. Soon Bear grew tired of watching, and snuffled closer, curious, and then she was licking, licking Orange all over, and then something like joy moved through Orange's body. Shudders of it.

Bo spent the morning getting to know Bear and trying to get her to do simple things—chase a string, stand on her back legs. He took her into the kitchen to fetch the Magic Bubbles, and then brought her back to Orange's room. He sat on the bed and held Orange on his lap.

"Now, be still," he said, holding her tight in the crook of his arm. "Let's see what Bear thinks, okay?"

He blew slowly into the little wand and tiny bubbles emerged. Bear sat and cocked her head and watched for a bit, but then she lunged at one and tried to bite it. It was too much for Orange. She flailed to get away from Bo, and Bear turned and ran to the corner of the room.

"No," said Bo. "Hush," but she wouldn't be still, so he said, "If you don't calm down, I'll take Bear to the back-yard and that will be it."

And he tried again to entice Bear, blowing bubbles until she began again to snap and then swat at them. Whenever Orange would wiggle, Bo would remind her: "Stay," he said.

After a while he tired of the game, put the lid on the bottle and picked the cub up. "I'll be right back," he said to Orange, and left.

He brought Bear out the back door and chained her to the porch. "Good girl," he said. "Go lie down." She watched him for a short time and then crawled into the blankets under the porch, so Bo went back inside. Down the hallway, he could hear voices, of his mother and someone else. It took him a second or two to realize it was Teacher. He stood by the door to Orange's room, listening.

"You can't keep breaking appointments, Rose."

He heard his mother mumble what might have been an apology.

"You need to do this for your children." Bo heard the front door squeak and then shut, and then the shuffling of feet on the floor. He wished Teacher would leave his mother be. She didn't like doctors and neither did he.

"Are you okay, Mum?" he called toward the kitchen. He waited for her answer and when it didn't come he ventured down the hall. "Mum?"

She was sitting at the table, and looked up when he came in the room. "Yes?" she said.

"Thank you for letting the bear stay," he said.

"You're welcome."

"Is everything okay? I heard Teacher here."

"She wants me to help with a play your class is putting on." Rose was not really looking at him. "It's to keep me busy."

"Why?"

"She thinks I'm unhappy."

He thought so too but he didn't say it. Instead, he said, "Are you going to help?"

"Yes, with costumes and with helping the students to remember lines," she said, and in that moment Bo thought she did not look unhappy so much as scared.

He heard the thump of Orange in her room, and was happy to have an excuse to go to her. He did not like to think of his mother being afraid.

CHAPTER SEVEN

TEACHER HAD WRITTEN the script for the play and given it to the class in early January, and after two months of studying it, and different versions of the poem, they knew the story well. All through January and February, Bo hurried home to be with Bear and train her, and time flew in a way he did not know it could. Bear could stand on her back legs and turn, the beginning of a dance, he thought. She could clap in a bearish way, and she was a brilliant, natural wrestler. And now, before Bo knew it, it was the week after March break, a Monday. The class began rehearsals today.

And here was Rose in the school to help out. Bo saw

her from down the school corridor, and cringed. She did
not look small; she looked smaller than that. She looked
like a drawing of a person. She stood outside the princi-
pal's office, hugging herself, as if to become even tinier.
She wore jeans and a big sweater under her winter coat.
The coat was shorter and less bulky than the sweater
and so she looked poor, and lost. Bo was happy the rest
of his class was gone or in rehearsals already so they
would not see her here looking tragic and scared.

"Mum," he said when he got closer, and she looked up.

"Bo."

"You didn't have to come."

"It's okay. I don't mind." Teacher had told Bo that
Rose was coming, and that she had organized it this way
to minimize his embarrassment at having his mother be
there, but Teacher had misunderstood. He wasn't embar-
rassed. He was ashamed. And he wasn't ashamed of
Rose. It was something deeper. It was the shame Teacher
conveyed, by trying to fix things. He wanted to shout
that these things were just broken. He wanted her to
understand about the pride of broken things.

Behind him, Bo heard the clack of heels and turned
to see Teacher.

"Rose," she said. "Thank you for coming." Teacher
made an awkward bow. "Is everything okay, Bo?"

"Yes."

He watched as Teacher handed Rose a script for the

play. "So you can read it when you have time," Teacher said, and his mother thanked her.

"I'd like to show you the stage too," said Teacher. "We are rehearsing by scene, so only some of the students come to each session. Can you stay until five?"

"Yes," Rose said, and turned to Bo. "Orange is sleeping. Are you going home?"

"Yes," he said. "I'm not in today's run-through."

He ran hard then, thinking of Bear, and how he would get home and there would be no one to tell him not to bring her inside. Bear would do things on command, but only sometimes. The rest of the time, Bear did what she wanted. She head-butted, and rolled, and fell asleep. She nipped, and chased her tail. She infuriated, and was beautiful.

When Bo arrived home, he saw that Orange had somehow opened her bedroom door. There was a trail of clothing, shit, shattered dishes; and the ancestor shrine was toppled. "Orange!" Bo said, and she looked toward him from amid the debris and cracked her strange smile. "Oh, Orange. Messy!"

He brought her to the living room, and went back to prop the Buddha and the sticks of incense back in the shrine. He found the broom and pushed the rest of the mess into a pile. He put a garbage bag over it and caught it up. When he had the bag tied, he got the mop and swabbed down the trail. Orange slumped on the living room floor, cocked her head and rocked back and forth on her hands.

"Naughty Orange," Bo said, a number of times, even if he kept glancing at her and half smiling, shaking his head. He breathed through his mouth to avoid smelling all the bad smells.

Bear whimpered out back, and Bo said, "Do you hear that, Orange? It's the bear. It's Bear."

Bo brought Orange into the kitchen and turned on the radio, holding her in one arm while he fiddled for the right station. And then he blasted it so that the house seemed to shake. He set Orange down and she swivelled on her butt along the linoleum floor. Bo told her to wait while he let Bear in. He went to the back and opened the door, unhooked Bear from her chain, a chain long enough that she could get beneath the porch and hide in the wooden cabinet he had found on a garbage day and turned into a kennel for her. He climbed back up the stairs and whistled for her to come.

The bear barrelled up the back steps and down the hallway, stopping short to somersault through the kitchen door. Bo pulled off Bear's collar and then stooped to take off his shoes. He glided in his socks all over the slick lino flooring.

"Dance!" Bo said—the music was loud—and Orange pushed her bum in the air so that on all fours she began to sway, and this is how she found the rhythm. The bear lunged up to standing and bounced from one foot to the other, following Bo's arms as if he were a conductor. When the music stopped, and the announcer talked weather, and sports, and news, Orange pounded the floor with her little hands until the next song made her sway again. This was happiness, Bo could see. This was a full-body smile when the mouth wouldn't do the work.

He turned the radio even louder, felt the music pulse through the floorboards. The walls breathed, and Bo danced like crazy, laughing at Orange's twisting ways, her bent, nutty self exploring the bass here, the drum there, until, closing his eyes for a time, it felt as if there were nothing else but song and pulse and sway.

And then the song ended. Ads were playing. Bear stopped to clean her paws. Bo doubled over. Between the wild swinging and the laughing, he was heaving for breath. He splayed himself on the floor and watched Bear lumber off down the hall to Orange's bedroom. Happy.

LATER, DARKNESS COMING, his mother still not home, and Orange asleep, Bo collared and leashed Bear to take her down the street. He did want some fresh air, but more, he wanted to feel the trains hurtle by, that violent shift of air. It was like he was in a dream, the bear sitting beside him, quivering nose up in the air, scenting Bo didn't know what, maybe the cattle at the stockyard a mile away, or maybe just spring rising from the earth. The train pulled him toward it as it raced downtown, and he imagined being sucked right into it, his body slammed. Bear recoiled from that same train's shattering wind, tugged on the leash, afraid. Bo let go and laughed, watching her bound back toward the house, then he followed.

Rose was home. She leaned over the table, the ceiling light giving her face a golden halo and illuminating the script, which she had clearly been reading. She looked up and Bo watched her pupils adjust.

"I was just gone for a few minutes," he said. "Orange was asleep."

"It's okay. She's still sleeping," Rose said, and then, "What is the underworld? The fairy place?" He thought she looked like a child when she asked this.

"It's just what it says," he answered, but he wasn't actually sure anymore. Teacher had said something about thresholds, and he had liked the word so much he had thought about it, and moved it around in his head, and felt it in his mouth, like food, and in doing this, he had stopped listening.

"No," said Rose. "It says: 'I rode into a rock, and went three miles or more.' How can this be? How can a person ride into a rock?" She poked herself when she said "person," to show her own solidity.

"Thresholds," Bo said, and looked at the wood trim of the doorway he stood in. "Teacher said something about doorways, and magic. We were talking about the play, and she said something about them being important."

"What did she mean?"

"I can't remember." He wondered if the thing he had forgotten happened in every doorway, and this began to stress him out. "I'll bring Bear out back," he said.

"When it's warm, you should bathe her. She stinks, Bo."

"Okay."

Then she looked back down at the script. "A castle! I see a castle over there!" She was reading his lines.

Bo knew them all, and had begun the work of making them come alive in the way Teacher wanted. He always imagined the castle made of blue paint—Orange's castle. He knocked on the doorway to the kitchen, just as he was supposed to knock in the play, and turned to his mother as if she played the porter. In fact, Sally was the porter.

"Listen," he said. "I am here to soothe the king with my music and stories. Let me in."

Then his mum said, "You have to say this?"

Bo nodded and recited, "Some stood without heads, and some had no arms, and some had wounds through the body and some lay mad, bound, and some sat on horses, and some choked as they ate, and some were drowned in water, and some were all shrivelled with fire, wives lay in childbirth—" and here he looked over and realized his mother was sobbing.

"Mum," he said. "Mum."

"What a sad play," she managed to say.

"Not really," Bo said. "It's about a hero. He rescues his beautiful queen from the underworld."

His mum looked up at him. "That never happens," she said.

He wanted to go to her, but he had already promised himself not to step through the doorway, so he turned and walked past Orange's room, careful not to wake her, and out to the backyard. He chained Bear to the metal floor of the porch. Bear hurled herself down the stairs and hid straightaway.

When he came back through the house, his mother was reading again. Maybe he had been mistaken about her sobbing. "I remember," he said. "The doorways mean change. Transformation. That's what Teacher said."

Rose looked up and then back to the script. She said, "You've got a lot of lines."

"Yes."

She didn't look up again, but he could see the tiniest smile at the edge of her mouth as she read, and he knew she was proud of this—that he could learn all these lines, that he'd been chosen for this hard part in the play.

THE NEXT DAY, after school, Ernie slammed Bo's face into the last of winter's snow in the yard, and then slammed it again. It was the same old thing only it had accelerated as spring approached. Bo didn't feel like fighting Ernie. He wanted only to play-grapple with Bear, or to be back again fighting for a paying audience. In some way, he didn't care to exist for Ernie anymore. It had become dull. A bunch of children gathered, forming a circle in motion around them, and the fight was on.

"Try harder, Bo," someone yelled.

The ground didn't hurt but it looked as if it might. Bo let Ernie think he'd won. It was uncanny that almost every afternoon after school a fight could break out and no one, not one teacher, janitor or parent seemed to notice. It was as if the kids cheering and yelling surrounded them in magic. Bo reached up as Ernie basked in his win, grabbed Ernie's face and pulled his cheeks down to his own face and bit him.

"You fuck," said Ernie. The cheek had reddened but the skin wasn't broken, and the fight was on again.

Ernie retaliated by pushing Bo's face away from his. A bad move, it turned out, since it forced him to let go of the grip he had on Bo, and gave Bo the opportunity to shove him off, then scissor-kick him in the ass, and get to standing. This riled the crowd. The rest of Ernie's face turned red now, out of embarrassment, and he ran at Bo. The impact of this should have hurt, and it did hurt, but not Bo, because he sidestepped and let a couple of the boys in the audience take the hit. Ernie turned, angry, and fisted Bo in the gut twice and then punched his nose. The blood dripping out of his nose cinched Ernie's triumph. Bo held his head back and limped off toward home. The entire episode lasted maybe three minutes.

"Wait up." Bo turned and there was Peter.

"I'm busy," he said, blood trailing from his nose.

"Yeah, I see that. Here." Peter handed Bo a Kleenex, and Bo made two wands and shoved one up each nostril. Red wicked along them.

"I gotta get home."

"Yeah." But when Bo started walking, Peter followed him. "The thing is," Peter said, "is that every day for years I've been betting on you. I figure you can beat him. You got the footwork, Bo. Why don't you give it to him for once?"

Bo stopped and stared at Peter. "You bet *for* me?"

"Yeah. You're better on your feet than he is. Anyone can see that."

Bo pulled the Kleenex out of one nostril, checked to see if the blood still flowed. It did. He put it back. "So, how much have you lost on me so far?"

"Maybe a hundred dollars."

"I didn't know you were so stupid, Peter."

Peter made puppy eyes, scrunched his mouth up to his nose, a plea, and when Bo started walking, Peter called, "Come on. Just win once, okay. You owe it to yourself, man. Ernie is a dick. We all know that."

But Bo wasn't listening. He had to get to Bear, then train. Because Rose wouldn't let Orange out to watch, he would bring Bear in for Orange. Bo had taught Orange to hold one end of a stick while Bear chewed and tugged on the other. With her instability, Orange got tossed side to side while Bear yanked, yanked and shook the stick like it was prey she'd hard-won. Gerry hadn't lied. With the table scraps they gave her, and the immense bags of kibble Gerry brought by, she was getting big.

When Bo got home, he slipped past his mum, who was sitting in the living room, and washed his face in the kitchen sink. He dried his face on a tea towel and went to his mother, watched her for a minute until she looked up at him.

"Mum," he said. "I'm gonna train in Orange's room."

"No bear shit," she said.

When he brought Bear into Orange's room, Orange woke to them mirroring each other, the bear clumsy and silly, the boy persistent. Bo sang the Prince song "Purple Rain," and made up a simple routine with hand and feet motions. The cub mimicked him clumsily, bored with her day under the porch, eager for treats. Orange clapped for them, contorted her strange little body, huffed when Bear huffed, and begged for treats too, not when she did something clever but when the bear did, as if she had something to do with Bear's ingenuity.

Bo heard the doorbell ring but ignored it. His mum could get it. He kept training, giving Bear and Orange each half a cookie, even as he heard the door close and then voices. He didn't dare bring Bear out, but after twenty minutes or so, he made her sit and stay, and brought Orange out into the hallway, and set her down, before closing the bedroom door and making his way to the kitchen. His mother was sitting behind her sewing machine, working on a costume for the play, and Teacher was about to leave.

"Miss Lily has asked me to sew more costumes," his mother said. She concentrated on pushing gold thread through the machine's needle. There was an abundance of material around her, so that it looked as if she were nestled in a golden cloud.

"Some of the other mothers dropped out—" Teacher began.

His mother cut her off. "This is Emily's dress for the final scene." She stopped threading and gestured at the bunched goldenness of it. "She will be beautiful."

Teacher said, "Yes!" and at the same time Bo said, "Emily?"

It was as if they had manifested her. When he turned toward the hallway door, there she was, holding Orange's hand.

"Hi, Bo." That wave again. "I was just in the bathroom."

"Hi, Emily." Bo looked back at Rose and she gave him an achingly tiny smile.

"We're fitting," Teacher said.

"Oh."

"Can you take Orange?" his mother said, and then rapidly, "Họ đột nhiên xuất hiện. Tôi có thể làm gì?" *They just showed up so what was I supposed to do?*

Orange clutched Emily's hand.

"It's okay." Emily squatted down to Orange's height. "We were just practising walking, right?" and then she picked Orange up and handed her to Bo. "All yours," she said.

Orange smelled of Bear.

Orange pulled away in Bo's arms and rocked her body such that he almost dropped her. "Orange!" Bo said and jostled her so that she crumpled against his shoulder.

"She likes Emily, it looks like," said Teacher.

"Đưa cô vào phòng cô, lam ơn," said Rose, not looking up, and Bo obeyed, taking Orange back to her room, but not before hearing Emily tell Rose that she loved to mind Orange.

He lay down on his back on Orange's mattress and let his sister slap him and bounce near him. Bear came and nuzzled his armpit. He pushed her gently away and when she came back for more, he pushed her again. After a while, he said, "Sleep now," to Orange, and like a miracle she curled up beside him.

He got up after she slept and wandered back to the murmurs in the kitchen. Emily now stood on a chair in the golden gown while his mother pinned the hem. Teacher was gone.

"Hi, Bo," Emily said, turning her head toward him.

"Hey." He tried not to stare and then, feeling awkward in the room with her, went back to Orange. He waited, listening for Emily to leave. Minutes later there were voices and then the door opening and closing. He heaved himself up and brought Bear into the yard.

When he was down the steps and about to chain her up, he noticed Emily smiling at him from the backyard gate.

"That's a big dog," she said. "Holy."

"Yeah," he said.

"Where did you get her?"

"That's the thing," he said. "It's sort of a secret. Her name is Bear. I'm training her to be a circus bear—a wrestling bear. That guy you saw my mum with? His name is Max and he's sorta my boss."

"Sorta?"

"Yeah."

Emily unlatched the gate and let herself in. "I've been smelling this scent on Orange for a month or more, every time I babysit. I didn't think she smelled like dog," she said. "But today it was super strong, so I decided to follow my nose. This is so cool." She came very close to Bo and Bear. "Can I pet her?"

Bo nodded, and Emily knelt, facing the bear at eye level. "Bear," she said. "You are very nice." She ran her fingers along the swirl of fur between Bear's eyes and Bear stayed very still and let this happen. "Oh, you are lovely."

"Promise not to tell," Bo said.

Emily looked up at him. "Promise," she said.

It was three weeks before the play and Bear strained at the leash, pulled Bo down the hallway and through the kitchen, past Rose, sitting in near darkness, her sadness like a force field, the tumbler rattling on the table to Orange's percussive angst. Orange ran her body against the door to her bedroom, and the house seemed to shake. The fact of the play was plaguing Bo. He had to get outside, into the dark, just to get away from his house. If he moved, he could stop thinking about it all.

Bo took Clendenan, then turned down through Ravina Park. There were dogs there, let loose to do their business, and Bear yanked Bo from scent to scent, sniffing and paw-swatting at the larger dogs. Bo and Bear did not linger, though—their destination was farther south. He sidled with his bear down shadowed streets until they came to High Park. The night brought strange rustlings but no trouble. In the park, Bo let the bear off-leash so the two of them could go freely cross-country.

Bo continued, silent, down the hill on Spring Road, where the brush hid them, and deeper into the park, Bear on his heels. There was some light from the half-moon, not much but enough to manage. The park was all but abandoned on the weeknights and in-between weather seasons, and what wild had made its home here had not ever thought of bear, had no natural fear of one, except from some primordial reflex—the smell suggesting some bigness. Raccoons and skunks waddled across their path and looked warily at Bo, but seemed to disregard Bear.

Each night since the trees had leafed out, Bo had done short training sessions in the backyard or in the dark and safety of the forest's opening canopy. He would have Bear sit and stay, or beg or roll over, and then give her freedom to climb a tree, or dig or upend a rock to look for grubs, things Bear loved doing. They had explored all over the park, but now they were in the dense brush in the northeastern edge, uphill from the reservoir pond.

"Up. Up," Bo said.

And Bear sprang up on her back legs and danced.

When Bo ran out of treats to give her, he scratched her behind the ears and rubbed her chest, and she was grateful and leaned into him. Bo showed her cartwheels and somersaults and the cub learned bearish versions. She would try most anything the boy showed her, like she was an extension of Bo. That is what Bo liked to think.

When Gerry visited every week, Bo demonstrated all she could do—a clumsy dance, a flip, how she wrestled his legs to topple him. "Oh-ho," Gerry would say. "I knew you were the man for it."

The *man* for it.

Bo heard something in the thicket next to them. "Crouch," said Bo. Bear did, compressing herself as best she could. She was a big girl, now, like Gerry had said— she was a full bear's head taller than Bo when she stood on her back legs. Bo gave the signal for quiet, and Bear nuzzled her nose under Bo's elbow by way of communicating she understood and then splayed like a carpet on the forest floor. Bo lay beside her, heart thumping.

"I seen you, kid." A strange voice, viscous and strangled.

Bo shook his head, gestured *stay* to Bear, and waited, meting his breath out long and slow to calm himself.

"I god-damned wasn't born yesterday."

Bo signalled again to Bear to stay, rolled away as far as he could, and stood, hoping to draw attention away from her. It was a vagrant. Bo tried to see if the man was crazy or drunk or both, and, if both, in what mixture. He was little, under five feet tall, his hair long and filthy with sticks and bits of forest debris in it. A wild man. He wore a green camouflage army jacket, stained, torn and several sizes too big. His nose was a gaping hole, and his chin was wrapped in a bandana.

"The rest of you," the man said. His words were slurred and wet.

The sight of the man froze him. Who was this? What was this? "Just me," Bo said. "A kid."

"Fuck off," the vagrant said. "If I didn't see a bear, I sure as fuck smelled one. Where'd he go?" The man was right up close to him now, and Bo stared at the inside of his face. A twist of pink flesh and bone, tooth, sinew where there should be nose, a damp bandana. "Stop staring, you ignoramus."

And stupidly, looking down, Bo gave Bear away.

Bear lifted, scenting the vagrant, her nose crinkling back, young fangs glinting white in the moonlight. "She's mine," Bo said.

"Nobody never owned a bear," the man said, "and nobody never will. A bear owns itself, just like any man owns hisself. One day, he'll tear your arm off to prove it."

"*She*. I'm her trainer," said Bo, chastened by the wreckage of the man's face, his poverty—his roughness.

The vagrant came a step closer and took a long look at Bear. "I can take her with me now and bring her to a place where she could really live."

Bo shook his head.

"What you got to lose, boy?"

Bo shook his head again. But there was a turning in his gut—dinner shifting—like a wrongness was being revealed to him.

"Who are you?" Bo asked.

"Who am I? Well, they call me Soldier Man. I run off and joined a war and it took my face. I'm ugly now, so I pretty much just hide in here." Then he said, "Come here, bear," and snapped his fingers at her.

Bear pulled up to beg and sucked in so much of the man's scent Bo felt air brush him. She was learning the vagrant, some part of him Bo would never catch. But she did not move. Instead, she glanced at Bo. The vagrant gestured, beckoned, and the cub pulled back fast. It would take some doing now to get her to come.

"You scared her," said Bo.

"Sure." And then there was a movement and the place where the man had stood was dark. A branch still swayed, but he was gone.

Within seconds, Bo moved on too, thinking how he would have to be more careful late at night with Bear. But mostly, he thought about *what war*, and *what soldier*, and then, before he could stop his mind, he thought about his father, sharks, water.

Bo got home to find Max sitting in the kitchen as if he'd never left, looking more serious than Bo had ever seen him. Rose flitted, picking Orange up and putting her down. Orange was sick, Bo could see. Mucus burbled at her nose and she looked overly pink. Bo hated it that she was even in the room, because it meant that Max could look upon her. But when Bo glowered toward Max, Max was looking at him, not at Orange. He was looking at Bo and at Bear, and he looked pleased.

Rose said, "Why don't you show Max what you've taught your bear?"

Max cleared his throat. "Circuit's starting up. Gerry must have mentioned."

"He said something to me last week when he stopped by. Millbrook Fair this Friday. But he's saving Bear for the Ex."

"Oh, he is, is he? I suppose it makes some sense. A novelty should have a special reveal, right?" He nodded at Bear, and reached out to pat her, but Bo pulled back on the lead.

"Bear's tired." Then he felt it himself, a cover of exhaustion being pulled over him. Soldier Man's destroyed face flashed in his mind, and then it was gone, just as he had disappeared. Bo needed to sleep.

He coaxed Bear to the back of the house and out the door to the yard. Bear did not want to be chained but she let it happen anyway. Bo scratched her between the eyes and went back to the kitchen.

"I'm taking Orange to bed," he said to his mother.

But it was Max who answered. "Good idea, son."

His mum smiled, and said, "Yes."

Bo made a face at Max and picked up Orange.

"What?" said Max, throwing his hands up in the air. "You don't like the bear I gave you?"

So, that was how it was supposed to work. In Max's mind it was a trade.

He hoisted Orange a little higher and shook his head. He could feel the rage rising in him, so to stop himself from hitting Max again, he took Orange to her room, then stayed with her until she slept so deeply that he felt for her pulse and the soft air releasing from her nose, to be sure she was not dead.

The door was cracked open and he heard snippets of conversation, but not enough to make sense of anything. He stood up and then sat again, this time with his back leaning against the wall near the door, to hear better.

"I'm so glad you're back," his mother said.

"I missed you, Thao."

And as much as he wanted to purely hate Max, this other thought was pressing against the rage: his mum was happy again. What if it were okay that Max was here? Maybe Max's feelings for Rose had somehow stopped him from preying on Orange. Maybe this was normal. Maybe everything would be okay.

"What stinks?" said Ernie. It was the Monday after the Millbrook Fair—first of the season and Bo had revelled in his fight with Loralei. He'd come home too tired to bother washing. Bo realized he smelled of adult bear.

Bo said, "Whoever smelt it, dealt it."

Peter and Ernie and he were waiting outside the

school for rehearsal. It was three-thirty, the afternoon sun hot. They had to practise the part just before the Fairy King steals Heurodis. In one week the play would go on, and in two, school would be over and it would be summer. Bo was glad to have had his lines memorized so long, because now they were just part of him. Still, he was nervous, and would be glad when the play was over and he could concentrate full-time on training Bear and getting ready for the Ex.

"Whoever denied it, supplied it," Peter said.

Bo got up and sat downwind from the others. He loved the way he smelled.

"Whoa," said Ernie. "What is that? Like a zoo or something. Like dead shit. Like the stockyards. You stink worse than the yards, you little asshole."

Bo did not mean to. It was Ernie calling him an asshole. It reminded him of Max calling him an asshole that time. His body reacted. He plowed Ernie's face so hard it jerked back and pulled him with it and then Bo was straddling Ernie and punching and punching, Peter just standing there, and Ernie too surprised to do much but take it, so that by the time Bo stopped, Ernie was a swollen bleeding mess.

Bo got to his feet, muttering, "Sorry, sorry," and stepped back.

Bo caught the edge of Peter's joy, as they both watched Ernie stumble off toward his house.

Then Bo started walking too. "Tell Miss Lily I got sick," he said.

"You're blowing off rehearsal?" said Peter.

"Yeah." He knew his part backwards and forwards and didn't want to explain to Teacher why his knuckle was bleeding, and why Ernie had left.

He stopped at the side of his house and ran the outdoor tap over his right fist, let the water pink and flow down the paved gully. Then he splashed his face and rubbed the water down his neck and chest and over his hair. He figured Ernie would wait a day or two to pay him back, that he had some breathing space. He walked up the metal porch stairs, looked down at Bear looking up at him, entered the back of the house. He could hear his mum crooning a Vietnamese love song from the kitchen, and knew she'd been drinking.

"Bo?" she called. "Is that you?"

He stopped in on Orange on the way by. She was bobbing her stuffed donkey up and down. He thought, new creature, and smiled.

"Bo?" His mum's voice was urgent.

"Yes, Mum. I'm here." He was at the kitchen door, and her back was to him, but now she turned and he saw she was not only drunk but also crying. "Oh, Mum," he said.

"I'm sorry," she said.

"It's okay. I don't mind."

Now, though, she shook her head. "Father Bart was here. We have to leave the house—we have until the end of July. He said the church group feels we need to find our own way. The diocese is selling the house. He said he knew we would understand."

"Leave to where?" asked Bo.

"I don't know."

And then the doorbell rang, and before he could answer it, Max was in the kitchen.

"Ready?" he said. He must have seen then that she had been crying. He said, "Hey, Thao, what's the matter?"

"We have to move," she said.

Rose stood and Bo saw then that his mum was wearing a new dress, and shoes with heels. "Mum!" he said. If her eyes weren't puffy from crying, she would be beautiful.

Max hugged his mum and said, "It's okay." He was patting her back. "We'll figure something out. Don't worry."

Rose went to the sink to run cool water over her face. She rummaged in a little pocket in her dress and pulled out a lipstick. Bo watched Max admiring her as she leaned toward a tiny mirror over the sink and applied a dark red to her mouth.

"We'll be back by ten," Rose said, then. "Okay, Bo?"

"Okay." Bo wasn't sure whether it was. He looked at Max and tried his hardest to smile, even while his heart raced.

After they left, Bo checked on Orange. She was awake and no longer so pink. He nestled her between cushions and tucked a sheet around her and then tightly under the mattress to restrain her. Her face was filthy with dried sweat and mucus, so that it was almost black in patches, and he left this, for fear if he tried to wipe her clean, he would upset her. There were bedclothes and diapers and odd assortments of clothing strewn throughout the space, all reeking of bear. He gently nudged these into a pile and pushed it out the door to be added to the laundry his mother tackled as infrequently as she could get away with. He could hear Bear moaning in the backyard, but he ignored her.

Bo sat in the green chair. The end of July was a long way away, he thought. They could find another place to live in by then. He was working again and they would manage. A flicker of movement at the kitchen window made him look up, and there was Emily waving something above her head. Then she ducked down and he heard her coming up the stairs and onto the porch. He jumped up.

"No," he said, and shook his head at her through the glass.

She ignored him and let herself in. "You missed rehearsal," she said.

He showed her his knuckles. "I hit a brick wall."

"Ernie?"

"Yeah."

"Well, Miss Lily had to call it short and when I was walking home I saw your mum leave with that Max guy," she said. "Guess what? My parents are away and— Have you noticed how warm it is today?"

She had a bundle of clothing in her hand, a dress that was just the right size for Orange and little sandals, and that was not all. There was a bathing suit, and outside on the sidewalk, an old blue pram.

"She's not a doll," said Bo, to stem the direction things were headed. "Emily, you can't just take her."

"Bo."

"No."

"You promised, and it's so warm."

"I didn't promise."

"We both made promises. And I've kept mine," she said. "It's just wrong that she never goes out. My mother says she'll get rickets. She needs some sun."

"You can't just take her."

Emily was already down the hall, pulling the sundress over Orange's sleepy head. "Oh, it's darling. Look, Bo!"

The dress managed to correct some of the torque in Orange's figure so that her torso looked fairly normal with it on. The problem was that her head was so over-large and her legs and arms so twisted that it was impossible to focus solely on the torso, and so, in the end, Orange looked more monstrous than ever.

"Freak show," he muttered, but Emily was already

busy strapping on the sandals. "She doesn't like this, you know? Plus, she's sick, otherwise she wouldn't let you do it. You're taking advantage—"

"No, Bo. I am not. I am taking her to cool off in my pool. You can stay here and suffer or you can come along." She put a sunbonnet on Orange and tied it under her chin. "Look how cute," said Emily. She went outside with Orange in her arms. "Going to the pool," she was saying, over and over, to cheer her, and she placed her gently in the pram.

Bo snorted. His sister looked ridiculous bent into the small space. "This is not a good idea."

"I don't care."

Orange lay staring up from the bed Emily had made in the pram, grabbing at the rim of her new bonnet. His mother would have a fit.

"No one had better see this," he said. "How are you going to get her in the pool without anyone seeing?"

"I'm not."

"What do you mean?"

"I mean people might see her."

"But—"

"Bo," said Emily. "She's going in."

She said this in such a way that Bo did not know how to argue against it. He imagined the water sucking his sister in, like a great liquid maw. Besides, Emily's house secretly terrified Bo, and now they were heading there, the pram bouncing over every bump it hit.

And then they were in front of the house—the ivy sweeping up to the roof and edging along it. Bo looked up and as he did, the ivy seemed to breathe, and then it bloomed in sharp downward wingbeats as hundreds of swallows emerged and swung into the air, billowing above the house like a black and dissipating cloud. Orange seemed to be watching them too.

Bo felt suddenly sick. It was terrible to see Orange out of the house in daylight. She would fall, she would drown, she would—something awful would happen. "Where are your parents?"

"They trust me."

"Lucky."

"Well, your mum is hardly around either."

"That isn't trust," said Bo. He tried to imagine what he would do with himself if he were truly alone and came up with: fighting, thinking about fighting, looking for a fight. He could also write in his journal, but without Orange, there would be no tower, no blue, no point. He didn't want to think about life without Orange, the ugly chasm that would be not-Orange.

"Bo," said Emily.

He looked from Orange, twisting about in the pram, into Emily's green eyes. They were shiny and smiling. She had eyes that could do that. Orange had flipped onto her belly and was bum up, rocking until she might pop out, so Bo grabbed her by the waist and swung her up and out of the pram. Tucked her under his arm like a football.

"Pool," he said, acting brave, and strode along the side of the house to the backyard.

"All right!" Emily said.

The pool was an egg-shaped concrete in-ground pool, and even though Emily maintained the water was clean, it had a green murkiness to it that reminded him too much of the sea.

"My parents are against chlorination," said Emily. "They like the pool to be reminiscent of a pond. Not everyone can afford a cottage, my father likes to say, so we have our cottage right in our backyard."

Bo could not see the bottom. He lowered himself to a squat and put Orange down.

"Come on." Emily lay down, leaned her arms and head over the edge and lightly trailed her fingers in the water.

The ripples seemed alive, but he followed her lead and helped Orange to do the same. He had to hold her tightly by her sundress when she realized what this was, for she began to slap the surface of the water, sending waves all about. The squirming brought her closer and closer to falling in.

"There is a little rubber dinghy," said Emily. "Do you think she would lie still?"

Bo shook his head. "You can't predict what she'll do." He thought of the worst thing that she could do and found his thinking could not stretch that far—he could not move.

"I'll show it to you and then you can decide." Emily stood up and strode off to a dilapidated shed in the back of the garden, brought back a pink blow-up boat, more or less round. "We'll put her in and hold the boat steady if she moves too much. Nothing can happen."

But Bo was thinking about having to get in the water, and water in general, so that now his head, and his whole body, were shaking, no.

"I think it'll be okay, Bo. The water will soothe her," said Emily. She pulled off her T-shirt and her shorts and she was already in her bathing suit. "Seriously, Bo. We got this far."

"Yeah."

Orange was skimming the water now gently with her palm, sending the tiniest waves out from herself. It seemed to please her, and she did it again and again. She was mesmerized, still, calm. Bo got up from the pool deck and complied with this insane request, pulling his shirt off and then his shoes and socks until he was in his shorts. "Okay," he said to Emily.

"What now?"

"If we disturb her she might get upset, so how are we going to get her in the boat?"

"It was your idea."

Emily gave him a look, then pulled the boat close to

the edge so she could dump it in the water. They watched as it bounced and then floated away from them. "Orange?" Emily said. "See that?"

Then she sat on the edge of the pool with her legs tucked into herself. "Watch," she said to Orange, and then slid down, the green water disappearing her, cutting her off.

"It looks like you are cut through the middle," said Bo. It was almost a whisper, windlike, coming across more like thought than sound, but he knew Emily heard because she turned and then lifted her feet—first one and then the other—to prove they were still there. And then she launched into the water and swam to the little boat. She grabbed the side and pulled herself up. She paddled it closer to Bo and Orange.

"A boat," she said, looking at Orange.

Emily pushed off the side of the pool and the boat spiralled and eddied. The little wavelets emerging from it met the water trails Orange had made with her hands, and disrupted them, making new configurations on the surface of the water. Orange was watching this as if she could read its meaning.

Emily was now at the far end of the pool, looking back. "Do you want a ride, Orange?"

Bo watched his sister slow the motion of her hand and wait for the ripples to broaden out into velvety green fabric, like the surface of the water was sighing, falling asleep. She looked toward the dinghy, her bulgy eyes askew, and her head now lolloping slowly back and forth, as if assessing.

"You do?"

"She doesn't," said Bo, though he wasn't sure.

"Yes, she does. Don't you, Orange?"

Orange pressed back from the edge and lifted her bum into the air. Bo grabbed her by the sundress again. "I wish your parents believed in chlorination," Bo called.

Emily laughed. "There are even frogs living in here. I've seen them." She was out of breath, paddling back toward them. "Orange," she said. "Your turn."

Bo was now holding Orange aloft as she tried to dive for the boat. "No, Orange."

"I got her," said Emily. "Let her go. I have her."

"You sure?"

"Yes." And there she was, his sister, cradled in Emily's lap, floating across the water, the dinghy rocking erratically. "Shh," said Emily. "Shh, Orange," and his sister began to calm, and the boat did too.

No one talked for some time and it was only the thick air, humid and still, and birdcall they had not noticed before, and a bumblebee, and some sounds Bo could not identify—city and nature all blended. Orange rotated along the water, her head resting on Emily's legs, a little strand of drool dangling from her mouth.

Bo squatted and then lay down so that he could watch his sister from almost the same level, and their eyes could lock—if Orange would even look, which she would not. Bo felt himself rocked by the pulse of the moving water, mesmerized, so that the splash completely surprised him. He looked up to see a plume of green and transparent water, as if the water itself were bucking and thrashing, and then he saw Orange's sundress billowing as she landed face down in the pool. He stood up before he knew he was standing up. And then he knew he had to jump in.

He looked to Emily, frozen in the moment. She leaned over the dinghy and grabbed the straps of the sundress and pulled. His sister sputtered as she came out of the water and began to flail her arms, like a crab, a caught lobster. Water streamed off Orange's protesting self. Back in the boat, she thumped about like a landed fish, and the boat rocked crazily.

"She's a floater!" Emily said triumphantly. She was laughing down at Orange, trying to keep her still so they wouldn't capsize. "She'll be swimming in no time."

"She almost drowned. She almost—"

"Nonsense. She's a natural. Come in and grab us, will you? Bring us to the shallow end so I can get us out and get a flutter board."

"What for?"

"Come on, Bo."

Orange was thumping wildly, and Bo was spinning back in time to an altercation between his parents right

before they got on the fishing boat, his mother shrieking, "Get on, please get on!" His father—what?—scared?

Emily had one arm curved under Orange's armpit.
Bo could hear his sister's frantic breathing; it was the
most noise she could make without a wall to throw herself against.

"Orange," Emily said. She sounded like Teacher, and
it soothed him, the authority of it. "If you want to go
back in the water, Orange, you will have to listen to me.
You have to stop squirming and I have to be absolutely
sure you will listen to me."

Orange thrashed for a little longer, then quieted, face
up now and panting, her eyes fixed on Emily's face. Bo
was slowly guiding the dinghy along the side of the
pool toward the shallow end. Once they arrived, Emily
explained to Orange that she had to go with Bo, and
again, that she had to listen. Emily jumped into the
water and then pulled herself up and out of the pool.
Again the surface gulped and the water spun in surpris-
ing ways, bubbles, fog, a kind of dance, and Bo found
himself unable to look away.

The flutter board was a rectangular bit of red foam.
Bo knew that the swimmer was meant to hold onto it,
and kick and so move about safely in the water.

"Emily," he said. "She hasn't got proper fingers."

"Shh," said Emily. "It doesn't matter. Come. Orange,
come. Jump."

"She can't," said Bo. His sister was twisting to get out of his grip. "I'm holding onto her."

"Then let her go, Bo. She's a floater," Emily said, as if this would be entirely obvious to anyone. "I have her."

She bit him then, and he let her go before he could think about it. She scuttled sideways and threw herself into the pool. The water reached out its wet hands and grabbed her, and then the hands were gone, as the water drank her. The water swallowed her, but she bobbed, face-up, jubilant, whipping her head back and forth. Emily pulled her over and slipped the foam under her belly.

"You can swim, Orange." She held her along the back and made a sound like "Wheeeee" as she swung the flutter board in a wide curve. "Kick! Kick! That's it. Harder. This leg, then this leg," and here Emily held one leg, and then the other, and began counting a rhythm she wanted Orange to follow.

Emily looked up at Bo. "Come on in, Bo."

"No," he said. "I can't." Even watching Orange, he thought he would die.

THAT WEEK HEATED THE CITY UP, but Bo and Orange did not go back to Emily's pool. The class was busy with rehearsals and fittings and finding last-minute props. And then it was the day of the play. They had made programs in art class. Two children from grade seven were going to hand them to the audience as they entered the auditorium.

Late that afternoon, after school, his mum fussing with a seam on his costume in the kitchen and Orange asleep, Bo heard the ice-cream truck bell, and scooped some change from the little box in his room. He intended to take the cone and go for a walk with it, but he was anxious, so instead he wandered to the yard, hung out with Bear. He'd forgotten about losing the house, he'd forgotten all of it. And later he would think how he should have been paying more attention, how there must have been details he missed, some explanation.

Instead he dripped ice cream into Bear's mouth, and later ate a tense meal, with Max holding forth about the new season, and all the opportunities a curiosity might have on the U.S. circuit—he meant Bear but he kept glancing at Orange and Rose.

Rose caught Bo staring at her, and made a face. "What is it, Bo?"

"Nothing."

"Are you nervous about tonight?"

"Nope." But of course he was. His stomach was churning and clenching and he had been to the bathroom three times since he got home from school.

At the school, after dinner, Teacher gave final instructions as Rose fussed with pins and Velcro. The insular feeling that had built around the play, the particular camaraderie that had formed as they rehearsed, was being challenged by the swelling noise of people chatting and laughing and moving chairs about on the other side of the curtain. Bo had a floating feeling, standing there in his silver braid and velvet costume, and he looked across to find his mother, who was fixing the hem of Emily's gown where she'd stepped on it and it had torn. She was too polite and quiet to tell Emily to stay still, and she struggled with the shaking fabric as Emily wiggled.

Teacher was suddenly in front of them. "You'll have to stop talking," she said, not seeming to notice that Rose and Emily had not been talking. "The curtain is about to rise." Bo had never seen her so flustered.

The curtain did not rise but pulled apart, Sally working the silken ropes to reveal Peter and Ernie playing the grafted tree, holding papier mâché limbs aloft, one with apples, the other with pears, all fruit the children had made and painted that term. They had been instructed to stay quiet until the audience stilled, and then take their cue from Rose, who sat on a chair just below them at midstage.

Bo felt air brush his face, watched the golden fabric of Emily's gown shimmer, and let his brain wander knowing there was some time until his cue. He thought of Bear, and Loralei. He thought of Gerry, who had told him that Max had put a great deal of stock in Bear. He wanted to prove something at the Ex, so that he would be invited back the following year.

"We gotta be our best every day," Gerry had said, and when Bo looked back quizzically, he growled, "A man has to earn a living," as if this should be self-evident. To Bo, it rang true. He would have to take care of his mother, and of Orange. He would have to take care of Orange for her whole life. He shuddered at the sudden image of the doctor saying how Orange's life expectancy was short, and that smug look that crossed his face. It was dishonourable to hit a doctor, but Bo wished he could go back in time and smack him.

And then he heard Emily screaming and the pounding of her feet across the stage and knew the scene was ending and he'd be on. And before too long, he was facing the audience, looking stage left and stage right for his queen. He looked behind him and there she was, her back to him, and then she turned. They were alone. Fake blood trickled down her face. Emily was very good at looking unhappy. She wailed and told him the story of how she'd fallen asleep and met the Fairy King in her dreams and how now she would have to go with him.

Bo summoned his army to stand guard against the Fairy King, and as they tromped around, the tree sidled back onstage, and Emily fell into a swoon, and he and the army stood guard while the lights dimmed, until it was so dark that no one could see. A single spotlight followed Michael as he rode in on the white hobbyhorse his father had carved. Its eyes gleamed so real. Bo stood right behind the action, and watched Emily follow Michael offstage, and felt an awful thickening anxiety that he could not name. He liked Michael well enough, but in this moment, he despised him.

When the lights rose and the guards realized she was gone, Sir Orfeo's rage and sudden emotional collapse merged with Bo's feelings, so that it felt good to rage and hate and swoon. He projected his lines so clearly and with such intention, he saw Teacher smile. He commanded his favourite baron: "Take care of my lands while I'm away. I will go into the wilderness, and live there evermore with wild beasts in grey woods."

The guards and ladies cried how they did not want him to leave. There was much weeping and lamentation. Even Peter and Ernie looked devastated, as they had been directed to look, though Bo saw their veiled amusement and tried not to laugh. Backstage, Bo stripped off his royal garments and donned a tunic his mother had fashioned from a potato sack. Before the crowd, he turned and turned and turned, and as he did, the others came back onstage dressed as trees and tried to tear at him.

When he had turned ten times or more, he bent over a cluster of the trees and fetched his disguise, and when he spun to face the audience, Ernie said, "Through wood and over heath, into the wilderness, Orfeo went. There was nothing there to give him comfort, and he lived in great distress. Where he had lain upon a bed of purple linen, now he had hard heather. He covered himself with leaves and branches, and in winter, he covered himself in moss to stay warm. For food he dug to find his fill of roots. Sir Orfeo suffered ten years and more with only his harp and the wild beasts to keep him company."

The fake grey beard and wig straggled down to Bo's waist and he attempted to look utterly despondent.

Act Two ended and Act Three began, the play un-spooling like a dream. Bo descended to the underworld and walked through its devastation. He sang to the Fairy King and won Heurodis from the dead. And then all was fine, and Orfeo and Heurodis ruled again in peace, and at last, like some truly strange magic, the audience erupted into applause.

Bo was stricken by how he must come away from being Orfeo and be himself, bowing and smiling out into the clapping darkness. Looking down, there was Rose, his mother, beaming up at him. She could look sad even in her pride. But still. He had not missed a line.

They walked home together, with Bo asking her if she had seen this and that small mistake they had made. His mother finally stopped him, saying, "Whatever happens, I will always be proud of you."

He did not ask because he wanted to think that it meant she loved him, and that no one knew the future, which she did mean. Bo smiled at her and said, "Thanks."

Max was minding Orange, and Bo spent the rest of the walk preparing how to avoid him once he got home.

The house was quiet when they arrived, and Max was in the kitchen. Orange must be asleep. Bo turned toward his bedroom, but Max called out to him.

"How did it go, Bo?"

"Okay," he said. And then, because he really did not want to talk to Max, he said to Rose, "I'm really tired, Mum. I'm going to go to bed."

She nodded. "You were very convincing as Sir Orfeo," she said. "You were a real hero with all those lines too." She hugged him.

Bo smiled and hugged her back. He had not hugged his mother in so long, it felt strange. He climbed into his bed and nestled his head into his pillow, listening to the murmurs of Max and his mother far off, and then it was morning. Nothing had disturbed his sleep, and he had not dreamt at all.

SOME STILLNESS, a vacancy, woke him early. He would go pee, he decided, and then fall back to sleep, but when he made his way to the bathroom, he could sense the not-breathing space of the house. He began turning on the lights, and in the brightness he discovered that they were gone. His mother had gone and his sister was not asleep in her room, and, save for the reiterative scraping from the backyard, which must be Bear, he was alone.

Bo went in his underwear to unchain Bear. He brought her in the house and sat in the kitchen with her for some time, Bear poking at his leg a few times and then, realizing Bo wasn't going to play, curling up under the table to sleep. The note in front of Bo read: *This is for the best. Call Gerry. We've arranged it. Love, Mum.* But Bo did not want to go to Gerry, and he sat there until it was too late to go to school. When the phone rang, he didn't answer it, figuring it was the school asking after his whereabouts. He sat beyond the sightlines of the window in the front door, so Emily couldn't see him when she came knocking after school. He fed the bear in between times, and by her moan, knew she had to go out—but he ignored her, until the house took on a smell and he knew Bear had done her business inside.

He couldn't cry. He didn't move. The phone rang, and he answered it this time, out of reflex.

"Bo Jangles," Gerry said, and Bo could not deny the sound of his voice comforted him. "How you doing?"

"Fine."

"Oh yeah?"

"Yeah." Bo imagined Grimsby, the sad truck, Loralei circumnavigating a corroded peg, an ugly peeling bungalow, and Gerry, standing in the doorway, scratching his belly. He whispered, "I'm fine."

"I've been calling and calling," said Gerry. "The plan is I come get you and you stay with me until the Ex. We work out the kinks in your act, get that bear in working order. Max agrees we should rest the animals until then. Forget the little fairs this summer; we have our sights on the big-time. So, you'll come here and you'll keep training Bear. I got all you need right here."

Gerry's optimism, and the fact of a plan, might have pleased Bo. But the letter sprang to mind:

We've arranged it. Meaning Max had arranged it.

Bo felt his throat close. "No," he managed to say into the accumulating silence. Bo could hear his own breath, his heartbeat, and already in his mind, he was running. "How long have you known?"

"Kid," said Gerry. "I'm really sorry. This can't be nice for you."

Bo tried latching onto just one thought. "Gerry," he said, "where did Max go with Orange? Where did he take her?"

"I'm not at liberty, kiddo."

"Say."

"Well, the fact is—" Bo could hear Gerry drawing greedily on a cigarette.

"The truth is I honestly don't know. All I can say is they came by here to sort out some paperwork. The kid and your mum were in Max's trailer, and the lot of them were happy."

"Orange—?"

"She was smiling, Bo Jangles. I won't lie to you."

Again Bo was quiet, only breathing.

"Max wouldn't say which direction they were headed."

Bo heard the pop of Gerry's jaw, and imagined a series of elegant smoke rings dancing within one another. It was a party trick of his. "You'll be happy here," he said. "Bear'll love it too. It's for the best, kid."

The peg, and there was Loralei sitting, and the scritch-scratch of her habitual rubbing. Bo imagined a doughnut of bare earth around the peg where Loralei had trod a path, bored, insanely bored.

"I'm staying here," said Bo, blood fleeing from his extremities. He might faint, he thought.

"Kid."

"I'm not coming." Bear sat in the hallway, her eyes lit and lively, watching. They could stay in the house until the end of July, he thought, despite how ludicrous he immediately realized this would be. Bo said, "*We're* not coming." And in his mind this new plan took some loose shape— he'd train Bear, not only to perform but also to protect him, and together they'd busk wherever they could. They'd rove the fairs until the Ex. Fuck Max. Fuck him.

"She's my bear, Bo Jangles," Gerry said, a warning entering his tone. "That's my fucking investment."

No, Bo thought, she's mine. And as he hung up, Bo could hear Gerry saying, "I'm on my way, Bo. You better be there for me, or I swear I'll find you. Jesus, kid. Don't do this—"

Bo stuffed into a rucksack an assortment of clothing, the tin from the fridge that now held only fifty dollars, his journal and the photographs he had taken of Orange those months ago. He looked around at the yellowed walls, the cracked, dirty linoleum, the ragged, dingy carpet running the length of the hall. Leaving this felt good. He'd finish training Bear and then he would find Orange, save her, and—then what? He felt so unequal to this task. What if he could not find her?

He stood at the window, paralyzed by all these thoughts pressing in, and watched Teacher come up the front steps. She saw him before he could duck. He opened the door and stepped outside so that she wouldn't see Bear, or smell her.

"Hi," he said, as if things were normal. His voice quivered at the lie of it.

"Hi, Bo." There were furrows between her eyebrows and he tried to assess whether she was worried or angry.

"I'm sorry I missed school," he said. "I overslept and then—"

"You weren't the only one," she interrupted, "but why didn't your mum call? Is she here? I'd like to speak with her."

"She's not home."

"That's impossible," she said. "She's known about this makeup doctor's appointment for weeks." Teacher checked her wristwatch, looked back up at him. "Do you know when she'll be back?"

He shook his head fast.

"What is it, Bo?"

"She went with someone. They took Orange."

"Oh," said Teacher. She made an odd face, like she couldn't take in this information. And then he realized it was more that she didn't want to meddle. "She'll have to make another appointment, as soon as possible, herself. It's very important. Do you understand, Bo?"

"Yes." He wanted to ask why it was important but he didn't. His mother didn't go to doctors.

"Bo," Teacher said. "You were very fine last night. I think you might be a born actor, you seemed so real up on the stage. I can't tell you how happy I was for you."

"Thank you," he said. He wished she would leave so he could go. He could hear the faint click of Bear treading through the house.

"Bo, there is something else I need to tell you," she said. She took a deep breath and held it for a beat, then sighed. She avoided his eyes, so that he wondered whether she would cry. "I'm leaving my job at the school, going back to my hometown. I won't be back in the fall." There was something more she wasn't saying, he knew.

Bo said, "Oh," and then, "Does my mother know that?" because he wondered whether she might come back if she knew no one would be there to try to get her to a doctor.

"She really needs to make that appointment," Teacher repeated, biting her lip.

"I'll tell her."

"Thank you, Bo."

When Teacher turned to go, he realized he would miss her, and wanted to say something about that, but instead he said just "Goodbye."

Bo went back through the house and stood in Orange's room, looking for some piece of her to take with him. And he knew right away. He went to the kitchen and found the sharpest knife, brought it back and slid it under the wallpaper, cutting a sizable piece. A knight on a massive blue steed, in full gallop, a jousting pole readied, and beneath it, his own drawing of a soldier pointing his pistol at another man whose hands were held up in surrender, and below that a great toothy fish coming to swallow it all. A bedtime story he had drawn for Orange.

He folded it carefully and tucked it between the pages of his journal in his rucksack. He sat at the kitchen table, the bear at his side. "We'll go, Bear," he said, "and then we'll come back every few days and check to see if they've come home." He missed Orange. He felt this missing like a hot stone beneath his rib cage. Bear looked up at him and then flopped down, tucked her head under her paw.

It was night when Bo left, hoping the darkness would hide Bear—ten months old, she stood over three feet at her shoulders and could never be mistaken for a dog. They were not far from the house, cutting behind the school toward Ravina Park, when Bo saw Father Bart, his black vestments crisply swinging, heading in the direction of Bo's house. Bo thought the priest had not seen him, and was surprised when he stopped and turned toward the maple tree where Bo had tried to hide with Bear.

"Bo?" he called. There were three street lights broken on this stretch of road and it was dark.

Bo did not move.

"Bo," the priest said. "What is that, son?" The priest's voice was pitched up with the birds. He spoke as a man who imagines himself to have gone crazy. "My God, is that a bear with you?"

Bo emerged from hiding, and stood with Bear on the end of the leash. He said nothing, did not really know what he was doing, and when the priest gawked, his gown fluttering in the evening breeze, his shoes polished so carefully, Bo merely turned and walked away at half speed. Father Bart called out that he was sorry about how things had gone, but Bo kept walking—the priest's calling meant nothing to him. He walked into the night, the park, that otherworld.

The way to the forest had never felt more strange. There were hard moments in the short journey from the house he had shared with his mother and sister, in which he considered what he was doing, so that the half hour or so it took him to get into the dimmest portion of the High Park woods, to the place he thought he might hide, took a spiralling lifetime. He was gutted by the time he arrived, so emptied, so cried out, finally, over all that had happened—his mother and sister leaving, and his father dying, all compiled into one pitted loss. He was alone with it all, and it hollowed him.

IN THE DAYS THAT FOLLOWED, Bo missed the fights with Ernie. He missed the shoving, hard-hitting anger of it. He took to baiting Bear, fighting her more than he should. He let it go too far, let her hurt him sometimes, so that he could feel the adrenaline surge and ebb.

Soldier Man found him in the bush, and disappeared, and found him again. Now he stood near the shelter Bo was building on an east-facing slope under the canopy of a young forest in the northeast corner of the park. Bo used deadfall and pine boughs he'd cut from trees farther south, decorated the lean-to with bits of cloth people had left or lost in the park.

"Make it with confidence, boy, and no one will see it. You try to hide, they'll find you, I swear." Soldier Man crouched down, trying to coax Bear with a treat.

"What happened to you?" Bo said.

"Shrapnel," said Soldier Man. "What happened to you?"

"Nothing," said Bo. And then he said, "Are you going to just hang around and watch me the whole time?"

"Maybe."

So Bo decided to show this guy how dangerous Bear was. Bo whistled to Bear, and she yawned and rolled herself to standing. He signalled for her to lunge and growl, and when she did this Soldier Man just stood there as if nothing had happened.

"What else can she do?" he asked.

Bo tapped on Bear's right front paw and then the other until she pranced. Then she stood on two legs—one front and one back—and bounced to the other two, an unwieldy ballerina, back and forth.

Soldier Man said, "Jeez." He folded his arms and nodded. "You know what you need? You need to get that bear a bicycle."

And the next night, he dragged up an old rusted stationary bike.

"Whoa!" said Bo.

"Well, you ain't going nowhere. You might as well bike there." Soldier Man had brought Bo a hot dog too—cold, a bit soggy, but still. Meat.

"Where'd you get this?" Bo said, eager to know where he might find more.

"People throw shit out at the concession stand all the time."

"You got this out of the garbage can?"

"Sure."

"Huh," said Bo, his mouth full, "pretty good."

Bo sat Bear on the grass and commanded her to stay. The animal waited, biding time, and Bo heaved himself up on the bike. He showed Bear how to do it, legs pumping hard. Bear cocked her head, learning, maybe, or perplexed, or wanting her turn, and so Bo dismounted.

"Okay," he said. "You try."

Bear sniffed the bike and tried to climb up, clumsy and reckless, so that Bo had to help her and hold her steady like he remembered his father helping him when he was little. It surprised him to remember so clearly— a paved road and veering off wildly into a green patch and falling, the cutting laughter of his dad. Bear kept on nudging his arms away, making it hard to help her.

"Bear," he said. "Quit that."

Bo held her back feet to the pedals. Her legs rotated, and her front body lounged over the bars. After a while he let go and watched her ride to nowhere. Bo needed to perfect this act, needed to feel they might have some sort of show, some way to make money. Bear could dance and she could fight, but that was useless without a ring.

"Tour de France," said Soldier Man, when Bear pushed herself off the bike and bounded a few metres away, panting. "Pretty smart bear." He took a sandwich wrapped in a greasy piece of waxed paper from his pocket. He pulled the corner of the sandwich off and tossed it to Bear. When she sniffed the ground and then ate the treat, he tossed another piece a little closer.

"Bo?" he said. "I got news. Some fella is looking for you, kid. Guy said he could smell bear, when I told him I didn't know anything about anything. He told me not to fuck with him."

Bo stared at Soldier Man, at his drenched and ragged bandana, and thought this through, how he would have to work harder, hurry, hide better. "When?"

"Evening before last. I guess your second day here," said Soldier Man, shrugging when Bo made a face. "Hey, don't shoot the messenger."

"Okay," said Bo. "What did you say to him?"

"I told him, 'Fuck you very much,'" and then Soldier Man was gone, not answering Bo's hushed calls for him to come back.

Bo turned to Bear, watched her sniff the grass where the scent of sandwich must still linger. "Come on," he said. He leashed her and they began walking. They had a routine already. Days, they slept, and under cover of night, they roamed and trained.

ONE VERY DARK NIGHT, two weeks in, they ventured back toward the old neighbourhood, Bo anxious and yearning. It was obsessive ghost stalking, of Emily's house, of the stockyards—a place where the sweet smell of cow pat drew the bear more than it drew him. Bo was homesick, and lonely, shifting in the shadows with Bear, and the risk of being seen was immense, even if Bo had never felt more invisible.

His house was dead and cold. The signs his family had lived there—a collapsed flowerpot, the begonias brown, their stems gnarled viscous limbs of some dead thing—insulted him. Junk mail, yellowed, piled up on the stoop.

He and Bear walked along the side of the house and up the metal back porch stairs. Bo had his key in the lock before he realized how crazy this was. He looked in the door window. A night-light burned ochre in a socket in the hallway. He could make out the peeling Naugahyde chair in the living room. No one had been in to clean. He looked in at that past for some time before he pushed the door open, and knew right away he couldn't go in.

The stale air was so potent with sorrow after the park's fresh air. His mother was really gone. He thought of her pride after the play when all the parents clapped, and he couldn't put it together with the fact that she had left him. He thought, he must stop trying to put things together. And then Bear yanked at the lead so hard he let go, and she was down the hall and moaning at a cabinet in the kitchen. The kibble was still in there.

He followed and scooped a big bowl for her, rolling the top of the bag down and shoving the rest in his rucksack. He had learned never to pass by food she might be able to eat. A full bear was a happy bear.

"Come on," he whispered, and they left by the back door, Bo pulling it shut and leaving the key stuck in the lock. He wouldn't come back. He turned to descend the stairs and head back through the shadows to the park and there was Emily in the yard, looking up.

"Bear!" she said.

Bo was filthy, he knew, and so was Bear. "Emily," he whispered. "How come you are here?" He brought Bear to heel and came down the steps.

"I was walking by, and I smelled her," said Emily, smiling. "She really stinks, Bo!" And then she smiled wider and reached her hands out toward Bear. "Some old guy's been around looking for you. Father Bart said a sermon for you too." She laughed a little, and looked at him. "Where have you been hiding?"

"High Park," Bo said.

"You can't keep hiding in one place, I don't think. That guy came around to my house asking if I knew where you were. He said he was your boss. I thought Max was your boss."

"Max is his boss too. His name is Gerry."

"Yeah, that's right," said Emily. "Teacher told him I knew you, he said. And he said something about getting the authorities involved, and that the newspapers are starting to talk about bear sightings in the park."

Bo thought he'd been so careful. "Oh, no."

"Gerry was scared that Max will find out he's lost you and Bear."

"We aren't lost. We just don't want to go to Grimsby," said Bo, thinking that Gerry couldn't lose something he didn't own in the first place. "Do you know where Max took my mum and Orange?"

Emily shook her head. "I'm really sorry," she added. "I miss Orange."

"Me too," said Bo. "I thought they might come back," but even as he said it he realized how babyish he sounded. "It's stupid. They aren't coming back for me." He told her how he'd been roaming by night and sleeping by day to avoid people. He told her about Soldier Man and how Max wanted to use Orange.

"You're kidding."

"No." He tugged on the lead and set off, the bear swaying beside him, snorting, chuffing. He didn't like to be still for long and neither did she. He would have to be more careful in the park, find a few more spots where he could camouflage the bear and hide himself, maybe off the paths, farther south where fewer people bothered to go.

"I've got to know if you hear anything," he said, turning back to face Emily. "Come find me, okay?"

"If you need to, you could hide in my pool shed." The shimmering image of green water came into his mind, and this must have shown on his face. "There's a back door from the alleyway. The key's under a fake stone right below the lock. We keep the poolside door locked too.

It's safe and you'd hear if someone was coming. I'll put a blanket or two in there in case," she said.

"I don't think that's a good idea."

"In case, is all," she said. "If you need to deke in anywhere." She gestured to the house. "No one would ever think of the pool shed."

Then the bear lunged. Bo let go of the lead, and she ducked under the porch to roll and face-snuffle into the dry warm dirt there, some memory smell of her own childhood enticing her. Bo climbed back up the grated stairs above her and stood looking toward the tracks, half hoping a train would rip through the night and give him awful sounds to cut the feelings he did not want to feel. He recalled ice cream oozing through his toes, Bear's tongue. When he looked, Emily was watching him, her eyes glinting.

"Thanks," he said.

"No problem, Bo."

Bo and Bear entered the park from the northwestern edge, crossed a creek and then followed it toward the marshes where it opened up into Grenadier Pond. Bear dug her paws into the path, refusing to move then, and Bo heard her rumbling growl. Bo tried to pull her into the rushes behind them, but she wouldn't budge. Bear rolled her head and scented, then let loose with a full roar when Soldier Man finally emerged from the green.

"Hey," he said, and Bo's breath caught in his throat. He had thought it might be Gerry.

"Jesus," said Bo.

"I scare you?"

Bo nodded.

"Well, you should be scared, I guess. Your friend was here. Right here," Soldier Man said. "Looking for you and your missus." He gestured to Bear. "He's the bear wrestling guy, right?"

Bo nodded.

"I told him you weren't here anymore. Told him you'd headed west by night down toward Grimsby to find him. I did good, right?"

Bo's heartbeat battered at his chest. "Yes," he said. "Thanks." But the screaming thought that ripped across his mind was, Where's my mother?

"He had something to tell you, he said, if you wanted to hear it—"

"Thanks," said Bo. "I don't want to hear it," surprised, as he said this, that Soldier Man had his back at all. He realized he would have to be even more careful.

He kept Bear still closer after that, and set about teaching her new commands: bare teeth, bite. No one would be able to take Bear from him. No one.

In the weeks that passed, Bear dug a hollow for herself a short distance away from the lean-to and raked grass and twigs into it for her bed. There was some bearness in her that led her to places that smelled good, where she could watch the night parade of fox and skunk and mole and rat. The pond below them tossed with fish, and she liked to watch that too.

Now, Bo could make out Bear's face peeking over the incline below him—the hill descended in a series of soft steps. The bear's back shuddered and then her head lifted. She had woken early, long before the sun crested in the east, and Bo woke then too. They'd been sleeping an hour at most.

Bear turned, orienting, noticing all there was to notice in the meagre light, and her nose twitched, taking in the musk of sewage that plagued them in that corner of the park—he had no indication she disliked this—and the particular odour of morning, its fresh greenness, the insects scuttling, earth smells—all the things Bo could neither smell nor see.

Bear emerged from her bed, and bumbled out along the slope. She rooted and tore up horsetail, pushed at deadfall in search of worms and woodlice. It amazed him how much she ate. Bear moved closer to the pond and scratched along the path, turning up what she could—

ants, Bo suspected. Then she seemed to hear or smell something farther down and was drawn there. Bo figured it must be close to six in the morning, a time when early risers might bring their dogs into the area, so he whistled for her to come back, but she ignored him and kept on.

He could hear her chuffing, and rattling the under-growth, and so he rose and made his way toward her. He could not see her. He began to worry about Gerry, worry that he would lose Bear too, and then he would be entirely, awfully, alone.

"Bear," he called, soft, soft. He needed her.

Nothing.

"Bear."

He heard her move again and located her, a fur line undulating at the shore of the pond. She looked back at him briefly, and then scooped at the water. The edge of the pond was mucky and grown up with bulrush and willow struggling against erosion. If she dug she might find a frog, but she did not dig. She slapped the water and scooped. Bo wondered if she knew instinctively to fish, if there were fish worth catching, and as he wondered, she forked a large glittering carp with her claws, watched it flop on the shore. Then, she seemed to smile as she tore into it.

Bo could only stare at this, the pink wetness sinking into her paw fur. Bo turned back toward the lean-to, worry rising again that they might be seen. He whistled low and insistent. Bear was up in her nest before he got back himself, curled in a ball. He wondered if she was faking sleep, trying to trick him, but she did not move from her bed again until night had fallen, and then she had to prod at him, he'd slept so deeply. Bear stood on her back legs and scented wildly. Bo jerked to his feet trying to see through the night and foliage to what she might have heard.

"Get down, kid."

It was Soldier Man, his smothered words. He pushed through the scrub, his hand welted from thorn slash. He was entirely filthy. They all were. Bo made an effort to bathe in the various ponds, keeping to the edges and splashing himself—the opaque water could hide anything. But without soap, it was futile. The grime and smell accrued upon him. Soldier Man was panting, aggravating the bear, who began to make little aborted charges, huffing, a low growl forming. Bo dropped to a crouch next to Bear.

"Down," Soldier Man murmured, and he reached over to Bo and solidly pushed him down by pressing on his head with the flat of his palm.

Bo hadn't felt the touch of another human for weeks, and this, more than the violence of the man's gesture, affected him. He felt grateful.

"They're coming," said Soldier Man.

Bo heard it then, a helicopter circling the park, a harsh line of light sweeping by them. The chopper was loud and Soldier Man was clearly spooked, wide-eyed and reliving some dream, or some past life.

"It's nothing," Bo said, too loudly.

"Shh." Soldier Man brought his finger up to his lips, craned toward him and handed him a rag. "Cover your head, put this over your nose and mouth. They're coming, dude."

Bo watched the yellow skis of the heli twist upward and away. He wondered if they'd spotted him, but figured no. They were looking for something else. A criminal on the run, a missing child who'd wandered off. The helicopter sliced up the sky, a swoop of searchlights, again and again. Soldier Man slammed flat to the ground, panting to calm himself, bring the tension down. And only when the helicopter putter was far away, when they could no longer hear it, did he let up his vigilance.

After, he was a brittle mess. "Oh, fuck," he said, the swear word like a sigh emerging from deep in his belly. "Fucking hell, kid. I'm sorry."

"It was nothing. Just city cops."

"I know. Yeah." He panted like an animal. "Shit."

Strange to watch someone leave himself like that. Bear tromped a tight circle around them, sensitive to Soldier Man's freak-out, going round and round, pawing at the dirt, lifting a stick with her fangs and shaking it, channelling some predatory neck-cracking technique that was so built in, she couldn't not do it.

Soldier Man stared at the ground. "In the war they flew over us and sprayed wherever they thought the enemy might be hiding. The shit billowed and wafted. The wind would take it. I'd have hated to be the VC. That shit stung even by the time it was dissipated in the wind. Better you get some bit blown off than breathe that shit. Man."

Bo was so still. His father gasping. His mother breathing it. "What was it?" he finally said. But he knew.

"Defoliant," said Soldier Man. "Agent Orange. Devil's handiwork."

In the dark, Bo imagined his father and mother crawling just below the fog as it roiled in and down. He stifled a sob, told himself he didn't care.

"You couldn't get away from that shit, kid." The Soldier Man quieted, sensed something, then, "Hey, what's the matter? I say something wrong?"

Bo shook his head, shook it to unwind the pressing tears and loosen the sense of desperation that was pushing at him. Then finally, when he could, he said, "No. I'm good."

"Hey, kid, how old were you in '75?"

"Six."

"Shit." Soldier Man got up to leave. It was dry out this night. He slurred his words. "I scared you pretty good, I guess," and then he was gone into the dark, the under-growth whispering his departure.

Such silence, then, as if the world had sucked itself deep into a hole. Bo couldn't even hear Bear huffing and snorting, nothing. No airflow, no beetle scuttle, no bird rustle, no water trickle, nothing.

"Bear," he said, and Bear jerked her head up at him. "Come." Bo slid on his belly. He shifted along the ground, imagining his father, and forced his face into the ugliness he had witnessed on Soldier Man's face and held this expression, so that he merged the two men—the veteran and his dad—and played them, shuffling through the undergrowth to the eastern reservoir. The bear ambled beside him not caring what game this was. She would plunge into the water for the wetness of it, and swipe her paw at any fish or frog that dared to jump near her.

"Down, Bear," Bo said, and flattened his hand toward the ground, until she hunkered, watching him for what was next. Bo pulled himself toward the water, down the incline, looking up periodically when he remembered the pluming threat of chemical descending. What that looked like, he could not recall, and so he substituted cumulus clouds and had them scud across and down. He pulled his shirt up over his mouth and gasped, and choked, and went into elaborate death throes. It should have been awful, real, some link to his dad, but he kept on until he was laughing at his game and guilty with it.

The last true memory he had of his father: a thin, sun-baked man, perched with his legs bent, his elbows propped upon them, on a bench along the prow of the fishing boat, looking out to the horizon. The sky was a deepening blue, and would become a storm, but this happened later, at least in his memory. His father's face had erupted with sores, and even his eyes were seeping some unholy wetness. His mother had told him not to disturb his father, that he was in pain and needed to stay still, let the sun bake the edges of these wounds and scab them over.

And so Bo stood at a hatch, in this memory, looking out at his father—had this happened? Yes. The sorepocked face turned toward him and stared for just too long, so that either of them might have smiled, though neither of them did. Eventually, his father saluted, sharp and perfect in its execution, and Bo saluted back, some boyish code for love. And then his father broke eye contact and went back to staring at the horizon.

"Growl," Bo said to Bear, and she did, low and resonant. He felt it up through the earth. Bo made the hand signal to go with it. "Bare teeth," and Bear pulled her lips back less in a snarl than a smile. Again, he had to laugh, because she seemed to know that they were playing. "Oh, Bear," he said, "come here," and when she did, he hugged her. But when he wrapped his arms around her neck, he felt the growing vibration of a real growl building deep in her body.

Six months and more since he'd first cradled her, and now they were nearly one creature. He listened for some primal stillness in the back of his head. Sometimes, he and Bear talked in huffs and snorts. He never knew whether this was real talk, of course. The talk was untranslatable, like talking to Orange, but deeper and thicker, as if the thoughts moved from the stomach and the heart rather than the brain. Bo sat still with her for a long time, listening to the park sounds.

There was nothing unusual, and he finally said, "It's okay, Bear."

But Bo was jumpy, and twice in the next week, he and Bear had rambled late at night into the Junction, when the feeling of being watched ate at him. They slept in Emily's pool shed, and both times, left before anyone noticed them. He couldn't say why he didn't want to see Emily, except it had made him lonely and anxious to have seen her. It began to feel like magic that they were never found. And he began to count on that magic.

CHAPTER EIGHT

ONE NIGHT IN EARLY AUGUST, Bo finessed Bear's wrestling skills in the middle of the park. He got her standing and then, huffing his intentions, he slammed his body into the bear's side. In the moonlit glade, they locked together, and when Bear's lips pulled back, so did Bo's, and so they were both smiling. Not the smile of people enjoying a good joke, but the smile that comes from the body gleefully expressing itself as a body. Bo grappled with Bear—himself, bear. And then Soldier Man showed up, the gleam of the moon dancing down his ragged clothes. Bear bounded recklessly at him.

"Stop, Bear. Stop," Bo called, and through his own prickling fear of what might be about to occur, Bear

checked and moved left into the trees behind Soldier
Man and disappeared.

"She's a big motherfucker," Soldier Man said.

Bear emerged from the brush, licked her belly, keeping busy until they would move again, and Bo saw burrs
clinging to her undercoat and saw how much dirt was
caked there. Soldier Man had a box of pizza he had
scavenged and they sat down to eat it.

"How long have you been in the park?" Bo asked,
wondering why he hadn't asked before.

"Oh, ten years, I'd say."

Bo remembered Sir Orfeo suddenly, and how Orfeo
had wandered in the forest for ten years before rescuing
Heurodis. And then Bo had to think of Orange and his
mum. A fury pierced him. It hurt behind the solar
plexus, as if he had punched himself.

"What day is it?" Bo asked, staring at the broken soldier. It was as if he had abandoned himself, in some
crucial way, these weeks in the woods.

"You forgot something important, kid?" Soldier Man
laughed at him. His eyes mocked Bo.

"My sister," Bo said, and already he was running, Bear
beside him.

"It's a dream, kid," Soldier Man called after him. "Get
used to it."

He would not get used to it.

Bo ran to his lean-to, and settled Bear. Then he pulled

out his journal, held it by the bindings and shook it until the wallpaper with the knight and the photographs fell out of it. He shuddered to see them. Orange must be changed by now, he thought. He imagined her behind a window somewhere in Max's sideshow, not knowing that people gawked at her, made jokes, felt pity, felt something, anything, then went home grateful they were normal—this last was the worst, he thought.

She did not look like herself in the photographs. If he only looked at the first photographs of his sister— the ones that weren't blurred—he could convince himself he was not a bad person. They were only curious views. One showed Orange settled back on the floor wondering what a camera might be; another caught her in the moment between wondering and grabbing at this new thing, so that her expression was strangely, beautifully, in flux. Her baby skin was porous and lively in the photographs in a way that was different, somehow more luxuriously real, than in life.

The pictures freaked him out. The bend of Orange's arms, the face, like someone had smeared it. And looking closely he saw shadowy spots. They looked like sores, and he recalled once seeing his mother half dressed, scrambling to pull a cheap cotton kimono up over herself, gasping. She had not wanted him to see the sores running the length of her torso.

"What—?" he had begun.

"Nothing." But they had been something and the recognition of that must have set upon his face. Rose added, "They don't hurt."

They must have, though. After that, when he heard her high-pitched moans in the night, he knew what it meant. She had rolled over, and the pain vexed her. And now in the pictures it was as if Orange had hints of something waiting to erupt. Photographs were supposed to hold people in time. He would not look at them again, he told himself, though he knew it was a lie.

Suddenly wanting an adult, someone to take care of him, Bo called out to Gerry. Stillness. The faintest echo of his own words bouncing back to him. His skin prickled, and defiantly he stood and lined the photos up on the bare earth outside his sleeping place so that they were like a film flickering along the ground. The last photo that came out of the stack disturbed him more than all the rest. It was the snapshot of Teacher, floating, that she had given him. The tape had gone brittle and it had come unstuck from the page in his journal.

He hadn't thought of her for weeks, hadn't thought she mattered until he saw the photograph, and her eyes. And then she was so important and so necessary that he was forced to keep her out of his view, so that even as he watched the jarring stop-action film of himself as a phantom pursuer snapping Orange, Teacher's grey eyes, her whole face called him.

"Miss Lily," he yelled, which was stupid. Guilt overcame him. He had betrayed his sister, and now he was sobbing. How stupid Bo had been for not heeding his mother's wishes for him. How stupid for thinking he could do anything on his own, that he could busk with a bear. He was a moron—a weak, little boy.

"Gerry?" he yelled into the dark. A futile waste of energy, but it felt good to yell. "Gerry!"

"Boy." It was later that night, Soldier Man calling from outside Bo's lean-to. "Kid?"

"Here."

"You okay?"

"Yeah."

"They're back," muttered Soldier Man. "Gooks."

Bo said, "I need to tell you something."

"You look like shit, kid. What's up?"

"My sister—"

"You really have a sister?"

"She's defective. From Agent Orange."

"Serious?"

Bo nodded. "That guy who's been looking for me? His boss wants her for his freak show."

"That's fucked up, kid." Not a heartbeat went by before Soldier Man was pointing. "You see that—?"

There was nothing. A shrubby plant struggling under a willow near the pond. If Bo swung his head quick he could imagine some movement, but if he kept still, there wasn't anything to see.

"There's nothing there."

"You got to get him before he gets you. If it looks like a kid. Or a woman, even an old lady, someone's grandmother. Don't be fooled. Fuckers all got machetes."

Bo pulled his bottom lip under his front teeth, chewed on it.

"Come on," and Soldier Man was off, elbowing the dirt down the incline toward the pond, day waking around them. Bo crawled after him. Soldier Man whispered, "We look out for each other, right, kid?" He said it like Bo would save him. "You got my back, right?"

"Sure," Bo said, but did not look him in the eye. Bo stared straight, squinting into the scene that he imagined was playing out in Soldier Man's mind. Crazy fuck. The trees, the undergrowth, danger lurking.

"See? Fuck—down, kid." And again the hand shoved Bo low to the ground.

From here he looked back over his shoulder to the shelter and saw Bear's nose rising, crinkling up, scenting. Maybe there was something after all. He stared where Soldier Man was looking, and sure enough, there was someone moving about, some early adventure-seeker, maybe some other vagrant who slept in the park too. Some no one.

"We got to—"

The interloper turned toward them.

"Shit."

"Stop—" said Bo, but Soldier Man was sliding left and beckoning him to follow, shushing him. Bear was on her haunches. She wasn't going to move anywhere. Bo signed for her to stay and Bear saw, but acted like she hadn't. He imagined a worst-case scenario, her bounding out to greet this stranger, blowing their cover, or worse, attacking—claws ripping body. Bo was terrified that his vivid thinking would make this happen, tried to stop it.

"Bear, come." She swung her head toward him, acknowledging but not budging. "Get," he said. Nothing.

The shadow below shifted through the green that grew around the pond. "Insurgent," said Soldier Man, and pulled out a gleaming knife.

"Put that back," said Bo. Jesus.

And Soldier Man turned on him, rustled his shirt collar, whisper-yelled, "Don't tell me what to do, boy," and then, "You cover my ass or leave. I never should have trusted a slant. You little fucker."

Soldier Man shimmied farther down the incline toward the shadow. Bo heard a thick "ugh" and a thump, and then nothing, his heart pumping too fast.

He stood and yelled, "No!" and then he saw a glimmer down the hill and realized what he was looking at— Gerry waving.

"No, Soldier Man," he yelled again. "It's nothing. It's Gerry. Please."

He did not know if Soldier Man could hear him. Bo felt fear heating him, so potent he could not halt it, and so he tore through the bramble until he was close enough to see the veteran. He lunged at him. He expected his fists to drive deep into Soldier Man, expected some emptying out of this fear. But it was like his body hit a wall, and then hit it again and again. He was a rag doll up against this force. Soldier Man was slamming him against the ground, grunting, wheezing. When the beating finally stopped and Soldier Man backed away, Bo turned his head and Bear was beside him, crouched—curious, worried. She licked him, along the cheek and nostrils.

"Ah. Ah," Bo said. It was good that was over. His body began to ache.

"Sorry, kid," Soldier Man said, and Bo could see the worst of it had rattled right out of him. Soldier Man rocked himself. "I'm real sorry."

There was a rustle and someone hooted, and Bo looked up moisture-wicked pant legs to Gerry's smiling face looming above him.

"Kid," he said. "At last! How you been?" Gesturing to Soldier Man, he added, "Who's this freak?"

Soldier Man stopped rocking to say, "Fuck you, asshole," and then stood, stooped, and ran off.

"He's a friend," said Bo. He stood, feeling for anything broken, but he was fine.

"Jesus, kid," said Gerry. "With friends like that, you don't need enemies."

"He just has some weird thing," said Bo. "And anyway, I'm okay." He rubbed his chest where Soldier Man had pummelled him, and he leaned against Bear. She swung her head and pulled her lips back, her nose going crazy as she scented Gerry.

"Bo Jangles, I missed you!" said Gerry. He looked down on Bo with the dumbest smile.

"Yeah?" said Bo.

"I've been looking all over hell's half acre for you, boy," Gerry said, and then he sat and stared at Bo and Bear for a bit. "How's the bear?" he finally said, and then, "Christ, it's good to see you, kid."

Bo hated to admit it but he was relieved to be found. "She's okay." He pursed his lips to stop from crying, shook his head. "How are you?" he said, instead of *What happened?* or *Why?* or *How?* or any of the things he wanted to know about his mother, because most of all, he did not want to cry.

"That's it, Jangles. That's the spirit. I'm excellent. Never felt better." Gerry smiled at him. "Bear learn any new tricks?"

And Bo couldn't help himself. "Yeah. She can ride a bicycle."

"No shit?"

Bo's chest was cinching, a band constricting him, holding his heart back from this, but the rest of him was won. Gerry at least knew him.

He said, "Where's Orange?"

Gerry rummaged in a grocery bag he had brought, evading the question. "Hell, Bo, you've made Max a happy man. Every newspaper in the city is talking about a series of mysterious bear sightings in High Park. Some people say it's hysteria, and some think bears are coming to the city because they've run out of food. But we—me and Max—we think it's money in the bank." He laughed.

"Where's my mother?"

"Yeah," Gerry said. "There's something—"

"What?"

"Forget it, kid. It's time to get the show on the road." Gerry waved his hands around. "The Canadian National Exhibition. It's showtime."

"How do we get there?"

"I sure as hell ain't going to piss her off by putting her in a cage right now. We'll walk. You still got the leash, right?" He reached over and let Bear sniff his hand. "Oh," he said. "She might need a bath."

So Bo packed his journal and the photographs into his rucksack, clipped Bear to the lead and headed for Grenadier Pond. There, he unleashed her and let her bound down toward the water. When she lingered in the marshy edges, Gerry threw a stick.

"She's not a dog," said Bo.

But Bear plunged after it and swam around in circles. In this way, most of the dirt came off her. When she was back on the shore, she shook, spraying them, and Gerry laughed and said to Bo, "Your turn."

"I'm good," said Bo.

"No, kid, you stink."

Bo made a face and, to appease Gerry, crouched at the water's edge and scooped water up to wash his face. He took his filthy T-shirt off, rinsed it, threw water into his armpits and then put his T-shirt back on. "Now I'm good."

Gerry said, "If you say so," and laughed. He handed Bo the leash, and also a muzzle he had brought.

"No way," said Bo.

"It won't bother her and she'll be safer with it. If she's freaked out by the noises and the cars, at least we don't have to worry about her biting anyone."

"She doesn't bite," said Bo, but he slipped it over her snout anyway, and watched her sniff it and then try to tug it off with her paws. "Good girl," he said. "It's okay."

"Here," said Gerry, handing him a box of Pop-Tarts. "Give her one."

Bo opened the box and broke a Pop-Tart, and fed Bear half through the muzzle. Then he ate the other half, enjoying the sweet of it. He watched Bear lick her lips.

"Let's go then," he said.

"Sure, kid," said Gerry.

The sun was rising, and though Bo was nervous after these weeks in the park, it was marvellous not to have to hide anymore. They took a paved path across the park and exited onto High Park Boulevard. The bear stopped periodically to scent, and worried garbage she found along the way. Children followed them. They pointed fingers and laughed. A crowd surged ahead through Parkdale, and then, whenever stoplights caught them and made them wait, they turned to gawk.

"The Ex," the children chanted. "The Ex. The Ex!"

"Step right up, folks," whispered Gerry.

As they approached the CNE grounds, Gerry said, "Jangles, this carnival is huge. She sprawls over 192 acres."

"Like High Park," Bo said.

"Yeah," said Gerry. "Except completely different."

Bear tugged the lead, bounding as if she knew their destination. She was entranced by the wild assortment of new people and creature smells, the rotting food she located along the gutter. She slipped her tongue through the muzzle's bars before they could scold her, and scarfed back what she found.

"She needs to build the fat back on, I guess," said Gerry.

And Bo saw then that Bear had become skinny. Her coat gleamed but her ribs rippled under it. Bear nuzzled a crust in the gutter.

"Where is Max?" said Bo. He tried to make it light, like no big deal.

Gerry didn't respond, just stared straight, a strange smile playing out upon his lips. Bo stared at him too long and almost tripped over a curb. Someone slapped Bo on the back, said, "Atta boy," and again, "The Ex!" Kids yelled, "Look! The Bear Boy!" to anyone they met, and in this way the crowd increased, young and old, so that their arrival at the Canadian National Exhibition became a small parade. A larger crowd undulated at the entrance and then parted to let them through. A great rolling sound of awe spread out as they were seen: a boy and a bear, the one the newspapers had been talking about.

But before they were allowed through the gates proper, a CNE official wanted proof from Gerry that Bo and Bear were, in fact, part of the midway. While Bo stood helpless, wishing for the cover and quiet of High Park, Gerry pulled out some papers and handed them over. The man tugged on his beard and stared at the papers and then at Bo.

"Animal needs immunization records."

"I've got those in my office," Gerry said.

"By the end of the day, then."

Gerry nodded, and they were in.

Tucked in alongside the grandstand to the southeast was the midway. The freak show was in full swing, a string of banners advertising THE CONGRESS OF FAT. For a dollar you could watch Baby Louis jiggle (*My, but he is fat*) while his twin sister played the banjo. Orange, Bo thought.

He tried to catch Gerry's eye, which avoided his. "Come on, Gerry. Where is my sister? Where is my mum?"

This is when Gerry stopped and took him by the shoulder. "She's dead, kid," he said. "Your mum died."

All around Bo, and Bear, and Gerry, the crowd seemed to contract and then expand, so that for forever, Bo would recall this moment, the moment he learned he was an orphan, amid a frenzy of coloured T-shirts and sickly carnival smells and spectacle.

"No," Bo said.

"I'm sorry."

"Wha—? How?"

"In good time, Bo Jangles. Look at this—" Here Gerry gestured widely, to break the tension, to change the subject, to run away from that story to the freak show. "The ten-in-one, just like I promised you. One kilometre of unique misshapen acts." He looked like a proud father. "I manage the whole shebang."

"I'll kill him," Bo said.

"No, you won't," and Gerry put a hand on his shoulder.

The crowd pressed through the corridor. The place smelled like ketchup and cotton candy, vinegar and sugar. Bear sat down and swatted wasps off her snout, snagging her claws in the muzzle, and Bo couldn't tell if she was upset or calmed by it. She tried to snap at the insects but her mouth was bound, an interesting new thing, and she tested this.

"Bear," Bo said. "It's okay, girl," but she didn't care. She was off in her bear head. Bo watched her for a bit then glared at Gerry. "Where is she?" he said.

"Who?"

Bo sneered at him. "Who do you think? Orange." He looked down the corridor of curiosities, to try to see if he could find the banner that belonged to his sister, but the banners snaked back and turned in a reverse loop and he knew he would have to walk the gauntlet to find her. And then what?

"She's not here, Bo." Gerry was back in the friend game.

Bo's lip quavered. His mum. And he had forgotten about Orange too long and now she was gone too.

Gerry said, "She isn't here."

"Well, where is she?" Was she dead too?

"Max promised to protect her—"

"Promised who?"

"It was an unusual sort of deal, especially for him. He's not that sentimental, as you know. But apparently, he and your mum got married."

"You're lying."

Gerry stopped to pull a pack of cigarettes out of his pocket. He shook one out and grabbed it with his mouth. He looked at Bo the whole time. "I'm a lot of things," he said, tilting his head to light his smoke. "But a liar isn't one of them."

"What happened to my mother?" He had visions of Max and his mum being married, his mum in a flouncy white dress he had once seen in an advertisement. Max killing her. Max watching her die. Max—

"I hate to be the one to tell you."

Bo saw how old Gerry was then, a man who was trying too hard to hold onto something born in another time, something that retained less and less meaning. People pointed at the bear and at Bo, but Bo let it blur, keeping his focus on this man, Gerry, who had given him a job, and whom he had once seen as a kind of saviour.

"I'm sorry," said Gerry.

"Tell me what happened."

"I don't do this sort of thing well."

"No, you don't," said Bo.

"Jesus, kid." He set a warm and tobacco-fragrant palm upon Bo's shoulder again. When Bo only stared back, Gerry lifted his palm and tapped once, twice in a little faux slap, and then, with a look that suggested Bo should follow, he sauntered ahead. "Let's get you settled first."

"I should have stayed in the park," Bo shrieked. He had been just fine. He wanted to go back in the quiet of that forest, with no one but Bear, the hush of the woods at night, and the forgetting.

"Yeah, but she's my damn bear, Jangles," said Gerry over his shoulder as he began to move again.

No—she was *his* god-damned bear.

Bo followed Gerry behind the twister and the roller coaster—the Ferris wheel loomed above them—to another gate, another security guard. Behind him was a grassy knoll dotted with caravans and trailers. Bo craned but saw no sign of Max or Orange or his mother. Rose was dead, Gerry had told him, and he couldn't believe it. He whispered, "Doctors," and saw Teacher's face the last time she came looking for Rose, recalled the way she had implored his mum to honour her appointments.

The guard let them into the carnie village. "Backstage," said Gerry.

People loitered at the metal fence, on the outer perimeter of the fairgrounds. Was there no end to people watching people?

"What do they want?" Bo asked, shooting his thumb toward those at the fence.

"A life, I guess."

This comment was meant to be funny, but Bo could only think of his mum, and whether she was really dead. He and Bear and Gerry moved among the many trailers, past assorted carnies who worked the Ex, who belonged here in this temporary world.

"Hi," said Gerry, and "Hey," when they passed someone he knew or liked. He did not introduce Bo to anyone, but kept moving even as he greeted people.

The bear pulled ahead, her nose pursuing what scents even Bo could not know. He could smell only the rank reminders of foot-longs and candy floss.

"First my place," said Gerry. They stood outside a dilapidated taupe caravan. "Home sweet home."

Bo could see his truck behind it. Gerry had detached the trailer and put it up on concrete blocks, like every other caravan. There was a huge crate in the bed of the truck.

"Loralei?" But Bo already knew, and couldn't pretend not to be happy about this one tiny thing, at least. Bear was yanking him toward the truck, and no amount of skidding and heel digging would stop her. Bo had to let go the leash. Bear lifted off the ground and stood swaying to the scent. Loralei. Had Bear ever smelled another bear? She seemed drunk on it now. "Is Lora in there?"

"Yup."

Bear jumped up to peer in the crate, swinging her head in recognition of her own kind. Loralei did not reciprocate. Bo heard her before he saw her, a chuffed warning that soon got louder. Bo picked up the leash and tugged Bear down, so that she would not present so large to the caged bear, but already Loralei was beyond caring.

She backed up in her crate, rubbing her ass hard, her chuffs turning growly, scared and ready. Bear was too stupid, too young, too un-bear to understand the warning. She pressed her face into the cage mesh, which brought the older bear to the edge of her patience.

Loralei threw herself at the door of her cage, jamming her snout and right paw through the spaces in the metal grating, teeth chattering, fierce. Which would have been the end of it, if the door to the crate had not swung open and left her briefly hanging there. She was furious. A clanging—then, the dangle of bear, tumbling and collapsing into a pissed-off mountain of fur. Loralei took no time to reorient and locate her main objective.

"Down, Loralei," said Gerry, through clenched teeth. There was nothing calm in the way he said it.

Bo wondered if Loralei might still recognize him— she never once looked in his direction.

She rose and leapt toward Bear, landing just in front of her on the ground, and then swiped her paw over Bear's muzzle. Bo pulled the leash taut, thinking he might have to let Bear go again if Loralei didn't back off. He'd have to give Bear a fighting chance.

Gerry backed away toward the caravan, muttering, "Crap!" Bo tried one last time to pull Bear back, but she wouldn't budge, so he dropped the leash and followed Gerry.

Bear batted at Loralei, lips pulled back, the muzzle now a big problem for her. They rose onto their back legs and began to twist and turn against one another, both creatures looking for a piece of neck to bite. It was beautiful and terrible, somewhere between a game and a fight. They bashed and whacked each other, low growls vibrating along the ground. Gerry waved a can of root beer above his head, futilely calling Loralei's name, overly shrill—the sound of fear. Loralei couldn't hear him, her ears and teeth and malice all attuned to Bear.

She clacked her teeth at Bear, and swatted, growling. Gerry just kept yelling and waving the can until Loralei at last cocked her head toward the root beer, softened her stance and backed off. Bear lowered to all fours and watched, head bobbing in lingering anxiety. Finally she sat. Gerry cracked the tab and let Loralei guzzle a little, then led her back into her cage.

"Up," he said. "Up," and she did this without too much trouble. "Atta," he said, and handed her the can. She hoisted it and chugged. "My lady," said Gerry, turning then to grin madly at Bo.

"She cut Bear," Bo said.

A red rivulet trailed down Bear's neck.

"She'll live."

Bear sidled up to Bo and tucked her head behind his legs, hiding, trying to turn her head so she could lick the blood. The wound was small, nothing to worry about, but she shook behind him.

"Loralei's getting feisty these days," said Gerry. "Gonna

have to retire her if she doesn't calm down and get with the program." He slammed his palm on the door of the crate, making Loralei start and cower.

A woman stepped out of Gerry's caravan. Spike-heeled sandals and an electric blue dress that ended in a little wavy hem above her perfect knees.

"Meet Beverley," Gerry said, not taking his eyes off her. "Beverley?" He beckoned to her. "Meet Bo and Bear."

"Nice to make your acquaintance," Beverley said. Her voice was octaves higher than any voice had a right to be. She put her hand out, to be shaken, or kissed, Bo did not know.

Gerry laughed at the expression on Bo's face.

"Hello," said Bo. He put his hand out, testing, and she took it, shook, with a tighter grip than he ever would have imagined.

"I've heard so much about you."

"Oh," he said.

There was pity in her smile.

"Come on," Gerry said to Bo. "I'll show you your sleeping quarters."

Beverley kept smiling as they led the bear away.

When they were out of earshot, Gerry said, "She hates what I do, so I don't expect it to last. Also, she's the smartest person I've ever met, so boredom is already setting in. The midgets are taking odds on when we'll have our first big argument—well, the second. We had a whopper two nights ago—but who will throw the first punch, eh? Morgana, who reads tea leaves and the crystal ball, and hasn't ever been wrong about anything, says it'll end badly, and I don't doubt it. What do you think, Jangles?"

"I don't think anything about it." Bear was riding up the back of his legs, her head down. Bo stopped, turning and crouching to cup her face in his hands, scratch her neck, careful to stay clear of the wound. "Good girl," he said. "We're almost there."

There was a crazy feeling racing through his body. "I need to know," he said, standing again. "I need to know what *exactly* happened to my mother."

"Kid." Gerry stopped outside a big canvas tent, and had Bo sit down in one of the folded wooden chairs set out on the grass. He sat down beside him, cleared his throat. "It's sad," he said. Gerry's face crumpled a bit and he nodded. "I'm sorry. It's just really shitty to have to tell you." A long silence passed between them. "She hanged herself, kid."

Bo's guts seemed to spin. "Where is Orange?" he managed.

"Safe." That was all Gerry would say, his brow furrowed so hard it was a wonder he could see.

"You're not gonna tell me."

"It's not my news to tell."

He saw his mother's feet dangling above a floor somewhere. Who had found her? He did not like to think that Orange might have witnessed it. Why had she done this, left them behind like this? There were too many questions and so he did what he had always done. He did not ask them. Instead he glanced around, biting his lip hard; the pain of it was good. Bo wished badly to hit something. He would pretend it was Max's face.

"When can I fight?" he said.

"That's the spirit." Gerry grinned wide. Bo had saved him from going deeper into that awful story. He gestured to the tent. "You'll be sleeping in here. Don't know what we're going to do with the bear."

"She can stay with me." Bo looked at Bear, who sat watching him.

It sickened Bo to imagine her crated, but that wasn't it. It sickened him to be alone.

INSIDE THE TENT, Gerry introduced him to Morgana. She was three and a half feet tall, of exquisite proportions, a walking doll. The most beautiful person Bo had ever seen.

"Enchantée," she said, and then she bowed to Bear and added, "How do you do," which made Bo laugh despite his sadness.

Morgana showed Bo his living quarters—a sectioned-off area of the industrial tent, with an army cot against one tent wall, a piece of dowelling hanging on ropes from a brace in the tent, for clothes.

"Normally we don't allow animals in the sleeping quarters," she said, looking over at Bear.

Gerry said, "It's okay, Morgana. I'll get the boys to bring in a bear crate for her."

"Thank you," said Bo. He had no intention of putting her in a cage.

Bo turned to Gerry after Morgana had walked away. "How old is she?"

"Old," and then Gerry pulled a suitcase out from under the cot, and handed it to Bo. When he looked perplexed, Gerry added, "Performance clothes. Something in there for you. Something in there for the beast."

Bo opened the suitcase and inside found a tutu, a couple of sparkly bodysuits, a pair of leather boots, and a suit made of black silk.

"The tutu's for the bear, Jangles. In case you were wondering."

"She's never been dressed. I never did that."

"You better get busy teaching her, then. You can't insult the crowd with a naked bear."

And then it was just this: the show going on.

WITHIN TWO DAYS, Bo was fighting Loralei. He was billed as Bear Boy because Gerry felt that would bring the crowds into the tent. The banner paint was wet that first fight. Gerry kept Bo busy, those first days, between perfecting Bear's act and wrestling, so he had scant time to look for Orange, and when he asked around, eyes glazed over.

"Anyone seen Max Jennings?" he said to a mingling of half-dressed clowns as he was returning to his tent from a fight.

"You think I pull the boss outta my ass, kid?"

He persisted. "Come on, where is he?"

"I saw him wandering the back of the freak show the other day."

"When?"

"Get out of here, kid," and then, "Hey, kid, did you hear about the leper hockey game?"

And one of the other clowns: "There was a face off in the corner."

Backslapping one another, they turned from him. "We'll keep an eye out, kid," said one, and another held a glass eye up over his shoulder like a periscope and rotated it back and forth. It was impossible for Bo to tell whether they were hiding information or just didn't have any. He went back to Bear and petted her to calm himself.

Bear had to spend time alone in the cage in Bo's quarters, the only time Bo would cage her. He would open it, and she would happily go in now. It was like a cave for her. Bo had filled it with towels and pillows in which she could bed down. She looked at him, then scented high and jealous, huffing at him because she smelled Loralei.

"Hey, kid!" It was Gerry calling him.

"I'm here," he called back.

Gerry pushed through the tarp door, came in and sat on the end of Bo's bed beside him. He cocked his chin at Bear. "How she doing?"

"I got her to wear the tutu yesterday, and she can ride the trike now."

"Fast work," said Gerry. "Good job, Jangles." He rubbed his face and yawned. No one had stopped working the whole time Bo had been there. "The plan from here is to get her in the tutu and up the ramp into the ring. I want her looking good for that first bout."

"First bout?"

"Yeah, she's gonna ride up and—"

Bo interrupted. "Ride up? I don't think she's ready for that."

And Gerry looked surprised. "Kid," he said. "It's not for another day or two. You got time."

It was true that Bear was talented. She was already bringing the crowd into the ten-in-one with the song and dance routine they put on there, but she wasn't a content bear. When Bo came back the next evening from a bout with Loralei, fur sticking to him, and welts where he hadn't been prudent, Bear whined and fussed.

Morgana called to him from the other side of the tarp wall. "Hey, kid, open the door, will you?"

He pulled the tarp door open, and went back to pet Bear.

"I just feel so closed in," Morgana said. She sat at a tiny, custom-built table, and waved her hands over the crystal ball set in front of her. She was quiet for a time, staring into it. Then she gestured to Bear and said, "She misses you when you leave."

Bo crouched in the cage with Bear and began to groom her with a dog brush. "I don't believe in crystal balls."

"Oh," Morgana said. "It doesn't work like that. You don't need to believe. It's just what I see, and—"

Bo watched her through the ball, a piece of her cheek distorted by its convexity, and thought of Orange. "What else do you see?"

"Please," said Morgana, as in, Please don't insult me. She thought he was mocking her, but he wasn't.

Bo pulled at the matted fur on Bear's rump and she swung back with her jaws open, warning. "Take it easy," he said to Bear.

"Take it easy, yourself," said Morgana.

"I meant the bear."

"Sure you did." She pulled a swath of red cloth over the ball, then swept up to the tent door and began to close it.

"Wait," he said, and watched the tarp flick and waver. Bo got out of the cage and closed its door.

Morgana's tiny hand slid through the opening, then pulled the canvas back. Her face peered in at him. "What?"

"I'm not just looking for Max."

"What?"

"Hang on," he said. Bo went to his cot, pulled the photos out of their envelope, took the least disturbing image of Orange from the pile and showed it to Morgana. "Look at this—"

"Phew," she said, holding the glossy as she came into his room. "I seen a pickle jar with a head like that in it once in Missouri but that was years and years ago." She looked away from the picture.

"Look at it closely," he said.

"Why should I?"

"Please." Bo chewed his lip. "That dead thing in the pickle jar, was it one of Max's oddities?"

Morgana shook her head, took a closer look. "You take that photo? Who is that?"

"Never mind," he said.

Morgana's body swayed a little, and then her face softened. She said, "Bo, tell me."

"She's my sister," Bo said. "I need to find her." Bear began to bash up against her cage, pushing her paws through the grating. "Can you help me?" he said.

"You don't think I'm really a clairvoyant, do you?"

Bo got up to unlatch the cage. Bear hesitated, then emerged to sprawl on the tutu lying on the floor. "Max Jennings stole her away."

"Max?" said Morgana, suddenly smiling. "If I know Max, he'll be taking good care of your sister. He'll want to protect his investment."

"I hate to think of her in a freak show."

"Pardon me?" Morgana made a face.

"That's different," said Bo.

"Oh?"

"My sister's disabled. She can't even talk. She didn't choose it."

"Nobody really chooses this, Bo," Morgana said. "It's just you try to fit in everywhere and then you find this, and there is a kind of sanctuary among the freaks, at least for freaks there is."

"Would you have been happier if you had been accepted in the real world?"

Morgana cocked her tiny head. It was like watching a figure on a television set come to life. She thought for a time before she said, "What do you mean by the real world?" She looked over at Bear and then back at Bo, and continued: "Most of the people around here, they mean well. Even Max Jennings, he means well. He pays us a decent wage and on time. He respects us, which is better than some I've worked for. Still, he's not perfect, and I wouldn't altogether trust him. I wish I could help you."

She reached up and patted Bo on the head before she left.

EARLY THE NEXT MORNING, Bo took the picture around to every aberration the carnival had to offer. No one had seen her, not the bearded lady, not the Siamese twins, not Frogman, not Mino the Giant.

No one would look long at it. "Jesus, ugly," one of the midgets said.

The Mule-Faced Woman threw the photograph up into the air and swooned onto her velvet settee she was so upset. "That's the nastiest human I have ever seen," she declared, and would not speak to Bo again.

And so he'd given up looking for his sister and gone back to his cot. The Ex was huge and chaotic and she could be anywhere.

"Bear, either they are lying or she isn't here, I can't tell which."

Bear was nestled at his feet, waiting. She lifted her eyebrows, one at a time. She was bored and wanted to train.

"Come on, then," Bo said, and leashed her to go out. He planned to take her around the perimeter of the carnie area, let her sniff some grass.

They were halfway to the fence when Gerry shouted and caught up with them, out of breath.

"Loralei's been jumpy this week," he said. "They say bears just get more and more mental as they get older and I guess they're right. You and Bear were scheduled to bout Thursday but I bumped it up to tomorrow."

What happened to old bears? Bo wondered, but said, "Will you bring her back to the woods?" Gerry looked sadly back at him. Bo blinked, hoped his face said, *Don't tell me the answer.*

"Jangles?" Gerry said. "I heard you've been asking around for Max, and showing a picture to some of the freaks."

"I just need to see her," he said.

"She'll be here soon. Max is on his way, I heard. He got delayed with things. I'll be sure to let you know when he gets here."

"What's Max done with Orange?" Bo said.

"You paint him badly."

"He is bad."

"Forget about it, kid. Your sister will be here soon. You think Bear can wrestle you for the show tomorrow, then?"

Forget about it. Forget about it. Forget.

"Bear?" he said. "We wrestled all the time in the park. She can do it."

"And the noise and audience?"

"She'll be fine." Bo stopped in the shade of a tree and turned to her. "Bear?" Bear looked at him, then lifted a paw and began to chew her claw. "You good to go?" And she leaned into the tree and rubbed her rear. Bo peered at the flank she was scratching. Sure enough, the fur was thinning and she had chafed her skin. "Don't rub, Bear. It's okay."

"They all do it," said Gerry.

Bear's tongue lapped out and slid down Bo's biceps. Tomorrow they would fight. "Come here, girl," he said, and pulled a Hershey hunk from his pocket. Bo took a bite himself and gave her the rest.

Gerry said, "You shouldn't give her treats unless she does something."

Bo stared blankly at him until Gerry added, "Well, I guess you know her best, right?" and then he left.

Bo brought Bear around the site and then back to their room. He watched her lie down and begin to snore, then twitch in her sleep as she rode some dream bicycle. He sat on his bed and cradled the photograph again, peered into the flat eyes of his sister. Monster. But after all the freaks and oddities, the ones who were born so, and the working acts who drove themselves into freakishness, was she so monstrous after all?

THAT AFTERNOON, as usual, people pushed and harassed their way into the ten-in-one. Bo watched the gawkers, watched them gawk and gawk, their brains not believing their eyes, until there came a threshold of satiety, and it looked normal. There were those in the tent, some of the midgets, and the twins, who craved being seen. They could not live without the regular feeling of being witnessed. They called it performance, but it was more than that and also less. Maybe they did not feel real unless people witnessed their bodies.

Bo wondered, as he cracked the whip and Bear toddled around on the tricycle in her fuchsia crinoline, whether the same was true for him. Maybe he needed to be seen too, or maybe he needed it more as it quickly became routine. There was a kind of reckless energy he got from it. It did not spin off him like the fights—that was different. But it fed something that he was not certain was altogether healthy.

Mino the Giant stood in front of Bo on the little stage because Gerry had insisted that one of the more seasoned acts help him out. Seven and a half feet tall, Mino was a crowd-pleaser. All he had to do was stand near them and people came.

"Bear Boy," Mino said, his voice a reverberating baritone. "Step right up!" He swung his huge body sideways to reveal Bo and Bear. Bo bowed deep, flourishing his arms.

Bo then signalled Bear to climb up onto the trike. The act wasn't perfect, but it was good enough. He held the back wheels for her, and she leaned over the bars and heaved herself up. He guided her back paws onto the pedals and she began circling around the small stage. Bo looked out, smiling at the applause that Bear got, and saw, bobbling through the crowd, farther and farther away, a hat—a black bowler—and he thought, Max.

He got Bear off the trike fast, clipped her chain and handed her off to Mino. "I'll be quick," he said. He jumped from the stage, and pushed and shoved his way to the end of the ten-and-one, trying to keep Max in view. Bo made it out the back of the ten-in-one. But the man was gone.

There was an Airstream trailer to his right—whatever its vendor sold, it was closed, the shiny aluminum awning shuttered tight—and to his left, the faux portico of a popcorn concession. A young boy was staring up at him.

"You see a guy in an old-fashioned black hat?" Bo asked, but the kid shook his head.

The boy shot a thumb at one of the trailers. "You know when this thing is supposed to open?"

It was the Blow-Off, the spectacle that pulled the crowd out of the tent so they could shove more people through the entrance. The trailer had a sign tucked into riveted brackets, positioned so that it loomed up into a kind of arch over the exit. On it was painted a worn image in greens—a hideous tiara-wearing toad.

"I don't know," said Bo. "I never come out this way."

"I've already seen it four times."

"Is it any good?"

"Naw," the kid said. "I just figure I should get my money's worth, is all."

"I guess you could complain," said Bo, and then he turned back into the ten-in-one to put Bear back to work. He would have her dancing and riding that trike until their shift ended, and then he'd find Max.

HE SOUGHT MAX AND ORANGE late into the night and got up early to look some more. Nothing, no Max.

Bear had been cooped up in her cage so long she was stir-crazy. She made it up the ramp with the tutu and the trike but as soon as her first live fight started, she cuffed Bo so broadly across the face, the hit spun him around before he fell. He hadn't expected it, and his ears were ringing, but he could hear Gerry yelling at her. Bo was too stunned to tell Gerry to quiet down. Bear had never responded well to loud noises, so screaming at her wouldn't help. He wondered if she was just feeding off his energy. His sweat mixed with the filth she'd brought in on her paws and rained down his face. Bear sat in centre ring licking between her stubby claws, cleaning herself, the tulle of her tutu twisted, ridiculous. Hanging from her, it seemed a bit of an insult.

He pressed his index finger to his mouth to signal to Gerry to shut up. "I'm okay," he muttered. Then, "Bear!"

People flanked the ring on all sides, pressed in tight, in ways they never could at the small agricultural fairs. Seats on all sides rose bleacher-style, made the space feel compressed. They would have to deal with sweat flung at them, the spittle of bear, that ungodly stink, and the flies.

Bo could see in Bear's eyes that the swat had been unintentional. She had had no idea of her strength in that moment. He pulled a dog treat from under the elastic waist of his trunks and palmed it so no one would see, wanting her to rise up on her back legs as they had practised. She did, and they lunged at one another—also practised.

"Good girl," he whispered, and when they went into a hug, he pinched spots on her he knew she liked. Maybe she was ticklish, but when he tugged at the fur around her muzzle and under her arms, she would roll over and play dead, a great party trick. She did this now, tulle rising to reveal her great underbelly.

"There, there!" he called out. The crowd loved it.

She swung her head back and forth, peering upside down at the people, curious, then at Bo, and then she flipped, in a way that gave Bo time to pretend he hadn't seen it coming. He walked the edge of the ring like he didn't know a thing.

The crowd's groans of fear warned him of some imminent danger, but he played dumb. "What?" he yelled, like he couldn't understand, Bear ambling behind him, swinging her head, her tight high roars wafting up to the rafters.

The rest of the show went smoothly. Bear pinned him tight in a corner with one flat paw upon his chest and shoved her head sideways into his neck. The referee came in for the count. Then they pranced her about, sat her on her little stool, and held aloft a root beer. The crowd loved this.

On the way back to their tent, Bear dawdled behind him so that she could scoop her snout under his bottom and try to upend him.

"Hey!" Bo said to her, and laughed. In the end, he stopped to give remedial training. He had her sit, lie down, stay. Bear, chastened, dipped her head and let it sink to the grass, apologizing. She flicked her tiny eyes in ways that made him fall in love with her again. "You're terrible," he said, and let her bound the rest of the way to the tent.

In their room, he crated her, something he thought she'd come to understand was for her sake. "You're a star, Bear," he said to her before he left again to look for Max.

CHAPTER NINE

BO WANDERED THROUGH the tent city and the labyrinth of caravans, knocking on doors. He did this for an hour and was about to give up when Max opened the door of the trailer Bo had been hammering at.

"Hold up, kid."

"Max."

"I was resting, kid. I have a bit of a migraine too." It was true he was red-eyed, dishevelled.

"Where is she?" Bo was already pushing into the trailer.

"What gives you the right—?"

"What doesn't?"

Max kept his arm extended and shoved hard to keep Bo back. It was like an act. Bo scrambling, trying to take a swing but just windmilling the air.

"Calm down, so as we can talk," Max said. "I know you hate me. I get that. But you don't know the whole story. You want to talk man to man?"

He wore a dressing gown over his trousers. Black patent leather shoes poked out under the cuffs—the man dressed like it was 1940, like he was a gentleman. Bo knew better.

The trailer was a different one from before, newer, brighter, bigger, but the same framed freaks were on the walls, the oddities and stage shots. He looked around for the glossy of Orange but did not see it. Max held the door open, the dressing gown flapping wide to reveal his muscled chest. He rewrapped the silken gown and then rummaged in a pile of paper on the counter on the other side of the door. He pulled out a small envelope that looked like it had seen better days. He handed this to Bo.

"What is it?"

"She would have wanted you to see it."

The air around the envelope seemed to shimmer with energy. "She" was his mother, his dead mother, who had hung herself in spite of how much she should have known he needed her. Bo's cheeks twitched like little creatures were crawling under his skin. He wanted to drive his body through Max's to get to the other side of this bad feeling.

But even as the thought crossed his mind, the fight went out of him, like a thick hard wind. He watched his own hand reach out and take the envelope.

He wasn't sure he could read what was inside it and then he wasn't sure he couldn't. The glue on the envelope had never been licked and had turned brittle and yellow. How long does that take? he wondered. Or maybe it had been old and brittle even before she'd tucked her note inside. It contained only a scrap torn off some larger piece of paper.

It read: *I'm done. Tell Bo I loved him. Rose.*

In pencil, as if it wasn't important enough for ink. Bo read it and then reread it, but there was no clue, no subtext, no way to read it except how it was meant to be read—*I am done.* How simple to be able to write that and then act upon it, as if the thought manifested the action directly. As if there weren't other people to consider. As if he meant nothing to her.

Bo looked up and there was Max shaking his head, his eyes so screwed up, it took a moment before Bo realized he was crying.

"I loved her," Max said. "I made promises to her. That Sister be kept inside. Heavens, what a promise to have to make. I don't make such a promise lightly."

Bo thought if Max had loved Rose, she would not have killed herself. He watched Max raise his palms to his face.

"Sure," Bo said. "The world's a stage."

And Max snarled, "This is not theatre." Then softened, pleading, "Look, why don't you just come in. It's private, and we can talk."

Bo thought that he would sooner drop dead than step foot in this man's home, but his legs carried him up the little aluminum pop-out stairs and over the threshold. The trailer smelled of floor cleaner—citrus and detergent, of his mother when she had worked at the hospital.

Max poured something amber into a glass tumbler and handed it to Bo. "Twelve-year-old single malt." Then he poured one for himself.

"Okay," said Bo. He'd never had a drink in his life. He smelled moss and earth and sour, and sipped the fire of it. It was like smoked grass going down.

After a time the quiet got weird, a kind of strangling quiet, and then Max said, "She was sick on and off all summer. We got married, you know?" And here he raised an eyebrow, as if to ask what Bo might think of this. "I loved her."

"She drank," said Bo, looking at his own glass. He wondered whether his mother really had married Max.

"No. Just to cope. We all do that," said Max, gesturing at the tumblers. "She'd been sick a long time. But she hid her illness from you. She didn't want to worry you, you see."

And Bo stared at the man. The sorrow, or the act of it, had given Max a purged look—he seemed goodly all of a sudden, even if Bo knew better. He spoke without thinking.

"She abandoned Orange to you," Bo said.

Max grimaced. "She thought you'd be better off without the burden."

"Orange is my sister." Bo slammed his palms down on the Formica table. But he had forgotten about her in the forest of High Park, he hadn't searched for her.

"Oh, hush," said Max. "Listen, people make all kinds of choices."

"She made a bad choice."

"Bo, she was— Listen, what made your sister like she is, the dioxins, they came from your father *and* your mother."

"Shut up!"

"Thao wasn't a drunk."

"Yes, she was."

"No. She was dying. I brought her to doctors all over the place, and they couldn't do a thing for her. They wanted her to stay in hospital, to die there. I didn't let that happen. She loved me and we got married. It's very simple, Bo. You've a very thick skull, but it's really very easy to understand. It's like her letter says. She was done." And then he thumbed a small photograph from his wallet, of his mother and Max, arm in arm leaning against the trailer, smiling. It was so rare to see his mother smile.

"She was beautiful, Bo."

Anger coursed through Bo's chest and up behind his

eyes—it was unbearable. "She could have told me," he said, swallowing air, trying to slow it. He would spurt tears soon, he knew.

Max watched him struggle with it. And there was this between them, shooting back and forth in the space of the trailer. Their unspoken thoughts just hung dead everywhere.

Bo looked around for the letter, which he had let drop. Max saw it, picked it up and tucked it under the Scotch.

Max finally said, "There was no medicine that could cure her. It was hard to watch and be so—helpless."And then Max told Bo what Rose had never told him. "She had sores," Max said. "They gave her horrible pain," he said. "She wanted to protect you."

Bo wanted to get up and find someone to fight, to hit until he felt better, but it was too late. He was sobbing, blubbering that he needed his sister, and where was she?

"She's been sick for the last few days," said Max. "But of course you should see her." And then he brought Bo past the kitchenette and the toilet, pushed a door with curved corners open, and there she was, sleeping, sheets and covers nesting her so that he could hardly see even the pink of her skin: Orange.

She was here, safe. There was very little space around the bed, six inches at the most, and as Bo edged closer to her, his knees banged the bed frame. She breathed; he could see her body rise and fall. He wanted her to wake and see him, wanted to snuggle into her. He wanted to wake her.

"Does she still hit and bite?" he asked, looking up at Max in the doorway.

"Sometimes," Max said.

Bo sat on the edge of the bed. He heard the door close and looked up to see that Max had gone. It was a while before Orange woke up. She did not start when she saw him. She pushed the covers off with her feet, her body all sweaty, red with fever, the flame of sores along her torso.

"Orange," he said, and she shook her head. And filling the unspeakable space between them—their mother, Max, time, Bear—she began to move her hands, making strange shapes with her stubby fingers. Bo watched, baffled. She signed for a very long time, forever, and he did not understand any of it. Where was the Orange who threw herself into walls? Where was his sister bashing her face, her fists? Bo got up and pushed the bedroom door open.

"Max!"

Max stood up, beaming. "She can talk a bit. With her hands. She's learning fast."

"What do you mean?"

"American Sign Language."

"For deaf people?"

"She's much happier now she can communicate."

"I'll take her to my tent. I'll look after her now." He

wanted her with him so badly, knew Max wouldn't like this, but still.

"Well, it's like this, kid," Max said, shaking his head. He took a sip from his tumbler to postpone the next bit. "When I made that last promise to your mother, I meant it. I told her I would look after Orange. I swore on my heart and on my own mother's grave I'd keep her safe. You wouldn't want to make me a liar, now, would you?"

Orange was hitting the mattress to get Bo's attention, and when he looked back, she began to sign.

"What's she saying?"

"Beats me, kid," said Max. "She goes too fast."

And then Bo asked the question that had been plaguing him. He said, "Did Orange see?"

"See what?" Max said, before he realized that Bo meant had she seen Rose, and then he bit his lip, said, "No, kid. God, no."

Bo found Gerry washing down Loralei's cage, the animal circling a stake off to the side, worrying the chain with a batting paw, making a game of it. Gerry aimed the nozzle at a spot caked with bear crud and fur, and opened fire.

"Loralei's getting so ugly, soon she'll be useless. The hairless bear," he muttered. "Alive!"

"Did you know my sister knows sign language?"

"Yep," said Gerry.

"Who taught her?" Bo felt like shit for not having taught Orange himself, for not thinking that she might be taught, for not knowing there was such a thing as sign language—it was so obvious now that he knew—and for thinking she was in any way smaller or lesser than she really was.

Gerry said, "Calm yourself," and walked off.

"What?" Bo called after Gerry. "Why can't I know?" He glared at Gerry's back. "Gerry, come on, tell me."

Gerry turned, his face creased up in a temper, and gestured at Bo. "You're getting too close to the bear, boy."

He was. He'd moved in far too close to Loralei, her snout near his feet. Bo waited for Gerry to turn back to his work, so that he could touch her muzzle.

"Loralei's not as easygoing as she used to be, Jangles. Be careful."

"She's fine."

"Sure. But move away, will you?"

Bo shifted out of range, squinted at Gerry. "Orange is my sister."

"Oh, for Chrissake. That teacher of yours bought a book, then hired some kid to teach her the basics. Back in October. What's the big deal?"

Bo stared at him until he turned back to his task, water ricocheting in all directions off the cage. The crud melted down the bars, Gerry coming in closer for the bits that clung, then spraying so wide he misted both Loralei and Bo. When the crud was blasted away, Bo could see that the floor of the cage was scratched in places, buffed in others. Painted steel. It had once been red, still was in the corners. Loralei watched the water arc, casting a rainbow in the air. She seemed to look lovingly at her cage. She pushed up and wandered to the end of her chain, tugging, then acquiescing, pulling back her lips, nostrils flaring at the reek of the cleaning session.

Gerry poured a cup of bleach into a bucket of warm sudsy water and sloshed that over the cage floor. The bear started at the noxious smell. "She doesn't like bleach, much," said Bo.

"No. She prefers the smell of her own fecal matter."

Gerry sprayed again, rinsing off the bleach, and then edged toward Loralei. She reacted with bearish joy to the water and light playing just out of her reach. She swatted at it, head rolled toward Gerry. She bobbed like a great brown seal does for fish treats from its trainer.

"Hang on," Gerry said to her. He went over to his trailer and inside, disappearing. Bo heard him call, "Beverley." No one answered. He came out again with a tin of tuna fish. "Here, kid, open this for her."

He tossed the can and a flimsy opener at Bo.

"I want to learn so I can talk to Orange too," he said as he cranked open the tin.

Gerry said, "Ah."

"Seriously."

"Don't hand-feed her. Jesus, kid."

"How else am I gonna give it to her?" He tossed the rest of the contents in Loralei's general direction.

"I was going to use it as bait to get her back in the cage."

"Oh," said Bo. "Sorry." Loralei finished up the tuna, and swiped her tongue along her lips, seeking out the last traces.

"If I could talk to her," said Bo.

"You've been talking to her for years."

"Sure, but I haven't understood a word of it."

Gerry thought that was funny. "Hang on." He went back in the trailer and came out with a book. *Picture Dictionary of Signs for the Deaf.* "Here," he said. "I can't hold onto any of it. I'm as stupid as I ever was. She's only, what, four? Five? And she goes too damned fast for me already."

"You've been trying to learn?"

"Yeah, well. I thought there might be something in there for the bears."

"Sign language for bears?" Bo laughed.

Loralei looked over, and then went back to delicately licking fish oil off single blades of grass. Then she ambled toward Bo. When she got to the end of her chain she hunkered down and made soft eyes at him. Begging.

"I got nothing else, Lora," he said. He looked down at the book, only half listening to the bear chirr for more. Gerry had gone in to get another tin, to use to get her back in the cage.

Bo flipped the book open, stared at the drawings of hands fluttering. He would learn this. *Go. Me. You. Love. Down. Up.* He tried one out, realized that speaking this way moved the air, sliced through it. Nice. Loralei watched him: cut, swoop, finish.

"Girl," called Gerry. "Come on." And she did, veering away from Bo so fast he was shocked at her speed. "Let her loose at that end, would you?"

Bo unhooked the chain from the stake, and she bounded straight into her cage. The second can of fish wasn't all the way down her gullet and she was rubbing, rubbing.

"Jeez," said Bo. The book fell. He picked it up from its sprawl, saw a name and number printed on the inside cover: *Emily*. He looked up. Gerry had seen him seeing it. "Okay," he said. "Thanks."

Gerry shrugged. He closed the door of the bear's cage, but Loralei didn't care. She was lost in a bear dream, licking her lips, rubbing her ass fur off. Bo couldn't watch. He pocketed the book and went back to Max's trailer, banged on the door until Max opened up.

"Kid," said Max. "What the—?"

Bo waved the book and pushed into the trailer. "Orange," he said, once he got in her room, and smiled at her. Then he fumbled through the pages. *You*, he signed.

Me, she said. Then something he did not catch. And she was off and he was helpless. She spoke so quickly.

THE NEXT MORNING, after exercising Bear along the back perimeter fence, Bo coaxed her into the crate and cooed, lying down beside her outside the grille, until she fell asleep. He loved listening to her suck her tongue and chirrup as she drifted off. She became a cub again.

When she was asleep, he headed west, out the Dufferin exit and then north, up Strachan, the book tucked into the back of his jeans. He had until noon, when he and Bear were set to perform again.

He noted the change in air quality from butter, cotton candy, animal, to fume and asphalt. He turned on Queen and then up Roncesvalles, through various neighbourhoods, their differences marked by how much junk accumulated on their front porches, how much garbage rolled down the gutter along the curb. It was already hot at 8 a.m., salty trickles sliding down his belly, wicking into his clothing. At Bloor, he turned west, climbing the hill at High Park toward Clendenan.

The park looked tired, summer weary. Bo half hoped to see Soldier Man guarding the periphery, but in this hope he was disappointed. He saw a fox, ears pricked and watching, then gone. He decided he would walk back through the park. Maybe he would find Soldier Man then, see how he was doing.

Clendenan, Annette, Laws, its ravine-hugging curves,

and then St. Johns and he was right outside Emily's house. It took him several minutes to work up the nerve to climb the porch stairs, and then he was listening to the trill of the doorbell on the other side of the door, and the sounds of someone stumbling down the stairs. Moments later Emily stood in the door, the breeze whirling her hair in an impossibly beautiful pattern.

"Hi," she said.

He pulled out the book from his pocket. *Picture Dictionary of Signs for the Deaf.* Held it up. "Teach me," he said.

She took a short step back. "Come in."

Bo's step over the broken weatherstripping and into the foyer was like a caught breath. He was a freak. He belonged here the least of anyplace he had ever been. "Maybe not," he said, and made to step back out. "How long were you teaching her?"

"Whenever I babysat. I thought you might get angry with me."

"Why?"

"I thought you might not want her learning to sign. And I knew your mother wouldn't like it. "

Bo felt sick. "I just never thought of it," he said.

"It was Miss Lily's idea. When she found out I could sign, she thought of it. But I didn't do it just for the money. I did it for Orange. You know that."

The door slammed shut behind him and she stood in front of it, not barring his way exactly, but making a quick exit awkward. She put her hand out and it took him a little too long to realize she wanted him to hand her the book.

He gestured with it. "Is it hard to learn?"

"I'm not that good," she said.

He handed it to her, and she riffled the pages, so that the illustrations seemed animated, hands opening and closing, in a language he did not know. A flip book in sign language.

She found the page she was looking for, and put the book down on the radiator in the hallway. "Do this," she said, fisting her hand and bringing it to her chin, then dropping her hand to meet her other hand, index fingers extended and touching.

Bo did it.

Then, she took her right palm and touched her fore-head, dropped that hand to meet the other one, again with index fingers extended, touching. "Do it."

"Again." He shook his head. He had not marked it well enough.

"Do this and then this." She showed him.

"What does it mean?"

"First learn it."

The foyer smelled dusty, old, brittle. Emily wore a pink blouse with a little lacy collar. He realized he wanted to kiss her. But instead he fisted his hand and made the first sign, and then unfurled it and made the other sign.

"Faster," she directed. "More emphatically. Not so sloppy. Make the motions distinct."

He began to stand taller, felt his muscles pulling along his belly, his butt, his thighs. He felt strong, in a way he didn't ever feel unless he was whacking someone, or wrestling.

"Again," Emily said.

And when he had done it over and over many times, she grabbed his hands in hers, stopping him, as he recalled doing to Orange to contain her, to hold her energy inside of his own energy.

"Enough," she said.

"Did I get it right?"

"You got it," she said.

"So, what does it mean?"

She handed him the book, open to the leaf for the visual of what he'd been signing. *Sister. Brother.* He had signed *sister* and *brother* over and over so that they rolled into a wave of thought.

"Will you keep teaching me?" he asked.

"The book can do that, can't it?"

"No," he said. "Can you?"

"Sure," she said. "But Orange learned from the pictures in the book mostly. She wanted to communicate really badly."

"I should have known she wanted to speak. I'm an idiot. I wasn't paying attention." But it wasn't that. It was worse, he knew. He had assumed she was stupid. Assumed her inside was as awkward and ugly and dumb and wrong as her outside. He was no better than anyone else.

"How could you have known?" said Emily.

"With all the hitting, I should have figured it out. But I didn't think she thought like I did."

They moved from the foyer through the house to the back porch, sat on aluminum chairs. Emily taught him to build some signs into sentences. *I am your brother. You are my sister.* After a while, Emily went inside to get them each a glass of lemonade. Bo looked out over the swimming pool, the shimmer of green. His father was everywhere and nowhere, death lurking in every flick of insect on the surface of the water. He shifted his gaze to the plants growing up the backyard fence, trying to stop these thoughts. And another memory: his father squatting with a gun, cleaning it, smiling at Bo. "It will all be over soon," his father said, "and we will be safe." The recollection was so awful, Bo went back to staring at the water's surface.

Emily had come back out of the house with the drinks. "What are you scared of, Bo?" she said.

"Nothing," he said, but thought this: when the man in the boathold had let him free, and he'd gone up to the deck, his mother had tried to shield his eyes, to turn him away, but in the end, by her frantic attempts to try to protect him, she had drawn attention to the fact that off in the distance sharks were feasting on something. There were plumes of blood. "What is that?" he asked his mother, and she told him to hush. But she was holding her belly, crying. And by this he knew it was his father's corpse.

Bo watched the wind unsettle the surface of the swimming pool. He blinked. He said, "I'm afraid of sharks."

Emily looked at the pool and laughed. She said, "Okay."

"You should come to the Ex," he said. "Give me some lessons."

"Okay, okay. I will." Emily's face screwed up. "I heard about your mum, Bo. Father Bart said a mass."

Bo looked away.

"It's shitty."

"Yeah."

Emily nodded, stared at the pool too. "If you ever need a place to stay," she said, "my mother takes in any odd stray, you know."

"No," Bo said.

"It's not pity," she said. "It's that I like you."

In the end, Bo did not go through the park on the way back, but skirted it, not wanting to see Soldier Man.

BO SNAPPED THE WHIP and let the crowd think his bear was cowed by it. The little whip was a prop and nothing more. He never struck Bear with it. Bo was alone with

Bear onstage. Mino had ducked out early. "You're fine, anyway," he had said. "I just stand there. It's boring."

He didn't need Mino. Bear did everything he asked her to. The trick, Bo was learning, was to guide her sightlines with the whip so she didn't get interested in anything else. *We do it so, we do it so,* so any worry the animal felt fell away. Bear didn't like to change direction.

It was the part in the performance when he sang. Bo modulated between a polka and a lament—the main body of the song was upbeat and fast and the refrain pulled down and in. He pumped a toy accordion along to the song and stomped his foot as Bear danced. She hopped about in the fast bits and swayed mournfully in the slow.

"Ooh-la-la," Bo called out, when Bear stuck her butt out.

Bo kept his eyes on the space between the whip and Bear's nose, as she followed it, turning in her tutu. People clapped to the beat of her steps. When Bo was done he kept her moving in a circular fashion toward the trike, which was the focus of their finale. He climbed on the back of it, after she'd settled in, and held an umbrella over her, as she spun them around the little stage for a turn before jumping off. He picked up the accordion again, and played fast, then slower and slower.

Bear was just running out of steam when a yelp of recognition made Bo look over at the crowd. And there, gaping at him, were Ernie and Peter. They were both taller than he remembered. Bo jammed the accordion faster, and Bear sensed him faltering—she dropped to the floor and waited for him to remember his place.

And then, he looked up and saw them jostling one another, sharing a joke. On him? The thought was enough to pull him so far out of the show he might never get back. Bear looked to him for guidance. Bo had none. His left hand let the squeeze-box fall—it made a sighing squeak as it landed.

"Show's over," he announced. Bear pulled up onto her back legs, trying to figure out what was wrong. This egged on the crowd.

"What the hell?" shouted someone. "Keep playing."

"Do something, kid."

Bo breathed deep and stayed calm for the bear, and she felt that, sat down and waited, head swinging from Bo to the people, and then she sank to the floor and stretched out for a rest.

"Rip-off," a kid in the crowd yelled.

"Check out the midget show next door," said Bo, pointing.

He watched the disgruntled crowd disperse, until all that was left were the two boys from his school.

"Hey, Chink," said Ernie, and all Bo could do was smile a little. It had been a lifetime. They stood opposite each other, just staring.

And then Peter cocked his chin over at the bear. "Where'd you get him?"

"Her. She's a she."

"Yeah, but where?"

"My boss."

"You coming back to school?"

Bo hadn't given that any thought. School was some far-off story that his character had exited. He shook his head. "Dunno," he said.

Ernie said, "We missed you this summer," and they all had a good laugh at that.

"Yeah," said Peter, eyes shifting. "Emily told us you were here. We came to watch you wrestle bears. When is that?"

"In an hour and a half," said Bo. He wanted to say it was fakery, but didn't. "I can get you in."

They had been hoping for this, he saw. Ernie and Peter nodded.

"Can you hang out?" said Peter, gesturing at Bear.

"Sure," Bo said. "What's your plan?"

"We thought we'd get you behind the Bandshell and beat the shit out of you," Ernie said—but he was joking, Bo saw.

Bo was stronger than he had ever been. No one would be beating anything out of him. "I have to get the bear home so she can rest before the fight. Then, I can take an hour or so."

He muzzled Bear, tugged at her lead. She hopped down off the stage. He turned to head out the ten-in-one entrance, but the boys wanted to see the Blow-Off so they parted the sea of gawkers, Bear in the lead, and went out the exit.

A huddle of people pressed up to the Airstream. They were so intent they did not notice Bear and so did not move. Ernie and Peter waited at the margins of the crowd for a time and then began to holler for a turn, people shushing, pointing to the sign that asked for quiet. In the end, the boys pissed off so many people that it took longer for them to find a spot in the front of the window and for that dark window to reveal its horror.

Its horror, Bo quickly saw, was Orange.

He could see that she did not know she was being watched. She lay on a bed that had been outfitted like a pond—with a green-blue coverlet and a few cloth lily pads, never mind that toads were land creatures. A couple of fake trees stood in the kitchenette. No expense had been spared to outfit her space, he saw. A tiara had been fitted to her head. She wore a green costume that had been rigged to look amphibious. Her feet were vaguely flippered anyway. Orange rolled onto her belly and used her stumpy hands to flip pages in a picture book.

He watched her shut her book and rock to standing, then lunge-walk to the little kitchen. She opened a fridge and took out a juice bottle that was already opened for her. She was so normal in her behaviour, it was a wonder to Bo why anyone would want to watch her, but then he was used to her bulging eyes and the unnatural bend of her frame, the pressed-back, distorted head, and her warped everything. The fury rising in Bo's throat was only exacerbated by the groans of pity and shock from the people around him. Bo couldn't move, or speak.

"What's the matter, Bo?" It was Peter.

Bo tried to talk, but he couldn't. His eyes wouldn't leave her.

"She's just a fucking retard. Come on," Ernie prodded him. "Let's go."

"Watch it," Bo said, at last.

"What the hell? Let's go." Again Ernie jostled him.

Orange sat splay-legged on the bed. She cocked the bottle and guzzled, rocking a bit like she might begin to hop if she felt up to it. People laughed, pointed. Bo looked to Bear, where she had slumped down. He signalled to her to growl. She looked a bit surprised at this, but began to rumble. The earth under them vibrated with it, and the crowd around the Airstream awakened and turned.

"Bear!" someone yelled, and then there was screaming, and running, and then there were just the three of them—Ernie, Peter and Bo, plus Bear, and Orange, who had set the bottle down and was flipping pages again.

"Wow," said Peter, nodding to the bear.

But Ernie was a smartass. "What's the big deal, Bo?" Ernie waved to Orange. "You got a crush or something?" and Bo, furious, was on him.

Peter tried to pull them apart, but failing, stepped back to watch. People coming out of the ten-in-one formed a crowd around them, and Bear, too, gawked, as Bo threw and pinned Ernie.

"Stop," Ernie kept pleading, and, "It's no big deal."

At last, Bo had spent himself. He had a knee on Ernie's chest and was heaving, his anger giving way to tears.

"She's my sister," he said, the awfulness of it gushing out of him. Bo stood and tried the Airstream door but it was locked. He would have kicked and bashed to get in but he didn't want to scare Orange. He turned back to Ernie and Peter. "Toad Girl is my sister."

"Jesus," said Ernie. "Jesus Christ on a stick." He held his hands up then and said simply, "Cool, man."

Bo had only forty-five minutes to get himself to the ring, not enough time to hang out with Ernie and Peter. Still, they followed Bo as he led Bear down Princes' Boulevard to the carnie tent village. They told him they would wait for him, when the security guard held them back from entering. Bo left them there and went to his tent, where he linked Bear's leash to her cage, giving her the choice to go in or stay out. She did both, before curling over onto her back and falling asleep.

Bo's deepest impulse was to find Max and kill him. He sat on the bed to think, to let the vision of his sister degraded in that display slide away. He rocked a bit, staring at the tent floor.

"There you are." Max's shoes glittered as if they never touched the earth; the piped legs of his trousers were pressed to a razor-sharp seam. Max wagged a finger at him.

It struck Bo that Max was not handsome at all, but pretty. His eyebrows arched perfectly over his wide-set, grey eyes. Slight, tall, exquisite, and furious with Bo for walking out of the ten-in-one and upsetting paying customers in front of the Blow-Off. "You do that again, I'll fire you, my boy. You'll never see that bear again, except in a zoo, or being struck by the whip of the trainer I hire to replace you—or stuffed! After all I've done for your family—"

Bo sucked in a thin long whistle to wake Bear as he rose from the bed. He was so mad he was shaking. "My sister," he managed.

"What about your sister?" Max protested. "She's happy."

"She's not."

"How would you know?" Max said. "You, who hides in the forest when things get tough. You, who—"

"You took them away from me," Bo yelled. "And Orange. She's not—" and here Bo floundered for the right word. "She's not—*yours.*"

Max grinned the grin of a man who knows he has

won. "The law is on my side, Bo. To be precise, according to the law, *son*, you are also mine." Max waited a breath to let this sink in, and then turned and walked out.

Bo signalled Bear to lunge and snarl, but the leash held her back and her attack was more comic than frightening.

When Bo re-emerged from the tight corridors between the caravans and tents with Bear, Ernie and Peter whooped, delighted in their new alliance, the way boys' friendships can turn on a dime.

Bo pointed southwest at the back of the Arena. "Meet me there," he called, but they preferred to follow along the other side of the fence that secured the carnies' homes.

"Can we pet her?"

"Better not," said Bo. He thought his teeth might crack from clenching them. "Maybe later."

Bear knew Bo was upset, and her gait suggested she was agitated too. Bo didn't want to risk her misbehaving, her weight a danger to anyone who might get in her way. She did not seem to even notice the boys, except to lift her snout briefly to scent them, mark the fence with a long splashing piss, and continue in the direction of the ring. She wore her sequined leotard, which Bo had struggled to clothe her in. It sparkled in the afternoon sun. She looked both beautiful and ridiculous. It was sure to get a laugh, even if it clearly upset her to wear it.

"It's okay, girl. Shh."

"She looks like a lady," said Peter.

"A hairy lady," Ernie qualified.

"Yeah. Nice."

And then they were inside the wrestling tent, and Bo had the creature sit, watched Gerry push through the crowd to him.

"Where the hell were you?"

"Gerry, I need to talk to you."

"Yeah, okay. Later. Let's get this going."

Gerry knew what he wanted to talk about. Bo could see it all over his face, the guilt, the excuses, the tiresome human weakness. So weak he would avoid it all if he could, and then he did. Gerry turned and spread his arms and shoved the people back, strung up velvet ropes to demarcate the ramp. Little kids tried to climb into the ring and Gerry shooed them away. Bo saw the telltale black bowler at the back of the room. Max was watching. It wasn't over, and Bo was on edge.

Bo signalled Bear to rise onto her back legs and then he walked backwards up the ramp, facing her, while she bounced from one foot to the other in a wayward dance, her sequins glinting, drool rolling from the corner of her mouth. He could see how concentrated she was, but also how vacant her eyes were, as if she were not really here at all but rather sunk deep in the glory of the crowd's scent—sweat, fear, excitement, and whatever else he hoped she might be able to locate: the lake, earth and its wormy prospect, clean air under it all, nature.

A part of Bo begged whatever powers there might be, God, gods, goddesses, that Bear could smell that too. That she could still smell the real of it, High Park, the past. Then they were in the ring.

Bo let Bear drop to all fours. There was a trike at centre ring for her, which she mounted without being told. Bo helped her paws find the pedals. He led her around the ring, around and around. She looked like any huge kid, rotating clumsily, fighting gravity and winning, and losing, and winning.

The crowd roared but Bear didn't care. She kept pumping around and around. When Gerry gave him a look, Bo slowed her down by lowering the lead, reminding her he was there. She glanced over at him and seemed to remember where she was, then shut down the pedalling. She fell off the back of the bike like a fast crap. That had them laughing. The referee pulled the trike out of the ring and sent it scuttling down the ramp to a carnie who was waiting for it.

"Bear!" shouted the announcer over the PA. "Bear and Bo! They found each other in a village in Vietnam and have never been separated. They are the most unlikely siblings. They understand each other perfectly, Bo having mastered the tongue of bears, and Bear learning enough English to make her the smartest bear in captivity. But, folks? This does not make her tame. Notice, if you will, the nasty wound along the boy's cheek!"

Bo flashed his face in each direction, to show them a tiny cut from the scuffle with Ernie, a scratch. He had learned to roll with the white lies in the carnival circuit. The announcer embellished the wound a hundred ways, all of them inflicted by Bear. "Sixteen stitches, inside and out." Any moron would know it was a lie, but any crowd was less than a moron. The crowd had paid, it leaned in, it wanted a story, wanted to be lied to.

He saw Ernie and Peter at the ring edge, their eyes on Bear's paws as she hopped. Bo gave them the thumbs-up, and first Ernie and then Peter gave a thumb back to him. The referee moved toward Bo and leaned down to fake-whisper. Then he turned and crouched to talk to Bear. Muffled laughter. Bo held his hand up in the air and Bear's paw rose. She linked her claws through his fingers. He could hear the crowd sigh—a breath of disbelief—as they collectively fell in love with the animal.

The ref held his arms out angled skyward like a priest readying for a sermon. Then he dropped them, indicating the fight should begin. Bear did not hesitate, and caught Bo off guard. He flew backwards onto his head as she hit him, to great audience approval. It was possible to see stars—Bo saw them now. Bear ambled over and licked the salty sweat from his knee. To the crowd it looked empathetic. But they had not practised this. It was all Bear.

Bo let her lick him long enough to catch his breath and get himself up again. He swayed there, a drunk puppet, barely conscious, trying to find his balance, his vision, himself. The fight with Ernie hadn't done him any favours, he thought, and saw Ernie smiling at him, mouthing, *Wake up*. Was it that simple? The bear was mid-ring, sitting, scenting up into the air, off in some smell reverie. Blissful.

Bo fell into her, cupped her under her armpits, made it looked like he had half a chance of jostling that great thing. Her hundreds of pounds were immovable, but her mind was agile, surprised by his sudden move.

She threw him again. He was a rag, but one that hung onto her for dear life. She shook and he was shaken. The audience thought this was pretty funny. His sweat arced into the crowd. Bear stilled, and licked him some more. There was some screaming at this, and in his peripheral vision, Bo saw Gerry looking concerned. He wondered whether this was, in fact, dangerous, decided it wasn't, and clutched Bear tightly. She was his mother, he thought. He was delirious.

"Go. Go. Go," the crowd was shouting.

His body wanted only to obey. To go forward. To do something. But what? He let Bear decide. His body became hers as he just held on, the bear trotting around the ring with him lurching alongside, clinging to her. The ref looked concerned too.

This was not right. He was having a hard time keeping a hold, had to press down under the leotard. There might have been a rip, he could not be sure, but one thing he did know for certain: the crowd was mesmerized. He might be in trouble but it did not matter. He watched their faces shirr by, a blur of colour, this one and then that one, pink, red, brown, and they were rapt. *Go. Go. Go.*

"Bear," he whispered. "Bear, save me."

But she did not stop. She kept on and on, even when Gerry shouted and the referee shouted, and the audience rose to their feet in alarm. Something was going wrong, he knew. Bear would save him from it. Gerry was crouching with a can of soda but Bear did not seem to notice. She was following something. A smell. A need.

"Goddammit," Gerry said.

"Stop her, for Chrissake." Was that Max?

"Jesus," said Ernie.

Around and around. Now they were opening the ramp, and there was screaming. His body thumped up and down as she ran down the ramp and he smelled the sick-sweet smells of the carnival, shit and bodies. Then it was only green, swaths of grass slipping beneath them, and then she stopped and he fell, hard, onto the ground. Above him, Bear was panting, a line of spittle running from her tongue to his face. And then Gerry was behind her.

"Jesus Christ," he said.

Bo grunted and turned. It felt like a truck had driven over him.

"Well, she sure as hell wasn't ready for that bout," Gerry said.

"She was scenting something."

"She could have killed you."

Bo let the gorgeous smell of the earth go in and out of him. He had never known how varied the earth was in its odour. It held decay, and wetness and dryness, and next year and last year. He breathed it in and out while Gerry muzzled Bear, who shied away from his roughness. Bo watched him lead her away, but he did not move for a while, waiting for his mind to come back to his body.

"You okay, Bo?" It was Ernie. Peter and Max loomed behind him.

He closed his eyes.

"Shit, man."

"Yeah," Bo said.

"We brought you something."

The boys set it down in front of his face, too close for him to really focus on it, and so it took him some time to see what it was.

"A beer. How'd you get that?" He reached for it, his neck muscles pulsating.

"Some guy who watched the fight felt sorry for you." The boys plunked themselves down in front of him. They each had one, and were laughing at their luck.

"Can you sit up?" Peter asked.

"Yep." He tried and got halfway there. "Nope." And sank onto his back again. "I'll be okay."

"Your bear," Ernie said.

"I trained her myself."

"That's a good one." They all laughed.

The boys joined three straws together, tucking the end of one into the end of the other to make one long straw, then bent it from the beer into Bo's mouth. The fizz and the cold felt good going in, and he sucked it back.

He hadn't wanted to look but he did. Max still stood there, worried.

HE WOKE UP IN MAX'S TRAILER, lying on a little couch opposite the table. He looked around, recognized the photographs, the geek show—a plump girl biting the head off a snake. His head hurt—everything hurt. He knew some days had gone by, that he'd been in and out of it. And now he was awake, his whole body wanted to run.

"What time is it?"

Max was sitting at the table. "The freaks are just waking up, kid."

He tried to shake his head but it was like his brain was going to and fro with it, clanking up against his skull, so he stopped.

Max got a mirror and held it up to him. Not good. It looked like things had been rearranged. "You must have hit the ground on that merry-go-round about twenty times," Max said.

He hadn't noticed hitting once, but he saw it must be true. There were welts and cuts all over his face.

"Bear," he said.

"*She's fine.*"

"I mean, where is she?"

"Back in your tent. Morgana has taken over feeding her until you're better. There's nothing broken and, as you would surmise, the show—"

"—must go on. Yeah, I know."

"Here—" Max dangled an ice pack in front of him.

He pressed it along his cheek and gloried in the cold seeping in, nullifying the throb there. An ice bath would be perfect. There was a banging, which he mistook for his head at first and then realized it was coming from the room down the hall. Orange was smashing the door, trying to get out.

"She wants to see you, I expect. You've been mostly out of it."

"I want to see her too."

So Max went to get Orange and she waddle-dragged her body toward him, her smile skewed but her hands flailing, her throat making grunts not unlike Bear's chirring when she was happy. He'd never heard Orange make any sound before.

You happy? He signed it for her, his wrist painfully rotating at his chin. He knew all of ten words by now.

She stopped, did a double-take, and made a face like squealing, though no sound came out—just an open mouth, all the energy of it playing out in her eyes.

"How'd you learn that, pal?" Max asked.

"That book. I've learned a few words." The book poked out of a bag of his things someone must have packed and brought over. He gestured to it. "Can you hand me that?"

Max slid the bag over, and smiled.

"We're not friends now, by the way," Bo said, not looking at Max.

"I don't expect so."

Orange plunked down in front of them, so she and Bo were eye to eye. My, she was ugly, he thought. He thought it with no judgment. She was. She was signing *Out* and pointing to the door.

"I'm taking her out," Bo said.

"People will look at her."

"That's odd coming from you."

"Your mother," Max said.

"Are you serious?"

"I promised she'd stay in."

"Look," Bo said. "She's signing she wants to go out." He was thinking how this guy lied all the time—his entire life was about lying—so why was he keeping such a promise?

"Tell her people will stare at her. Ask her if she minds."

Bo just glared at Max. "Why should you care?" meaning the Toad Girl exhibit.

"That's different," said Max. "She has no idea."

"Really?"

"The Airstream is soundproofed. And there is always music playing for her, to muffle whatever sound might penetrate. I call it the daytime trailer. She loves it, hardly ever bangs around in there." Max shrugged and added, "Though the gawkers love it when she does—the spectacle of it."

"Eventually she'll figure it out."

"I prefer not to imagine that time."

Bo pulled out the book and flipped through. *People*, he signed to Orange, then, flipping some more, *stare*, a lunging V, his head bobbing toward her.

Out, she said. *Out*.

Bo pushed himself to sitting, ignoring the pounding head. "See?" he said to Max. "She wants to be normal." Then to Orange he said, "Okay, hold your horses." He signed, *Okay*.

She signed something back to him. She crossed her wrists and clawed them at her shoulders. What was she signing? He looked to Max but Max had no idea.

"Never seen that one before," he said.

She kept at it. Scratch, hands crossed over. Bo pushed the book toward her. "I don't understand," he said.

She tried again, making a face, her cheeks wrinkled up with her awful misshapen mouth pursing, and the hands scratching emphatically.

Bo shook his head. "Here—" he said, pointing at the book. "Find it for me."

He turned the pages and watched her watch the pictures, watched her *read*! They were well into the book before she banged her hand on the floor in glee, and pointed, jabbing the image. *Bear. Bear. Bear.* She signed and signed it.

"Bear," said Max.

Bo signed it back to her. *Bear?*

Bear. She made the sign: *To see.* She wanted to see Bear.

Max looked appalled. "You can't take her there."

"Why not?"

"She's never been out."

"You've never let her out. But I have."

"It's my decision," said Max. But he said it in a way that indicated he wouldn't stop Bo from doing this. He would find a way to turn a blind eye, act like it wasn't his idea. Well, it wasn't his idea.

Bo tried to get up but his legs would not obey. He rubbed them and placed them for easier standing. Bo was laughing and so was Orange by the time he got himself up. He would walk through the trailer site with her. He would carry her if she couldn't make it.

Orange was leaning back, laughing, drawing her fingers into crooks in a crossover in front of her face. *Ugly,* she signed, and pointed to him.

"Me?" Bo said, and she nodded fiercely.

Ugly, ugly, ugly.

"What's she saying?" said Max.

"None of your business," he said. "You coming?"

"I made a promise, and I'm keeping it. If she's going, you take her." But he held the door for them.

It took some doing to get out the door, Bo in pain, and Orange never in her life having moved over anything less flat than a floor. Her muscles were untrained to the task. Bo had to catch her to prevent her falling a number of times, steady her, compensate. But they did it. When she got down the trailer stairs, she slumped to the ground, and Bo worried she was hurt, but no.

She caressed the grass, smoothing her fingers over it, letting the blades run through them, playing the grass like she could hear something gorgeous coming out of it. When she looked up at him, he signed *Okay* and she pulled herself up using his pant leg, letting him help her too.

"This way," he said.

They moved through the tight alleys between the caravans and trailers, the tents and the laundry. He saw freaks everywhere. Self-made freaks with full-body tattoos, and in clown getups, people who had defined themselves by the carnival's terms. And the natural-born monsters—the tiny and the giant, the thin and the fat, the conjoined and the limbless, chatting, drinking, joking, being people, and then, like a wave, they turned toward this new sight. He wondered what Orange saw as they gawked at her, at Toad Girl, Max's prize, whom they had seen only through the darkened glass.

These freaks were being out-freaked.

"Jesus, where'd you unearth that?" the Mule-Faced Woman screeched. She tried to run but Mino held her.

Bo heard his bass rumble, "Respect."

"Respect." The word flowed like a sudden acclamation on the lips of the tent city freaks. "Respect," and "It's Alive!" and then laughter, even joy.

And then Bo and Orange were in front of Morgana.

"You found her."

"I found her."

"She looks worse than in her photographs."

"I'm sure she'd be happy to know that. She *can* hear, you know."

"Well, I meant it as a compliment."

Orange walk-hopped over to Morgana and stood swaying, looking at her eye to eye. If Orange weren't so crooked she'd be taller than Morgana. She was signing like crazy and looking back at Bo. She wanted a translator.

Bo felt useless, especially when Morgana said, "What the hell is she saying?"

Bo pulled the book from his back pocket, crouched and drew his sister's face toward him. *Help*, he signed. And they went through the pages again.

Tiny, she mimed. *Witch*, she pointed.

"Oh," said Bo, and laughed. "She's calling you a tiny witch."

Morgana looked pissed at first, then smiled wide and curtseyed. "It's not the first time I've been called that."

"Hey, kid." Mino was striding toward them. When he got close he waved his hands over them as if they were his puppets. It was a joke he liked to make. "She okay?"

"So far. You okay, Orange?"

She nodded, twisted her hand side to side. To show *so-so*. Mino crouched, said something about the air quality down there, and even still he was monstrous beside Orange.

"Little girl," he said. "Hello."

She signed her greeting.

"You're a whole new category," Mino said.

Orange cocked her head.

Mino swept his hand toward the loose grouping of freaks who had come out to see her. "I'm God-made," he said to Orange. "Some of them there are self-made, like him and him." He pointed to the tattooed man and the sword swallower. "You—" he said, and Morgana finished for him, "She's man-made."

The freaks nodded, and Orange watched them. To Bo, in that moment, she looked like a baby bird, something almost cute in its crushing strangeness, its wide-open eyes, its purity. She seemed to have given up on talking, having wrapped her fingers around two tussocks of grass. He did not know and could not imagine what she was taking in, but he was happy to watch. To be a part of this. She crumpled to the ground then and rolled, and began to sign *Bear*.

Morgana patted her. "There, there."

Bear, she signed, *Bear, Bear, Bear.*

"She wants to see Bear," Bo said.

Morgana's eyes lifted from Orange to Bo. "Well, what are you waiting for?"

"The last time I saw Bear—"

"Ach," said Morgana. "You never had a bad day?"

Morgana's response gave him the permission he needed. "I'll bring her out," he said. "Hang on." He peered down at Orange, her signing now frantic and obsessive: *Bear, Bear, Bear.* "Hang on," he said. "Hang on."

He looked sharply at Morgana and then walk-ran, until the pain reminded him to slow down. He found Bear's snout pressed between the bars. If she could have pushed through on the strength of her desire, she would have, she was so happy to see him.

Bo said, "Field trip." He pulled out her harness and collar, and opened the cage so he could put them on her.

She wanted out. She was chirring with pleasure and gently head-butting, burying her snout in his T-shirt.

"That's Orange you smell," said Bo. "You know that, don't you?"

The bear looked at him, pushed her ears down and proceeded to shove him two feet with the force of her excitement.

"No!"

She sat and bounced, yawning to calm down. She lifted a paw and scratched the air as if by way of apology. Bo thought of Orange signing.

By the time they got outside, he had Bear well in control. She knew to stay calm even if she quivered with the constraint. And then there was Orange, all askew, sitting beside Morgana. The day was clear, a wide pale blue sky and no clouds, so that Morgana and Orange seemed etched into the scene, a picture. Orange signed; she was not calling for the bear anymore, she was acknowledging Bear, showing the creature she had learned her name, that she could now speak to her.

Bear shook to the point she had to sit to calm herself. She raised her paw and held it in the air to mimic Orange. And then she slid to lying and snuffled the grass wherever Orange had been. She rolled and slid her snout along it, bathing in Orange, loving her. Hello, she seemed to say, Hello.

Orange stopped signing. Her body tilted sideways—

bearwards—and she looked as if held by a string, but she never fell. She just held herself all bent and wrong and ugly and man-made, and she watched the bear.

"I never," said Morgana. "Look." The bear had slid so she could sniff at Orange's knee.

And then Max was calling to Bo. "It's time, kid."

And Bo turned. He watched Max striding over to them.

"Time to get back to work." Max looked both resolute and pained. He was holding a tiara, twirling it. "The show, kid. The show."

Bo looked from Bear and Orange to Max, then caught Morgana's eye and saw the flit of shame in her gaze, and then to Mino, who hunched over the girl and the Bear, and who seemed to be avoiding eye contact. Bo figured it was nine or nine-thirty and the Ex would be opening soon. Max had a point, he knew. It was a job, and for all kinds of reasons they had all signed on; they owed a debt to this work and to this lifestyle too, for making them less freakish, for giving them something like home. But still.

"Stop calling me kid," Bo said. "My name is Bo."

"Come on, kid."

"No," said Bo, and he spread his arms out in front of Bear and Orange as if by this gesture he could offer protection. He was a kid, he was as good as owned. He had nothing. "No," he repeated.

Max's eye twitch turned into a squint. "Bo," he said pointedly. Then, "Oh, for crying out loud," and then,

with Gerry until the local fairs dried up and make enough to carry himself and Orange through the winter.

"Where're you going after the season ends, Gerry?"

"Back to my farm." Gerry looked hard at him. "You're always welcome."

Bo thought about the bears circling stakes beside a farmhouse, pacing, pacing. That would be him, too, restless and running in circles. One thought persisted: if he managed to save up enough to look after Orange, what would he do then? Maybe he could ask Emily for help, or the church group; maybe someone would take them in.

Max wanted them to head south with him. "Even if she wobbles around the local fairs down there, she'll draw folks," he said.

"You never give up, do you?"

"No, I don't."

Bo stood outside the deflated midway watching carnies moving poles and material all around him, and he stared down the carnival corridor; the three weeks they'd spent there had felt like a lifetime. The path on which so many thrill-seekers had trod, had laughed and argued and eaten, that path was strewn now with cigarette butts, and straws, the remnants of cotton candy cones. Mud intermingled with the mess too, where the sod had been so trodden it had given up for the season. The CNE caretakers would come in and rake the earth flat again for next year, re-sod. It wasn't the concession's responsibility to leave it as they had found it.

Bo needed to find Gerry and figure out when Bear would be loaded onto the trucks. The plan was that he would ride in Max's trailer with Orange. They had two vehicles, ten-tons, and Gerry and he would drive ahead in his pickup. Gerry was king of the world now. He'd paid off his farm, Beverley had agreed to be his fiancée, there was a rumour she was expecting. "Half-child, half-bear" had been the joke, and Gerry didn't seem to mind.

The breakdown action got louder, more frenzied, as Bo moved toward where he hoped to find Gerry. The hammers, yells, drills, and the clatter of aluminum sliding against aluminum, the canvas swish of awnings and tents, that pop of air when tents were folded, carnies shouting over one another. But under it all something thin was rising—a scream, a series of screams.

Where to look—no one could fathom this. The sound became dire, and then everyone seemed to be running in its direction. Cries of "Loralei" preceded the awful thing, so that by the time Bo pushed through the wall of carnies, some crying and some spitting "Fuck," he knew, or half knew, what he might see. Flesh—but whose? Beverley was leaning against Gerry's trailer with one hand covering her mouth, to hold in a shriek so deep it made no sound. And then it came. She screamed again and again.

Loralei stood on her back legs, clawing at some invisible wall that she would never again be allowed to breach. She kept batting her own nose to calm herself, her tongue pink with what she had done. Gerry was in pieces, strewn across the grassy knoll in front of the trailer. Gerry. Bo's gaze landed on Loralei, and the sight of her made him cry.

"Gerry," he whispered. Already there were flies. Already grief wrenched at his throat. He looked at Gerry's body and thought of his mother leaning into the water. He thought of his dead father. He couldn't breathe.

"Loralei," Max was saying. "Why'd you have to do that?" A bluebottle settled on her jowl. "Heel, girl." She did not budge. Max's face streamed with tears. "Lora," he said. "Oh, geez, Lora."

Bo turned and pushed past Beverley, who was sobbing. He tried the trailer door and found it locked.

"Beverley," he said, but she was too grief-stricken to help, so instead he ran out to the midway in the hope of finding someone willing to sell or give him a root beer. If they could lure her back into the cage, maybe there was some hope.

He stood at a pop machine, the can dropping in that second after he had shoved the coin in and pushed the button. The sound of gunshots sliced through him. The clunk reinforced the realization. Cold can wrapped in his palm, Bo walked back, weeping now for Loralei and Gerry. For the waste, and for himself.

He could barely stand to look at the heap of Loralei's body. Bo sat down beside Max on the stoop of the trailer, and watched the cops milling, the carnies gawking.

"I wish people would stop staring," he said, though he himself could not look away.

And Max said, "All the world's a stage." Then he turned to Bo, as if he were only then waking, and said, "Hey, kid, you know they won't stop with Loralei."

Bo ran. Let the sun set, he was thinking, let me go under cover of night, let me take my bear and go. He found Bear in a dream, her paws scurrying nowhere, fast.

BO LEASHED BEAR and they hustled south, the sun setting—a huge red ball spewing colour to the west. The bear lolloped alongside him, looking forward, scenting. The land sloped down in a subtle way, but she seemed to know they were heading to nature. It didn't take them long to cross the Lake Shore, so few cars at dusk—though a truck driver craned to get a look at what he thought he couldn't possibly be seeing—and with the sun a thin crease of light at the horizon, they made it to Lake Ontario. The beach.

Bo was so deeply in his head, knowing what he was walking away from—Orange, some duty he didn't know exactly how to fulfill—that he did not sense the shuffling of Soldier Man behind him. But the vet was beside him when he stopped to scan the shore—a kind of magic. It wouldn't be long before the news that Bo had run off with a bear would be widely known. He had to avoid people. Again.

"Kid." His voice sputtering, liquid, weird.

"Hey."

Bear glanced and then turned away. She would have known he was there all along. She sat politely at the end of the leash, snuffing and looking up at Bo, swinging her head around to the water. Bo crouched and looked her in the eye, leaned in to unclasp her leash.

"Go," he said. He didn't need to say it. She bounded sideways in crazy bear glee and was up to her flanks in lake before Bo had even stood up. She popped her head under the water, slammed the surface with her great paw, delighting in the splash, the arc of water droplets as they sprayed back at her. Bo pulled off his clothes, thinking hard about Gerry, that flayed body, and wanting some kind of cleansing. It was all he could think of, watching Bear cavort, the bear seeming to invite him in.

"Take it easy, kid."

Bo was down to his underwear, cramming his clothing into a canvas satchel Morgana had handed him as he left. He waded in, the water cold but velvet-smooth against his skin. The bear was in deep by now, and swimming.

"Not too deep," Soldier Man shouted from the shore.

"I can't swim," Bo shouted back. "I'm scared of water." He plunked himself down, shivering, and sat chest-deep in the shallows. He sat so that he could watch the bear in one direction, Soldier Man in the other. Bear was coming back, fast, first swimming and then, when she bottomed out, running. Soon she would be on him. He started clucking, talking soft, trying to talk her down. Could she see who it was?

"It's okay," he said, putting his palms up in the water so that they created a visual wall around him. He was afraid she couldn't see his body below the surface. "Easy," he said.

"Get the fuck out of the way," shouted Soldier Man. He looked like he was going to step into the lake to save him.

Bo could see Bear already shifting her energy. "It's okay."

"Jesus."

"It's okay. Look." Bear came right up and head-butted him gently, and then she was turning and turning to find a seat. She circled five or six times, enjoying the water swirling around her. Every turn, Bo noted where she had fully scratched a patch of fur off her rump, right down to the skin. There were nasty scabs scattered through the baldness. "Sit, girl." But she did better. She lounged flat, her body so huge she could lie down and still keep her head above the surface. She swayed her head and dipped it, playing at wave making, keeping him in the game whenever he looked away. There were no treacherous fish in fresh water, Bo told himself.

The night had fully fallen. There was only the merest sliver of moon, and Bo could barely see her now, and best when she was in motion, bear eye glinting. Bo pulled his hand out of the water and plowed the surface.

"Take that," he said, real soft, and watched the splash hit her. She recoiled, assessing this. He did it again.

"Come out, now, kid," Soldier Man called.

But Bo arced water at Bear faster and faster. She rolled away and sat watching him, and then, before he knew what she was doing, she threw her body up out of the water and slapped the surface so hard, he choked on the wave that hit him. She finished him off by swiping her huge paw sideways along the water, and he was briefly submerged, and then he was up, sputtering, and then retaliating, throwing as much water in the bear's direction as he could.

"Bo!"

Soldier Man's voice was plaintive. But in the night there was only Bo and Bear and water and laughing. Pure pleasure.

Finally Bo staggered toward shore, out of breath, saying, "I'm here, Soldier Man. I'm here." The bear took a few more languid swipes at the water and ambled after him, chuffing, lips pulled back into an insane bear smile.

"She's okay?" Soldier Man said.

"Yep."

They discussed the dark then, Bo telling Soldier Man all that had happened, and Soldier Man reminding him how each night the moon would grow and with it visibility. They would have to keep moving, keep to green spaces, and waterways, to allow themselves and the bear cover, and hope of food and water.

"Down below Baby Point. It's safe all along the Humber at night. There's fish for the bear right now. The salmon run is on."

"Okay," Bo said.

They crept along the lake until they reached the mouth of the river and then followed it north for a time. The glint of curious animal eyes met them here and there, along the bank, and Bo had to regularly whistle Bear to heel, stopping her from chasing after every smell and rustle of bush. The undercover was lively with night sounds, and they caught whiffs of skunk, which they wanted to avoid.

The whole area smelled of dead fish too—a stench to Bo and Soldier Man, but to the bear, an enticement. She pulled Bo toward the bank and plunged into the water wherever she could, luxuriating in the salmon stink. They walked for an hour until Soldier Man insisted they hide for the rest of the night and catch some sleep. He knew a crevice in the hillside tucked below an overhanging rock. "It used to be an Indian place but now people live in mansions up there and sleep under silk sheets."

"We have dirt," said Bo.

"We have dirt."

The slit in the earth Soldier Man found opened up into a cavern. Soldier Man was asleep and snoring before the bear even made it into the cave. But she settled fast too, and left Bo wondering where they would go the next night, if they could hide and run forever. As he fell asleep he thought how Soldier Man had suggested he set Bear free. He wondered if this is what he was doing. He did not want to be free of Bear.

When he woke up again, it was dark, the bear was snoring deep and loud, and the soldier was gone. He wasn't surprised. That man came and went. He couldn't be relied upon.

CHAPTER ELEVEN

FOR WEEKS, Bo stayed below Baby Point. He was held there where Soldier Man had left him. It was easy living. In the thick of night, Bear would amble into the river and wait for salmon to jump, and catch them mid-air. Bo wondered what the fish were thinking, if they thought, and how that split second of flying in the air must feel to them, unable to breathe, and then failure and a quick death. Bear ate more fish in an hour than Bo could count. She never shared her catch, though she was happy to share Bo's when he was swift enough to catch one.

There was already a chill in the air—the bear was readying her body for winter sleep, even if she might not get it. From newspapers he had salvaged from a bin, Bo knew that because Loralei had killed Gerry, bear wrestling would be banned in the province. There was probably no future for Bear in any sideshow circuit. Max's carnival had hit Woodstock, and was heading to Elmira.

Then, in late September, the first leaves began to fall, and Bo woke one morning to a memory. He was six or seven, it was sultry out. He was in Vietnam, a place he never thought of anymore, except in connection with some fantasy about his father. Yet here he was, opening the front door of the house they'd lived in. He looked outside. It was morning. The world had transformed. Every green thing that had grown around their house the night before was gone. The world had blackened and dripped with an acrid stench. The earth was sending up water.

"Dead," said his father, standing behind him. He wore his uniform, so he must have been on furlough.

It didn't feel dead to Bo, though, just strange, a kind of powerful magic that could take everything away, that could turn the whole world into another world. He was too young to be afraid. It had no deeper meaning than this: change. He ran out into the forest, through the long grasses all dead around the house. He touched a tree, watching the leaves fall around him. With the foliage all gone, he could see farther than he had ever thought possible. He could see the houses of his friends and his grandfather down the incline from his house.

He stood with his hand protecting his eyes from the sun, marvelling for a long time, oblivious to the bad smell. Then he ran farther even though he could hear his father and his mother calling him back, such alertness in their voices that he should have been alarmed. But how wondrous this not-green world was, where you could see through the jungle—where you could see *everything*!

There were other children wandering through the strange landscape, lost, as if without the markers—this shrub, that knoll—they could never begin to know where they were. They began a game. Someone touched someone else, and then they were all running, howling through the devastation, tagging each other and tearing away again, the ruined flora swiping their legs and arms.

When he came back in to eat, his father yelled at him. "You didn't listen!"

Bo hardly ever saw this man, and so had made him large in his mind, a hero, to be sure, but something even more—an epic character in the story of the war, of his family, of his own position. But now his father was home, and scolding him. His father was the opposite of the father he had created.

"Sorry," Bo said. But he wasn't really.

"You can't run and play in the jungle when it's been sprayed. It's poison. Look," and here he pulled his khaki shirt up to reveal an oozing wound.

Then Bo's mother pulled him to a tub, stripped off his

clothes, and began to scrub all the dirt and jungle debris from him. Bo watched his arms turn red in swaths where the brush she used scraped him.

"Ow," he said, but she did not stop.

His father did not speak at all while she did this. He sang. Bo did not recall the song except that it was a lament. His father sang it often. Perhaps it had become his song. Sometimes, Bo heard him whistling it, sometimes he hummed it—always it seemed to be part of him, coming out with his breath. His mother hated this.

"Stop singing that awful song," she said now. His father had not known he'd been singing, which made it worse.

It was Rose who decided they must leave Vietnam, that they must take the risk to get out. They argued at the shore before they boarded the fishing boat. Bo could recall his father protesting, saying, "I'm too sick." Rose spoke to Bo's father as if he were a child.

These recollections had no continuity. They were vignettes added to some story he'd told himself about his parents' marriage, about the circumstances of his father's death. And then this memory brought him to another more recent one. He and his mother were in their kitchen. They were always in the kitchen. The walls pulsed with her anger but she wouldn't say a word. She took a sweater off, and under it she wore a T-shirt, something donated certainly, but she looked beautiful no matter what she wore. Even when she was tired, she was radiant. Sometimes he did not know how she could be his mother. There on her arm, along the soft skin on the inside was a long sore. It festered, he saw. She put her hand over it when she noticed him staring.

"From work," she said. "A cut. It will heal."

Now he wondered about that. His mouth fell open. He recalled the sore on his father's chest, the frenzy of hungry fish. Wondered about the way he had lined up his memories. That his father did not want to get on the boat. Forever it had meant that she had had a hand in his death. Forever he had blamed her for the sharks and the fear. Forever he had blamed her for every bad and sad thing. Now he wondered.

A few nights later, on the river, Bo watched Bear concentrating so hard on the water it looked like she was willing those fish up into her mouth. One after the other. He knew he did not really exist for her. She did not look up to find him. She did not need him. She was fishing, fish filled her thoughts. They leapt to her mouth as if they knew their fate, and delighted in it.

He whistled for her, to make himself known from time to time, but she didn't seem to notice. He thought about Orange, and how much he missed her. It was an ache through his body to be away from her again.

That night, he began to walk.

He looked back at Bear once, twice, and stopped, whistled. He turned around and waited half a dozen times or more. He watched Bear move upstream as he moved down. Day was dawning. It was time for him to call her in, so they could hide, but he didn't. He walked south, toward the lake, and hoped to hear her lumbering behind him, but she did not follow. He imagined Bear— *his* bear—circumnavigating the city, for years and years, protecting him, and he knew it was nonsense, a fairy tale, but still he wished it would be true. He walked south along the riverbank. The tears came unexpectedly sometime around Old Mill, and they did not let up until he heard the lapping waves of the lake.

THE END

THEY WERE IN ELMIRA, Teacher's hometown, at the end of the last gig of the season.
The tents had been pulled down and put away.
Max had found a spot in the carnival for Bo, without
Bear. "It was never about the bear, you know," he said,
always revising. "You got spark. You'll always have a
home with me."

He became Max's "Boy Who Had Wrestled Bears,"
running games, running bingo, rigging here and there,
making himself indispensable, making himself money.

Bo was talking up the ring-toss one day and there she
was. Miss Lily. She wore those white boots, but had
darkened her hair. As soon as he saw her he knew he'd

been hoping she'd show up. He had smelled her before he spotted her, some airy perfume mingling into what he knew he'd see before he looked. Teacher.

"Miss Lily." Bo smiled, wondering how he looked to her. Fuzz on his lip now, and he was taller, he figured.

"Hello, Bo."

He handed her a set of rings. "Three ringers wins the stuffed toy, Miss."

She laughed like her voice was catching in her throat. "Bo, I'm terrible at games!" she said. There was already a line of people behind her. She hesitated and went to hand the rings back to him.

"Come on, Teacher," he said, and she smiled at that, and got into position, swinging one arm back and aiming.

She was way wide. She seemed to know it too, and closed her eyes and threw wildly, all three at once. The crowd cracked up. Teacher's hair swung with her.

Bo put his hand out and said, "Wait."

The others hurried through their turns, or seemed to, knowing they were in the way of something. When they were gone, it was quiet; they were in a bubble. Bo swung his legs over the table, and stood opposite her.

"Where's Orange?" Teacher said.

And he became suddenly sorrowful not because of Orange, but because the question reminded him of his mother. He did not want the conversation to go in that direction.

"Orange can talk now," he said.

"Oh?"

"You—Emily—taught her how to sign. Thank you."

"I'm pleased."

"Yeah. She likes pink, likes closing doors—slamming them, actually. She wants to be a clown when she grows up."

"Can you leave the booth for a while?" Teacher asked, and he nodded.

Teacher walked with him past the midway and then through the town, its red-brick Victorians kept up, gardens tended. "My house—" She pointed, and they walked by that too.

Soon they were crossing a track. He could see a silo in the distance, a creek of rust and green sludge flowing slow and ugly. This was the factory that made Agent Orange, he supposed.

"I worked there before I became a teacher," Miss Lily said.

He could see this confession meant a great deal to her. She expected a reaction, he knew, but it was nothing to him, or almost nothing.

He said, "Why did you leave the school?"

"I quit," she said. "I followed my heart. I teach in this town now. I needed to be closer, to fight this." She gestured to the factory—a low warehouse, windowless, with a chimney, a great stink coming from it.

A logo: Uniroyal. Men and women in blue coveralls going in, coming out. "Because they still make those chemicals."

"Why are you—?" he said, and then stopped himself. "I should get back to work."

Teacher said, "I thought you should see, Bo," as if seeing changed a thing.

"I don't need to see. I'm not angry."

She laughed then, and said, "I've never known an angrier person than you."

Now, at the end of the fair, Orange told him she would join the finale parade, insisting she sit on the float. When he said no, she bludgeoned him. She would have her way.

"Max," Bo said.

"What?"

"Orange says she's coming on the parade." He pointed to the red mark on his cheek.

"Should get her in the ring, boy-o."

"No, thanks."

In every town there was a finale parade, in every town people waved, in every town some kid wailed, freaked out by the freakery of it all—and for Bo these had all merged into a single pageant of people passing by. He wondered what it was like for those boys and girls who spent their time shifting hay from field to barn. Farmers. The county fair must be the only time in the year they saw anything but green fields turning brown.

The floats were hay wagons festooned with bunting, decorated for this one occasion. In the first car, the mayor waved his pudgy fingers, and in the next, the Corn Queen—prettiest girl to enter the competition—smiled and swayed, and then the Lion's Den people, and onward to the freaks.

From the float, Bo saw Teacher up ahead, saw her laugh, saw her wave to the Corn Queen. He wondered if Teacher taught this girl, what their relationship was. And then he and Orange were alongside Teacher, about to pass her.

"Miss Lily," he called.

Orange saw Teacher then, and waved, crooked-smiled. All around, people began to notice Orange. They stopped waving and stared before they realized how rude that was. They glanced all over the float, at the blue and white paint, at the way the artist had gone too far with the turrets and towers, but they avoided Orange, her manic smile and wild rocking. They had never seen anything like Orange. Then, they started up waving again, to compensate for all they had just thought.

But not Teacher.

She lifted her arm and swung it in a wide wave. She beamed at Orange.

Bo stood behind his sister, thinking how they would go back to the city, how they would find their way somehow, and he turned and smiled back at Teacher. He looked at Orange waving.

She waved at everyone. Orange waved and waved.

ACKNOWLEDGEMENTS

I have indebted myself to many people during the process
of researching and writing this novel. Sarah Henstra for
cheering and reminding. Ky Anh Do, Thao and Van
Nguyen, Hoa, and Adam Arshinoff for sharing life
experiences with me. Norm Perrin at Four Winds Library
for trusting me with all his out-of-print Vietnamese
fairy-tale books. Linda Cobon for her knowledge of the
CNE archive. Susan Bryant for answering endless questions
about the manufacture of Agent Orange in Elmira.
Miriam Toews for riding the Ferris wheel and the Swing
with me. Naomi Duguid for information about the refugee
process post Vietnam War. William Robins for introducing
me to Sir Orfeo and all things spectacular. Bethany Gibson

for her astute editorial. Alissa York for reminding me to follow my instincts. Thuy Morgulis for translation. Adam Sol for his helpful fixer skills. Catherine Bush for dog walks and animal talks. Dawne McFarlane for providing an early ear and talking through the Orpheus myth with me. Julia Cooper for providing reading prowess and for her beautiful singularity. Martha Magor Webb and Anne McDermid for loving the ugly, early draft, and believing. Anne Collins for smiling upon this with her brilliant mind. Amanda Betts for smart considerations and keeping time in all manner of ways. Ken Woroner for making me beautiful. My husband and sons for keeping everything real. And the staff at The Good Neighbour for their hospitality. Thank you.

KATHRYN KUITENBROUWER is the author of the novels *Perfecting* and *The Nettle Spinner*, which was a finalist for the Amazon.ca First Novel Award, and the short-story collection *Way Up*, which won a Danuta Gleed Award and was a finalist for the ReLit Award. Her short fiction has been published in *Granta*, *The Walrus*, *Numéro Cinq*, *Joyland* and *Storyville*. She won the Sidney Prize for her story "Will You Staunch the Wound?" Kuitenbrouwer lives in Toronto with her family.

All the Broken Things is set in Adobe Jenson (aka "antique" Jenson), a modern face which captures the essence of Nicolas Jenson's roman and Ludovico degli Arrighi's italic typeface designs. The combined strength and beauty of these two icons of Renaissance type result in an elegant typeface suited to a broad spectrum of applications.